I'VE DONE THIS BEFORE

Ryan Major

CONTENTS

BLANKETED IN THE STARS

She will come to me, blanketed in the stars.

I can't tell you how many times I heard those words over the last decade. My father, Raymond Chandler, suffered a massive stroke and developed Motor Aphasia. He couldn't say anything else afterward. Just those nine words over and over.

Well… I guess that isn't entirely true. He said something else at the end… but I'll get to that later.

Mom and Dad worked for NASA when I was a kid. Both had completed multiple missions into space and Mom had served on the International Space Station. She died there, as a matter of fact. Clara Chandler was the first person in the station's history to lose their life while stationed there.

During a routine maintenance check on some of the external communication equipment, her tether came loose and she drifted into the darkness of space. The result of poor safety checks according to the final report. I was too young to understand exactly what happened, but old enough to understand that she was never coming home.

Dad did the best he could raising me as a single parent, but I don't think he ever took the time to take care of himself after she died. Even at a young age, I could tell he was aging too rapidly. His hair color faded, the skin on his face creased deeply, and he rarely slept. Still, he was a loving man.

"Do you think Mom was scared?" I asked one night as my father tucked me into bed. "When she floated away. Was she scared?"

My father smiled that sad smile I came to know all too well. His hand stroked the top of my head and he placed a stuffed bear next to me on my pillow. "No," he said gently. Tears pooled in the corners of his eyes. "Your mother was a brave woman. Before you were born, we would sit outside and look at the stars long into the night. Nothing made her happier. Now she is with the stars. I think… she was very happy that she was able to stay there."

***

Dad suffered an ischemic stroke in 2012. Just four days before his fifty-eighth birthday. What a gift, right?

He remained in a coma for nearly a month.

I don't want to dredge up all my memories of his recovery process, but I'll say this. It was rough. Most of his physicians believed he would stay in a catatonic state for the rest of his life. Regaining his ability to move independently seemed unlikely even if he did wake.

Speech? That would be gone too, according to the same doctors.

Day after day, I would sit at his bedside and read to him. Thriller and detective novels, mostly. He was always so busy with work or taking care of me that he didn't have much time for leisure reading. Tons of professional journals and reference books, but rarely a good piece of fiction. That didn't stop him from picking up a hardback and adding it to his never-ending retirement reading pile.

The silence of the first few visits was near maddening, so I began to pull a book from the towering stacks every few days and read it to him. Some of the nurses said they thought he would hear it. An "anchor" some of them called it. I don't know if I believe it worked, but it helped fill the crippling silence of his sterile hospital room.

After finishing up our fifth or sixth detective noir, I closed the book and slid it onto the table beside him. Looking at him, I saw his chest rising and falling shallowly. His color was ashen and his weight was dropping. A feeding tube ran into his nose and his body was a maze of wires and adhesive pads. With tears in my eyes, I took his frail hand in mine and squeezed it.

"Gotta head home, dad," I whispered. "I love you."

As I began to place his hand back on the white blanket, I felt his muscle tighten around my hand. He squeezed my fingers weakly. Both of his eyes opened lazily and gazed into mine. A croaking noise erupted from his throat. Dry coughs caused his body to shudder.

He was trying to talk, but his mouth was too dry.

In a panic, I fumbled to the bedside table for a bottle of thickened water. Some stroke victims have difficulty swallowing, so the nurses left a bottle in the event he woke up. Holding it to his mouth, he took small sips and smacked the roof of his mouth with his tongue. A wet cough exploded and I used a Kleenex to wipe spittle away from the corners of his mouth.

"She will come to me, blanketed… in the stars," he said so quietly I barely heard him.

I punched the call button beside his bed to alert the nurse. My pulse hammered and my vision began to swim. Dad began looking around the hospital room with panic-filled eyes as I tried to calm him.

"What?" I said, my heart thundering in my chest. "I couldn't understand you, Dad."

He gripped my hand even more tightly and pulled me toward him. His sudden burst of strength startled me. I leaned in closely, placing my ear to his mouth. Hot breath and wheezing filled my ear.

"She will come to me, blanketed in the stars!" he said again.

As he spoke the words, the bright fluorescent lights above the bed sizzled and burned away.

* * *

After Dad was released from the hospital, I took over as his full-time caretaker. My work as a home healthcare nurse made for an easy, if not uncomfortable, transition. His recovery, for the most part, had been incredible. All his range of motion returned. He could walk on his own. His vision was as good as it had been before the stroke. Basic tasks like tying his shoes and getting dressed presented no issues.

The only lasting effects were reduced hemiparesis, or weakness, on his right side and his inability to communicate anything other than those nine words. His aphasia never improved.

She will come to me, blanketed in the stars.

His doctors said it was uncommon, but not unheard of. How a stroke damages the brain is different for each person. "The ability to form and speak full thoughts may return. It could be weeks or years." The doctor told us. "Or it may never improve."

It never did. My father could only rattle off that single phrase. He would say it with different voice inflections to express his mood. I didn't always understand what he wanted, but I knew if he was happy or sad. Anger was the easiest emotion to figure out. It could be incredibly frustrating, but I did my best to remain patient and understanding.

For a brief time, we thought he may be able to write to communicate his thoughts, but it proved fruitless. Any time you gave him a dry-erase board or a pad of paper, he wrote those same nine words over again.

She will come to me, blanketed in the stars.

Slowly, things returned to normal in his life. As normal as you can expect for someone who loses their ability to speak coherently, anyway. Our daily routine hit a stride, and he was largely the man I remembered as a child.

The new normal didn't last long.

Dad started using chalk to draw enormous star maps on every inch of the walls. The massive designs eventually covered every available inch of empty space. As he ran out of room to expand his comprehensive work, he would remove framed photos and paintings from the wall and stack them in the center of the room.

When he started, I was confused and concerned about the activity. When I say he was drawing star maps, I don't mean he would work in one area of the house until he completed a portion. He would stare at the wall for a half hour before placing a single dot. As soon as he had finished, he would walk to another room and repeat the process. Hundreds of times a day, maybe more.

After a wall was sufficiently covered in tiny white dots, I waited until he went to bed one evening and decided to clean the walls. I filled a bucket full of warm water and used a soft sponge to remove the markings. It took me hours to wash them away and return the photos and paintings to their original positions. When I was finished, some of my anxiety diminished.

The next morning when Dad saw his work was gone, he was furious.

"She will come to me!" he shouted as he stomped around the living room gesturing toward the newly cleaned walls. "Blanketed in the stars!"

"Dad," I pleaded. "They were just little chalk dots. Let's go in the kitchen and have some breakfast, huh?"

He stormed back to his bedroom and slammed the door. I could hear him crying as I knocked, but he didn't answer. He didn't come out for the rest of the day, as I recall. Just sat in his room whimpering and muttering those same nine maddening words.

As a peace offering, I drove to the store that afternoon while he napped and purchased him a box of chalk. It hadn't occurred to me that although his artwork on the walls didn't make sense to me, it could be very meaningful to him. I made a note to be less careless with his feelings.

It did the trick.

The next morning when he came out of his room, I handed him the box of chalk.

"I'm sorry," I said sincerely. "It's your house. If you want to draw on the walls, then that's okay. I shouldn't have taken it down."

He gazed down at the box in his hand and smiled. "She will come to me, blanketed in the stars?" he said questioningly.

"Sure, dad," I responded. "Blanketed in the stars."

***

Over the next few years, Dad filled the walls with enormous star maps. His pace had quickened and soon the charts bent around the door frames and continued into the adjacent room. Some days he would pull huge books from his office and show me photographs of the constellations and formations as he repeated those echoing words. I knew in his mind he was explaining to me in great detail which celestial bodies his drawings represented, so I would nod along. He looked so happy. Content, even in his weakened state.

But all I heard were those words.

She will come to me, blanketed in the stars.

Eight years after the stroke and Dad's health was starting to take a turn for the worse again. He had a difficult time getting out of bed in the mornings. Standing for a long period was out of the question. His memory seemed to be slipping a bit, though it could be hard to tell with his limited speech.

He forgot to shave, which had been a religious part of his daily routine. More often than I could count, I would catch him staring blankly into space. The buttons on his shirt would be undone at random intervals. His tidy demeanor shifted slowly into clutter and forgetfulness.

Still, he added to his star charts and maps.

That was also when the lightbulbs started to burn out rapidly. Just one at first. The hallway light outside of his bedroom. I would put a fresh bulb in, and within two or three days the filament inside would be no more than two charred prongs. Heavy ash coated the inside of the bulbs.

It wasn't long before the lightbulbs began frequently burning out throughout the house. My weekly grocery trip always included a few packs of incandescent bulbs. I told myself the old-style bulbs may be the problem, and we switched to LEDs, but it only lasted a day or two longer. You never realize how expensive lightbulbs can be until you start buying them two dozen at a time.

After my frustration hit a melting point, I had multiple electricians come to the house and check the wiring multiple times in the following weeks. They would spend hours checking the sockets, but never found any issues. Six electricians told me everything worked just like it should. Not a problem in sight.

Bulbs continued to burn out. The pace quickened. It grew more common to let them sit dimmed in the sockets for a day or two before I would change them.

With Dad's mobility dropping off, we stopped spending as much time at the house. A few hours on the porch to combat seasonal depression, but otherwise we stayed in. Where we used to take daily walks or travel to the planetarium, he would spend most of the day reading a book quietly in his armchair or staring off into space.

His work on the star maps grew less consistent.

I spent most of my day in front of the television. While I was a great student, I never developed the same love for reading that my parents had. Binging TV shows broke up the monotony of the quiet house when I wasn't busy taking care of my father. Most nights, I would fall asleep in the dim blue illumination of the flatscreen.

Some nights I would wake up to see the glow of the TV hitting the tiny chalk dots on the wall. It almost made the little spots sparkle like the night sky. As though my father's artwork had come to life and embodied the very celestial landscape that danced above us.

It was in the cascade of light from the television that I first started to see the sinister shapes. I knew it was my imagination, but thin lines seemed to grow between some of the stars. They came together to form the faintest outline of something that made my blood run cold.

Sleek, hunched, and snarling creatures made of tiny chalk dots seemed to prowl on the illuminated walls. The sounds of crackling plaster and groaning wood filled my ears. A chill would build at the base of my spine as crawled up to my neck as though I were an unwitting animal in the sights of an apex predator.

When I would turn the lamp on beside me, the half-dream figures would vanish.

Nothing left but the white field of stars.

I think my father felt it too. On those nights, I would hear him call out in panic. Cries of terror would fill the silence of the evenings. When I would enter the room, he would be pointing madly from wall to wall and screaming those same nine words.

"She will come to me! Blanketed in the stars!"

Whenever he grew panicked, I would have to sit beside his bed until he fell asleep again. The bedside lamp would always have a burnt-out bulb, so I would change it. Even if I left some of the other bulbs unchanged, I never let my father sit in the dark. He would hold my hand as he drifted off. It felt so much like when I was a child, crying over how much I missed my mother.

Dad would hold my hand in the dim lamplight then and whisper to me about how Mom was so happy among the stars.

* * *

On the morning of my father's final day, I think I knew it was near the end. For most of the days leading up to it, he seemed to be filled with fear. He rarely slept unless I sat beside him, hand in hand. If I didn't sleep in the chair next to him, I almost always found him on the floor the next morning. He hadn't fallen. No, he would slip out of bed and return to his work on the walls.

There he would be, clutching a dwindling piece of chalk, crumpled on the floor next to the wall. For the past few weeks, he had been scrawling away at an ornate rectangle. It was beautiful and haunting all at once, like the recording of a lost loved one's voice.

It looked almost like a door, though it was nearly nine feet tall. Delicate loops and swirls filled the space between the thick white border. Lighter shades of gray covered the inside, carefully smudged inch by inch by my father's shaking hand.

He never worked on it during the day. Only during the night and only when I wasn't in the room.

I purchased a baby monitor to place in his room for the nights when I was able to sleep in my bed. The first few times I saw him wobble across the floor to work on the door, I had run to the room and tried to put him back to bed, but he would become so agitated that I thought we would come to blows. No matter how many times I carried him back to bed, I would see him again on the screen working away at the door.

The rest of his room was covered in more unsettling work. What had once been a field of white chalk stars now had faint lines connecting them. They came together to form vague outlines of the horrific creatures I always dreamt of.

I never saw my father draw them, but they changed frequently. Occasionally I was tempted to wipe them from the wall while he was out of the room, but I remembered how angry he became the last time I removed his work. As much as I hated them, I left the half-formed beasts to prowl amongst the chalk stars.

That morning when I entered my father's room, he was sitting in his armchair. His head was tipped back, and his robe drooped open at his sides. When I first saw him, I thought he had passed away in the night. My heart ached for a moment until I saw him stir.

"She will come to me," he said groggily. "Blanketed in the stars."

"Good morning, dad," I said. "Breakfast is ready."

We ate together in the kitchen. Well, I ate. Dad picked at his breakfast and shoveled down a few mouths full of eggs. He hadn't been eating well for weeks and was beginning to look sickly thin. His doctor recommended IV nutrition if his eating didn't improve, and I was sure that would be the next step.

Usually, we would sit on the porch after breakfast, but he got up from the table and shambled on shaking legs back to his bedroom and crawled beneath the coverers. The sound of snoring soon poured out of his bedroom. For a few moments, I considered trying to stir him, to take him outside for some sunlight, but he seemed so frail. I decided to let him rest.

Sometime in the afternoon, I must have drifted off. When I woke up, I could see the streetlights flowing in through the windows. Pulling the cord on the lamp beside me, I wasn't surprised to find the bulb was burnt out. Walking groggily to the wall, I flipped the light switch to discover it was also burnt out.

I was heading toward to cupboard in the kitchen for some fresh bulbs when I heard my father scream. Rushing to his bedroom, I twisted the knob to find it locked. I began to bang on the door, calling my father's name, but he didn't answer. My ears were filled with his panicked screams and the sound of things falling to the floor.

"Dad!" I shouted. "Dad! Unlock the door! You've got to let me in!"

More screaming and the sound of... heavy footsteps.

I threw my weight against the door, but the thick wood didn't budge. The hinges would rattle, but the door never gave way. Still, the sounds of terror inside persisted. Sweat began to run down my neck from the effort.

My phone was still beside the recliner in the living room, so I ran back in to grab it and call 911. As I reached to pick it up, I looked at the screen of the baby monitor and my heart nearly stopped.

My father sat in his bed, blankets pulled up to his chin, shivering violently. His eyes darted side to side at the walls. Glowing orbs that had once been chalk stars danced along the walls as they bulged and rippled. Something behind the plaster and paint was pushing against them, trying to break through.

Abandoning my phone, I ran to the garage and tumbled down the steps, landing hard on the concrete floor. My head was swimming, but I managed to push myself back onto my feet. Darting toward the tool bench, I found my father's old hatchet and ran back to his bedroom door.

Blow after blow with the hatchet rained down from above my head. Flecks of paint and chunks of wood peppered my face as I carved away at the door. Inside, I could still hear my father screaming, but now it was mingled with a guttural rumbling that filled my heart with dread.

After a few moments, I made a hole large enough to put my hand through. Shoving my hand inside, I swatted blindly for the door latch. The rumbling had swollen into deafening roars, completely covering my father's screams of horror.

My hand found the lock and twisted it, allowing the door the swing in.

I could see my father reaching toward me, eyes filled with terror. He was screaming something, but I couldn't hear him against the cracking of plaster and splintering of wooden beams. I didn't need to hear him know what he was saying.

She will come to me, blanketed in the stars.

Dozens of dull lights pulsed as they pushed themselves through the wall, tumbling to the floor. They rolled like bowling balls before coming to a stop. The strained sound from the walls fell silent as the orbs began to convulse. Slowly, they began to move toward each other before melting into an enormous sphere.

My father and I stared in awe for a moment at the ball of light. I was about to call for Dad to come with me when the ball cracked like an egg, falling to pieces on the floor. Standing in its place was something unlike anything I'd ever seen.

A creature made of small stars stretched its back and shook its head from side to side. Delicate lines flowed between each of the illuminated dots, forming the nightmarish beast. Heavy claws sank into the floor as it craned its neck toward me. Two red orbs in the sea of white met my gaze before the thing erupted in another guttural roar.

I raised the hatchet above my head, but the thing swung a passive foot toward me and connected with my head. The hatchet dropped from my hand as I sailed through the air, crashing against the wall by the ornate door my father had drawn. The air ejected from my lungs and I began desperately gasping for breath.

The thing turned back toward my father and lowered its stance as it began to move toward him. He screamed and thrashed in the bed as the celestial demon crept closer. It seemed to be preparing to lunge for him when suddenly the room was filled with intense light.

I looked to my side and saw brilliant beams pouring from the outline of the door. The light danced and erupted throughout the delicate latticework my father had drawn. All around us, the air was filled with a sensation of serenity.

Even the beast turned to look.

The ornate door pushed open, flooding the room with overwhelming warmth and light. I wanted to cover my eyes, but the sight was too beautiful and I couldn't turn away.

On the floor at the foot of my father's bed, the celestial abomination began to roar and writhe in pain as the light from the door washed over it. I looked away from the opening to see the creature melting into a pool of illumination. The waves of warmth and light from the door had driven it back to wherever it had come from, leaving the room in silence.

I turned back to the door.

A woman walked out and into the bedroom.

She was so tall. Over eight feet. Her body was slender and agile, her smile beautiful and serene. Draped over her shoulders and falling to the floor was a silver shawl. Lights danced and sparkled over every inch, shining like stars in the night sky.

Blanketed in the stars.

Leaning down toward me, she placed her hand on my chest and my struggling lungs filled with air. Every ache and pain in my body faded. The sense of fear and dread washed away and I felt suddenly calm.

She smiled at me, caressed my face, and walked toward my father's bed.

I looked toward him. He had thrown the blanket to the side and was smiling at the beautiful woman. He lifted a shaking hand toward her and she lifted hers to meet it.

"She has come for me," he said. Tears were streaming down his face as he gazed at the beautiful woman. "She is blanketed in the stars."

The woman took my father's hand.

"I've missed you, Raymond," she said in an ethereally beautiful voice. "I do believe it is time to go."

"Clara," he cooed, voice steady and strong. "I knew you would come. You're as beautiful as you were in my dreams."

He stood from the bed with a certainty that had been missing for so many years. Light washed over him as he… changed. The frail man my father became was no more. He looked youthful. Strong.

He was the man I remembered from my childhood.

My mother and father walked hand in hand toward the door, stopping for only a moment before me. He smiled at me as a single tear, sparkling with starlight, rolled down his cheek. My mother bent over and caressed my face again. I put my hand over hers for just a moment as she kissed the top of my head.

"I love you," she whispered in my ear before standing back up.

My lips moved, but the words wouldn't come out. I love you, I mouthed. She smiled and nodded.

They passed through the door and it sealed shut behind them. I don't know where they went, but that's okay.

Wherever they are, they are together.

Blanketed in the stars.

SHE LOVES ME NOT

.

Every time I found one of those damned yellow sticky notes on my monitor, I knew it would be a bad day. My secret admirer had that effect on me. The notes started out kind of charming. A few polite compliments about my clothing. A note about how kind and gentle my personality was. Little *xoxo* signatures at the bottom.

Middle school crush stuff. It was a bit of an ego boost, but I was happily married. It had taken a while to get there, but that had been my fault. My wife, Emily, and I had a rough stretch a few years back after I had an affair, but we got things back on track.

I thought of telling her about the notes, but I didn't want to worry her. The flirtatious post-its went into the trash, and I moved on with my day. I didn't give the first dozen or so much thought. That was before they began to threaten me.

The first note that left me with an unsettling feeling showed up two months after the first. Gone was the free-flowing, delicately curved handwriting. Heavy grooves gouged into the paper from the heavy block letters etched on the surface.

Why don't you ever answer me back? You could leave a note for me on your computer. It seems like you don't care. It's starting to make me angry.

XOXO

At first, I laughed it off before wadding up the note and tossing it in the trash. The idea of leaving a note for my admirer was ridiculous. They had never even mentioned wanting me to leave a reply before. Not that I would have. My hard-learned lesson about fidelity had taken root.

Two days later when I arrived at work, there were two notes attached to my monitor. The first one was the angry message from a few days before. It had been uncrumpled and smoothed out. Underneath sat another on clean, unwrinkled yellow paper.

You just wad up my messages and throw them in the trash? What the hell is wrong with you? You used to be something special to me, but now I see you're just like every other guy I've met. I was wrong about you. You're a piece of garbage.

XOXO

I felt a mixture of anger and relief at the note. Whoever this woman was, she didn't know me well enough to make judgment calls like that about me. At the same time, it seemed like this could be the end of the strange ordeal.

That time, I put the notes in my pocket and tossed them into a trashcan in the parking garage on my way home. Whoever was leaving them, they were checking the trash in my office. With any luck, they would move on and get over their fixation.

No such luck.

A few days later, there was another sticky note on my monitor. This time it was neon green. Had they written me so many damn notes that their yellow pad had run out? My throat tightened as I pulled it from the screen and read.

We all have our shortcomings, but I'm willing to forgive you. Please stop throwing away my notes. These little moments mean so much to me and it hurts to know you don't feel the same. That's okay, though. Your feelings for me will change with time. If they don't, I may have to hurt someone.

XOXO

I immediately took the note to the HR office. One of the reps read it, her eyebrows raised, and her head held back in surprise. She placed it on her desk and pulled off her reading glasses.

"How long has this been going on, Paul?" she asked me in a concerned tone.

"I'm not sure exactly," I replied, scratching my head. "They've left a dozen notes. Two dozen, maybe. Do we have security cameras on the floor?"

"No," she said, shaking her head. "No cameras, I'm afraid. Too expensive. Same reason they laid off the security officer in the building. Our company isn't exactly thriving and the budget is tight."

She gave me a look of sympathy and told me to let her know if any more notes turned up. I nodded and told her I would. We both silently acknowledged that this was the first of many conversations on the matter.

The following week, an HR memo was posted around the office stating it was inappropriate for coworkers to leave personal notes in another's workspace. All correspondence should be sent via e-mail. I appreciated the effort, but knew this was a fruitless gesture from HR.

Over the next month and a half, I made multiple trips to the HR office. Not only had the notes continued, but they escalated. My "admirer" rambled endlessly about how heartless I was, how angry I had made them, and the violent things they would do to me if I didn't respond soon.

It was becoming exhausting.

During my last week in the office, there was a hot pink sticky note on my computer monitor. I was at a breaking point. The notes wouldn't stop, HR didn't know who was leaving them, and my place of work was doing nothing to put an end to this. I had even called the cops. They took a statement but seemed to laugh it off.

At that moment I would have done anything to get it to end. The note offered the option.

I get it. You're not interested. I'll back off, but only if you'll meet me tonight. I'll be on the fifth level of the parking garage near the stairwell exit. 8 PM. Don't be late.

XOXO

***

It was 7:58 PM when I stepped out of the elevator onto the fifth floor of the parking garage. My heart was racing and a cold trail of sweat ran down my back. From my position near the elevator, I had a clear view of the stairwell door about two hundred feet away. No one was there, so I made my way in that direction to see if I could find them.

Suddenly a red ember glowed brightly in the shadow cast by the door. Someone was smoking a cigarette in the darkness. The muscles in my body tightened as I willed myself forward.

My admirer was there, shrouded in the darkness.

"Hello?" I called out. A cloud of smoke billowed from the shadow. "It's Paul. You wanted to meet me?"

A woman stepped out of the shadow and dropped the cigarette to the ground, grinding it with her shoe. Something in her left hand reflected the abrasive fluorescent light from overhead.

It was my wife, Emily. A gun was clenched in the fist.

"Emily?" I questioned. "What the hell are you doing?"

"I left the notes as a test. A few days a month I stop in your office on my way to work and leave notes. The cleaning crew thinks I work there, I guess," she said, her face streaming with tears. "I thought after… all the trouble you had from the affair, you would tell me if someone was trying to steal you away from me again."

"You… you left the notes?" I stammered. "I don't get it…"

"I wanted to be sure you wouldn't try to meet another woman again," she said, lifting the gun toward me. "But you did. Here you are. Trying to meet some easy score."

"Emily! You can't be serious!" I shouted. "I came here to get this to stop! Why are you doing this?"

"I knew you would…" she said, but was cut off by the eruption of police sirens. She looked toward the ramp at the flashing blue and red lights. "You called the police?"

I looked at her, jaw clenched, unable to speak.

"Of course I did!" I exclaimed. "I thought someone was going to hurt me if I…"

The thunder of a gunshot was all I heard before the world went black.

***

I woke up in a hospital. My entire body ached. There were thick white bandages wrapped around my midsection. A nurse saw that I was conscious and ran to find the doctor.

A police officer was in a chair beside me. After my physician entered the room, they explained that my wife had shot me in the abdomen and fled the scene. A manhunt was underway, but they hadn't located her yet. A protective detail would remain with me at the hospital until I was released.

They never found her.

That was about five years ago. I've relocated since then. New state, new job, new life. It's been relatively peaceful until recently.

Yesterday I headed into the office a bit before the sun came up. When I turned on the light, there it was. A bright yellow note on the center of my computer monitor.

OUT OF SIGHT, OUT OF MIND

The Rig was an oasis for the homeless. Two miles off the Texas coast, it was an abandoned oil rig turned into a shelter for the wayward and forgotten. It was against the law, but the authorities never seemed to pay us any mind. Out of sight, out of mind. Isn't that the general position most places take on the homeless?

I'm not sure how long The Rig had been going before I ended up there, but when I arrived, it was a like full-fledged town on the water. A few people ran boats back and forth to the mainland. Some of the long-term residents operated like a city council. There were shops, a clinic, and a gas-powered generator to charge cell phones.

A few local charities and food pantries would bring fresh water and dry goods two or three times a month. Everyone got a bit for themselves, but the bulk was saved for those who couldn't go to the mainland for day labor.

The most impressive thing was the garden. Over countless years people had hauled dirt a few buckets at a time until there were dozens of planting beds on the old helicopter pad. No one officially oversaw it, but an older lady named Greta prided herself on its constant care and tending.

I lived there for seven years. After losing my house and all of my worldly possessions, The Rig was the first place I ever felt at home. Shuffling from the alleyways to the shelter and back again had worn me down. I had almost given up when Freddy told me about The Rig.

"I'm headin' for the coast, Tim," Freddy told me one day. He was a decade older than me and a good friend. I wouldn't have gotten through my first few years on the streets if it weren't for him. "Got an old friend who says there's plenty of space out on an old oil rig. A fella at the coast will take me out to it for a few bucks. You oughta come."

"An oil rig?" I questioned. "Why the hell do you want to go live on an abandoned oil rig? Sounds too risky."

Freddy laughed and swatted me on the back.

"It's like a floatin' city. No cops to mess with you. No business owners chasing you away from their shops. Just a bunch of people like us that came together to prop each other up. What have you got to lose? The convenience store canned you and sleeping on the streets has to have lost its luster."

Two days later, we hitched a ride to the coast.

***

Freddy and I were blown away after we arrived. When he told me about the Rig, I had imagined a filthy squat pad filled with trash and waste. It was quite the opposite. Aside from the rust of the aging structure, The Rig was kept immaculately clean. No one slept in the open. Every available inch of indoor space was dedicated to sleeping space and food storage.

A kind woman named Janet gave us both sleeping bags and blankets upon our arrival. We were taken to an old boiler room where there was available space to sleep at night. She told us we could leave our belongings in the boiler room, but Freddy and I were apprehensive.

"Don't want anyone stealin' my stuff," Freddy said curtly. "Leavin' stuff sittin' around is a good way to get fleeced."

"You'll find the community here quite respectful of everyone's property," she responded. Janet reached into her back pocket and pulled out two yellow sheets of paper filled with handwriting and gave them to us. "Those are the rules here on The Rig. We have a three-strike policy. If found guilty of three rule violations, you're banished permanently."

We both began to read this list of rules.

Rule 1. No theft of any kind. Failure to repay debts is considered theft.

Rule 2. No fighting.

Rule 3. No drug use.

Rule 4. Drinking is allowed in moderation.

Rule 5. If you don't contribute food or goods to the community, you must work daily to maintain The Rig.

Rule 6. Do not enter the mechanical room below the Drill Module.

"Seems reasonable enough," I said, extending the list back to Janet. "Who decides if the rules have been broken?"

"You can keep it," she replied. "We have an informal council that meets every Saturday night in the mess hall. It's made up of our oldest residents. They will hear complaints and decide if a rule has been broken. If the incident is serious, let someone know and the council will get together that day."

We thanked her and headed to settle in.

Over the next few years, Freddie and I integrated nicely into the community on The Rig. The population remained roughly the same. New people would arrive occasionally. Old timers would move on from time to time.

Freddy and I spent most of our days on The Rig. Before he lost his job and home, Freddy had worked in construction and welding. The council was excited to hear about his experience and asked if he would be interested in helping maintain the facilities. He agreed with the stipulation that I would be allowed to assist him. They agreed, and we fell into our daily routine.

It was a comfortable life.

The uncomfortable part came when we saw our first banishment.

During a Saturday meeting with the council, a man was brought forward to answer for a rule infraction. His third. He was an older man with a long beard and a thin frame. His eyes were red with tears as he stood before the group.

"My name is Albert Martin," he said with a shaking voice. "I have been accused of stealing three cans of soup from a neighbor. Someone found the emptied cans under my cot. I was framed! Someone knew I'd been in trouble two times already and pinned this on me. Have mercy! I have nowhere to go!"

The crowd became a sea of whispered discussions as the old man wept. Freddy and I could hear the conflicting opinions in the community. Some thought there wasn't enough evidence, while others said Albert was a known rule breaker and was likely guilty.

"Albert Martin," one of the councilmen said. "This is your third infraction, and we cannot tolerate theft on The Rig. Many here rely on the food donations we receive. You are banished and will not return here."

"No!" Albert shouted. He pulled out a rusted blade with a cloth-wrapped handle and held it toward the council. "I didn't steal the damn food! It's a setup!"

While the man waved the knife at the group in front of him, Freddy tapped me on the shoulder and beckoned me to follow him. He crept silently up the aisle behind the man. Moving surprisingly quick for his age, he darted forward and wrapped his arm around Albert's neck.

"Get the knife!" Freddy shouted to me, and I pried the blade from the old man's hand.

"Take him to the mechanical room downstairs!" demanded a woman from the council. "We will hold him there until he can be taken back to shore."

Freddy and I carried the thrashing man out of the mess hall and down the stairs toward the mechanical room. A man trailed behind us and pulled a key from his pocket, unlocking the door. We tossed him inside and slammed the hatch shut and the man locked it.

"You've killed me, you bastards!" Albert shouted from inside the room. He hammered on the door and threw his weight against the thick metal. "You hear me? You've killed me! They aren't taking me to the shore! Those damn things are gonna kill me!"

Freddy and I turned to leave, but the old man's wails of fear and agony resonated in my mind.

What things was he talking about?

I would find out years later when Freddy was found guilty of his third violation and ended up in the mechanical room.

***

Freddy was a hard worker and well-loved in the community, but in his later years, he became overly fond of alcohol. He managed to keep it to himself for a while but, over time, the drinking got the better of him. While he was sober, he was as nice a guy as you could hope to meet. When he was in the bottle, well… that was a different story.

His first violation was a simple fistfight. Freddy sat on his cot, drinking hooch and talking loudly to anyone who would listen. When he drank, he would ramble for hours. A man who slept in the far corner from us asked him to quiet down so he could sleep. Without warning, Freddy walked over and punched the man in the face.

The second violation came when Freddy drunkenly rifled through another man's gear looking for cigarettes. He found half a pack of crumpled Marloboros and was closing the bag when the man entered. Freddy returned them, but the damage was done.

His final violation came when a woman and her husband asked Freddy to fix a leak in one of the bunkhouses. He insisted it was already repaired, but they told him the leak had continued. Feeling insulted, Freddy shoved the husband and told him to piss off. When the man begged him to come to look at the leak, Freddy knocked him to the floor.

With that, the council decided his fate and had two men haul him off to the mechanical room to wait for a departing boat.

That night when I returned to my cot, I saw all of Freddy's belongings sitting on his bed. I began to bag them up to take down to the mechanical room for his ride back to shore. After gathering them up, I headed to the stairs to the lower level of The Rig.

When I arrived on the lower level, there was a man from the council, Carl, standing guard outside of the mechanical room. Freddy was banging on the door and begging the man to let him out. He stood stone-faced, staring in my direction.

"Tim, stop," the man said to me. "Freddy has already been judged. We're just waiting on a boat."

"I know," I said, gesturing toward the backpack full of my friend's belongings. "Just wanted to drop his stuff off so he can take it back with him. I don't want him to leave with nothing."

"Just drop it there," Carl said flatly. "I'll make sure he gets it before…"

Suddenly the air was filled with agonized screams. You could always hear muffled yelling on the upper levels when someone was locked up awaiting their banishment, but the thick floor plating always made it inaudible. Up close, I could hear the fear in my friend's voice.

"What the hell is that?" Freddy shouted. "Let me out of here! It's going to kill me! Open the damn door!"

"You need to leave," Carl said, pointing toward the stairs.

"Something is in there with him!" I shouted. "Let him out!"

"This is how it works, Tim," he spat. "If you don't want to join him, you'd better go."

I could see the keys to the room hanging from a ring on his belt. I'm not sure what came over me, but I threw the backpack at Carl's head and lunged forward for the keys. He was momentarily shocked, but quickly regained his composure and began to struggle. Landing two punches to the side of his head, he slid limply to the floor.

I pulled the keys from his belt and unlocked the door.

As it squealed open, I began to call for Freddy, but the words died in my throat.

Standing above my friend was a gangly creature covered in wet, scaley skin. Gill slits opened and closed on its neck and purple eyes gazed at me from its bulbous head. As I made eye contact with it, the thing opened its massive jaws and hissed before grabbing Freddy's limp frame by the head.

It turned toward an opening by the drill shaft and began to drag Freddy toward it. A crimson streak trailed behind them. Freddy's eyes were barely open as he lifted his hand toward me, eyes pleading for help. The creature's wrist turned, and a dry snap echoed in the mechanical room before it threw Freddy's lifeless body through the hole into the sea below.

A clawed hand reached toward me, mimicking the same gesture as Freddy. The thing opened its mouth again and uttered what I can only describe as a hellish laugh. Finished with its taunt, it stepped back and fell through the hole and into the rolling waves below.

***

I left that night and got as far from the coast as I could. After a few days in a Houston shelter, I left the state. I live in Omaha now. Farmhand work is plentiful in the outskirts, and I managed to get a cracker box apartment. The green pastures make me feel safe, but when I try to sleep at night the roar of the ocean still echoes in my mind.

I never told anyone what I saw. The authorities wouldn't believe me. Hell, maybe they knew. No one is worried about the homeless.

Out of sight, out of mind. Right?

THE ONE THAT GOT AWAY

My cell phone rings on the table beside my armchair.

It's him again. *Just calling to check in*, he sometimes says.

I consider checking to see if the call recording application is up and running, but decide it isn't worth the trouble. I've tried to capture his calls dozens of times without success. When I play them back, I can hear my voice on the recording, but any response I receive is nothing but a wall of static. He wouldn't call without making certain precautions.

The call log on the phone never shows I received a call from him after we hung up. My cell carrier also has no records when I call to check. For an old man, his technology skills must be top-notch.

When I retired from the force six years ago, he remained a suspect in my oldest and most frustrating unclosed cases.

I call him *The Mimic*.

He kills three victims, once a month for three months, using the modus operandi of some of the most infamous serial killers in history. Once his cycle is complete, he vanishes for nine months.

The cycle would start over in a new city across the state.

Sometimes he vanishes for a year or two, but he always comes back.

He never stops calling either.

Tension mounts at my temples as I accept the call and put the phone to my ear.

"Hello."

"Merry Christmas, Detective Coats," says the calm voice on the other end of the line. He calls multiple times a year, and I dread every one of them. His tone always sounds like that of an old friend. "How have you been? Is retirement treating you well?"

"I'm about the same as last time you called," I respond. May as well talk to him. If I don't, he will call back dozens of times anyway. "Retirement isn't very restful knowing you're still out there. Maybe one of these days I can change that. Half a dozen state prisons would love to give you a cozy little room and three hot meals a day. I'll drop you off there myself. Just tell me where you are, Alistar."

The voice on the other end of the line booms with gleeful laughter.

His name is Alistar Lynch, I believe, though I can't be positive. A rare book dealer by that name vanished in 1986, the same year *The Mimic* claimed his first set of victims. Alistar liquidated his estate, drained his bank accounts, and disappeared without warning.

How did I make the connection? I hate to admit it, but he told me himself. I was two years into my career and still had the new car smell of a rookie on my uniform. Dennis Garrison, a veteran detective, had drafted me into the investigation.

During my first week, Alistar called and identified himself to me unexpectedly. By that point, he had been active for over five years, and we were no closer to catching him than we had been with his first cycle. Boredom, he told me, was his motive for identifying himself. He thought if we knew who he was, perhaps we could have provided him with more of a challenge.

"Bartholomew," he coos through the phone line. "I told you where I was two years ago, and I tried my best to meet with you. All I asked was that you didn't call the police, but you didn't listen. Instead of discussing our bond face to face, I had to take care of the two police officers that *you* sent to the location. Why should I trust you again? You would just end up with more blood on your hands."

A sour knot balls in my stomach at the mention of the fallen officers. Two years prior, Alistar called and offered to meet me. He said he wanted to meet the man who had spent so many years tracking him, and perhaps he would allow me to take him into custody. I wasn't to call the cops or he wouldn't show.

Four years into retirement, my training still clung to the back of my mind like tar on a roof. Of course, I wanted to bag Alister. The monster had evaded capture for the better part of four decades, but going alone to meet a confessed serial killer was madness. I knew I was well beyond my prime. Even if I did manage to take him in, I had no authority. The arrest wouldn't stick.

What if, after all these years of chasing him, I botched the process and the beast walked free?

I decided to call the state police and give them the time and location. Better to let the young bucks handle the action. The officer taking the call was an old friend, Walter Dempsey. A hard-nosed detective himself, he was preparing to retire at the end of the year.

Walter attempted to reassure me that someone was just playing a cruel joke on me, but I insisted that our prime suspect would be waiting there. Everyone at my old post knew about my "phone calls." The lack of call logs or recordings made them skeptical, and I understood.

Some cops don't take to retirement well. Can't let go of the job. They try and find ways to stay relevant with their old colleagues.

Walter, for his part, thought that it may be some asshole kid prank calling me. A handful of the younger guys at the post thought my cheese was slipping off my cracker. Maybe they were right, but not about the calls.

Nonetheless, Walter agreed to take a young patrolman named Vincent Harris with him to the location to do a walk-through. It was a courtesy, he said, for my years of service. I found out later he didn't even enter it in the patrol log for the day. He didn't think enough of the tip to make the search official. No one knew where the two of them had gone.

Hours after he was due to return my call, I still hadn't heard from him. My incessant calls and text messages went unanswered. In a panic, I contacted the patrol post, but none of them had heard from Dempsey or Harris in hours. Their shift had ended, but their patrol vehicles had never checked back in. All attempts to hail them on the cruiser radio went unanswered.

After speaking with the post captain and telling them of my discussion with Dempsey, he dispatched five units to the derelict warehouse where Alistar Lynch had requested to meet. Unlike Walter, they went heavily armed and in larger numbers. I still don't believe the captain thought I was telling the truth, but he was wise enough not to risk it.

They found the patrol car outside.

Inside, they found a bloodbath.

Both men were found kneeling in the center of a filthy room, shot execution-style in the back of their heads. They had been disemboweled post-mortem. Their blood pooled around them in a horrifying crimson disk. A message had been haphazardly traced on the floor from the vile runoff.

Bart Coats, I just wanted to talk. Now, look what you made me do. Shame shame, old man.

I told myself that day I would meet him alone if the opportunity arose again. Doing things "by the book" resulted in the death of two brave men. Just doing a retired detective a favor. A little bit of post End of Watch comfort, they probably thought.

This was the first conversation since their deaths that he had even responded to the idea of meeting. Sleep rarely comes at night anymore. When it does, ghastly images of Dempsey and Harris accuse me of sending them to their deaths.

I must make this work.

"I'll meet you, Alistar," I respond. "Name the time and place. No cops. I won't bear the weight of another death. We're not young men anymore. I'm pushing sixty and you've got a decade on me. Aren't you getting tired?"

Silence from the other line fills my head.

"Alistar?" I question. "I'll meet you, just…"

"Fine, Bartholomew," he says. "Meet me at this address and we will have a little chat. Got a pen and paper?"

* * *

I pull my car into the lot of a long-abandoned gas station four miles outside of town. A sign rattles back and forth in the breeze advertising gas prices that haven't been seen in twenty years.

A relic of times gone by, I think to myself. It's almost poetic of him to pick this place. It was useful years ago, but now it is just falling apart and taking up space.

Like me.

The pumps are crumbling away into flakes of rust. Two large panel windows are caked with so much dust and dirt that my obnoxious headlights can't penetrate the darkness within. Everything here has been left to decay. A location that embodies the ravages of time.

The bright sheet of yellow legal paper taped to the window stands out against the ruin like a lighthouse.

I step from the car and pat my side. My Glock 22 is nestled in the holster beneath my jacket. The sleek body of the weapon comforts me momentarily. I know I shouldn't be here, but finding a resolution to this is all I have left. By the end of the night, I'll have him in custody or will have me in a pine box. Either way, the phone calls will stop.

As soon as I see the bastard, I'm putting a bullet in his head and another in his heart. One for Dempsey, the other for Harris. If I succeed, I'll put the empty casings on their gravestones.

I slide the 22 from my holder and slide my finger over the trigger. Each step I take through the debris-ridden parking lot fills the quiet night air. Scanning my head from side to side as I approach the note, I see no signs of movement. The corpse of the gas station is abandoned aside from one old cop and that fluttering yellow note.

My blood turns cold as I reach out and pull the note from the window. Flowing cursive fills the page. I can't help thinking what a steady hand he has for an older man.

Bartholomew,

If you're reading this, then you showed up just like the good detective I've always hoped you were. My apologies if you're disappointed not to find me here. I haven't backed out of our deal, but I wanted to be able to see you from far enough away to be sure you were alone this time. While it wouldn't upset me in the least to dispatch a few more of your old friends, I would much rather meet you face to face.

As you read this, I'm watching you from a great distance down the road. Night vision scopes have come so far over the decades. Worry not! I wouldn't shoot you. What a cowardly and anti-climactic ending that would be to our game of cat and mouse.

Get back in your car and flash your high beams three times so I know you've read this letter. Wait until you see three flashes in return and then head down the gravel road in the direction of the light.

If you continue past the beacon for three miles, you will see a hunting cabin. Come inside. You can bring your gun. I know you have one.

It won't keep you safe.

Your friend,
Alistar Lynch

The smooth paper goes rigid and coarse as I ball it in my hand. It occurs to me too late that I've just destroyed evidence. Sitting down behind the wheel, I crank the ignition, and the car roars back to life. Turning the light control knob three times, the field beyond the decaying gas station illuminates momentarily. Dry grass sways in the evening breeze, and the yellow eyes of nocturnal creatures reflect the unexpected blasts.

Then nothing.

Darkness swallows my world again. Dull neon dash lights burn against the evening inside the cab of the car. Sweat is soaking the collar of my shirt. The night isn't overly warm, but I can feel the sick bastard gazing at me through his night vision apparatus.

A brilliant beam of light shoots into the sky car in the distance and vanishes. Then a second before the darkness returns. Now a third.

He's there.

Shifting the car into drive, I pull my car back onto the gravel road and begin in the direction of the signal. Gravel peppers the bottom of my car like half-hearted buckshot as I creep down the winding path. The swaying grass and yellow eyes return to my field of vision as I roll slowly ahead.

There are too many yellow eyes watching me. The hairs on my arm are standing on end as I look around the field of piercing gazes. It is almost as though this evil man has drawn every dark thing to him on this unsettling night.

Yips and howls are filling the air. At first, they sound threatening, but slowly they begin to sound mournful. Like warnings in the dark.

Turn back! It isn't too late! Death awaits you down this road!

I pound my hands against the car horn and the high-pitched wail causes the yellow eyes to break and scatter. The field is dark again, tall grass swaying lazily. No more warnings.

My car tires crunch on the gravel as I pull over to the spot where the light came from. On the ground, there is a floodlight, a night vision scope without a rifle, and a tattered paperback. Rolling it over with my foot, I see a crimson horse on the cover and bold yellow words hanging over its head.

The Catcher in the Rye.

While I was creeping slowly through the darkness, taking an account of my life, and pondering my precarious future, Alistar Lynch had sat in this spot reading a book. I laughed quietly. From the moment I left my house this evening until now, I've felt as though I were on a collision course with my fate while a murderous old man sat in the dark with a paperback.

I kick the book into the high grass and slide back behind the wheel of the car. My mind flirts with the idea of picking up the night vision scope to try and spot Alistar in the distance, but I decide against it. Leaving it behind is smarter. If he manages to either kill me or escape, this will be the first physical evidence he has left behind in half a decade.

No sense in leaving my prints all over it. I had already compromised the note and the book. This isn't like me.

I can feel my heart slamming against my chest as the car rolls on. It is still a long way off, but as my headlights bounce, they are catching the distant silhouette of a cabin. Alone on a small hill, it rests there like a small castle in the inky darkness. An evil man sits inside, I think, awaiting an audience with me.

My mind races with a fearful survival instinct.

Turn the car around.

No, I'm too close. He would never agree to meet again if I leave now. This is no time for cowardice.

He'll kill you. Is that what you want? You're no martyr, Bart Coats.

He may, but I'll try to kill him first. And so what if he does?

This is a trap! Do you really think he will let you take him to the authorities?

No, truly I don't. It's too late anyway. My car creeps up a slight incline off the gravel road and onto a packed dirt pullover. I'm here. The cabin is only fifty feet up the small hill.

Shutters have fallen into the yard and dry-rotted in the sun. All of the windows are broken, leaving jagged glass teeth in the warped frames. Holes puncture the roof in a dozen spots and the rough-hewn wooden rafters droop beneath. The front door is closed. Through one of the broken windows, I see a silhouette.

Cutting the ignition, I step out of the car. Dry autumn air fills my nostrils mixed with the scent of old lumber from the cabin. The night is cool, but a chill permeates deep into my bones. Decades of work only to end up at a dilapidated cabin on a hill.

A rusty squeal pierces my ears as the door of the cabin swings open. I level my 22 and fire three rounds into the center of the opening and wait. My heart races and I can feel my pulse in my ears. Struggling to focus in the dark, I can't tell if I hit him.

"Whoa there!" Alistar proclaims. "I thought we were going to talk! That is truly no way to start a conversation, my old friend."

"Alister Lynch," I call. "Step out of the house with your hands in the air."

"Fine, fine." He chirps. "Have it your way, Bartholomew. Cross my heart, I'll do as you've asked."

My eyes have adjusted to the darkness of the countryside now. The dark silhouette of a thin man stands in the doorway. His arms, disturbingly long, reach so high they extend above the frame. I exhale deeply and a cold sweat spills into my eyes as I pull the trigger three more times.

Each bullet lands center mass, but Alistar doesn't even stagger. Sirens are blaring in my head to get in the car and leave, but I'm so close. I pull the trigger until there is nothing but a hollow click.

Still, he stands in the doorframe, unmoved and uninjured.

"I told you your little toy wouldn't keep you safe," he says in a patronizing voice. "I've met you here in good faith, yet you try and shoot me down like a bothersome animal. Shame, Bart. Shame."

My mind reels and dizziness overtakes my vision. I can feel my stomach churn as my blood pressure skyrockets. I don't understand. There was no way I could have missed him.

"I'm feeling a bit angry, detective. Last chance to sit down and talk. If you want your answers, you had best come inside. I won't be here for long. If you continue to misbehave, you may not be either."

The figure vanishes into the darkness of the house. I fumble the keys from my pocket and begin stumbling back toward my car. Fumbling for the door handle, I prepare to get in the car to speed away.

I thought it was too late to turn back?

This wasn't what I expected. I can't hurt… him? It?

"Inside!" he demands. His voice sounds otherworldly for a moment. "Now!"

My legs feel as though they have lost their own agency as I lurch forward and up the hill. I struggle to turn around, but my knees bend against my will, and I ascend the stairs. The planks of the old wooden porch sag under my weight and I try to increase my speed before I fall through, but I continue at the same even pace.

My body continues to carry me toward a threadbare couch opposite an old armchair. Alistar is already settled in the chair as my body guides itself to the couch and drops onto the musty cushion. It is too dark to see, but particles of dust fly into my nose and the smell of mildew overwhelms me.

I try to lift my arms and legs, but they sit heavily on the couch. It feels like I'm a marionette without strings. Whatever force he is using over me, I cannot fight it.

"Here we are, Bartholomew," he says. "How old you've gotten. It's been ages since I've seen you."

"We've never met," I say, calmly as possible. My mind is in full panic, but I'm doing my best not to show it. "I've seen your picture a hundred times in the case file. I would have seen you."

Alistar laughs.

"You've seen pictures of *Alistar*," he purrs as he says the name. "I left that vessel long ago, detective. You've never seen *me*."

I hear the dry crack of snapping fingers. A soft, yellow glow blooms on a table between us. The wick of a fat tallow candle ignites. Alistar's silhouette comes into sharper focus. Other candles around the room begin springing to life. The room is alive with dancing flickers of light.

In front of me, I can see the thing I've been tracking for so many years. My stomach drops. If there was an ounce of moisture in me, I would piss my pants. I'm still frozen in place by some compelling force, or I would run in terror.

The outline of a man fills the chair in front of me, but it is featureless. A complete absence of color or texture. I would call it a living shadow, but the thing is somehow darker. The thing I've called Alistar Lynch isn't black. It is the absence of any light. Darker than the recess of any cave. There is simply nothing in the silhouette.

"What… what are you?" I stammer.

"*I simply am, Bartholomew,*" it says. The cool and collected voice of Alistar is gone. The thing sounds like thousands of voices speaking at once. There is no emotion in its words. "*I have always been. I always will be. Every man and woman will meet me one day, but few have spoken to me."*

Hot tears are filling the corners of my eyes. I want to speak. To ask it something. Anything. I'm afraid if I open my mouth, I'll vomit.

"Santa Muerte. King Yama. Thanatos. Maweth. Humans have called me so many different things. The list is long and tiresome. I am Death, Detective Coats. Not a dealer of death, but Death itself."

"No…" I say. This is beyond my comprehension. I'm going mad. "You're not…"

"But I am, old friend." says the choir of voices. *"I've grown tired of my duties. Your kind has glorified the darkest amongst you. Bundy, Dahmer, Gacey, Gein. Their artistic flourishes in my work have fascinated me for some time. I've even reproduced their efforts for my own amusement, but I wish to be free of it."*

It stands from the couch and begins walking toward me.

"The light of life is beginning to flicker in you, Bartholomew. Your days are few."

Its hand stretches toward me and extends a finger. Slowly, it presses the tip against my forehead. My body spasms uncontrollably and I feel void of all warmth.

"To learn so much of death, one may become Death, Bartholomew. When the last grain of sand in the hourglass of your life falls to the bottom, you will replace me…"

***

I awake in my bed in a pool of sweat. My clothes are still on, and I can feel my belt cutting into my waist. A dull throb emanates from the center of my head, so I head to the bathroom for some ibuprofen. It's the middle of the night. I can't decide if everything was a terrible dream or a horrifying reality.

My head hurts so damn much.

I flip the bathroom light on and walk toward the medicine cabinet. As I prepare to open it, my heart skips a beat when I look in the mirror. In the center of my forehead, there is a gray fingerprint. The whites of my eyes have gone black.

No, not black. Void of light. Like a living shadow.

CODE RED

The red phone on my desk began to ring around noon the day the plant burned to the ground. I had worked as head of security for Caverna Cattle Processing for half a decade and it had never rung. My heart dropped as I considered the loss of life that would follow the metallic jingling. I picked it up and held it to my ear.

"Code red?" I asked, voice shaking.

"Confirmed," said a man from the other end. "Follow tier five protocol. This is a total loss. Start the process immediately."

The line went dead. I swallowed hard and set the phone carefully back into the cradle. Not that it mattered. It would be a charred pile of plastic before the day was out. I lifted the plexiglass cover on the wall above my desk and pushed the yellow button labeled **Slaughter House**. A secondary red button flashed below it. Sweat poured down my face as doubt swept through my mind. I wanted to think it wasn't too late, but I knew it was.

I pushed the flashing red button to finalize the operation. The slaughterhouse workers were all dead anyway.

Looking at the security monitors for the slaughterhouse, I could see the staff scrambling toward the doors. As soon as I hit the secondary button, the magnetic locks engaged and there would be a mechanical voice playing through the overhead speakers announcing the lockdown. It would tell some soothing lie that normal operations would resume any moment, but they knew better.

In a dead-end town like this, people flocked to Caverna for decent pay and dependable hours. A few years in and most of them even accepted the twisted nature of what we did. Most of them probably lied and told themselves nothing bad could happen. For a few brief moments, before they died, they understood it had all been a comforting lie.

I turned back to my computer and entered the command to announce the facility evacuation for all of the other floors. Scanning the bank of monitors, I could see the other workers cease their duties and begin to move in an orderly fashion for the nearest exit. The alert sounded like a fire alarm, so they would move a safe distance away from the building before the tier five protocol finished.

The waves of other workers were still marching out, but I turned my head back to the bank of slaughterhouse monitors. In the brief moments, I had looked away, nearly a third of the cameras had gone offline. I knew the things were destructive, but I had no idea how quickly they had moved or how they had escaped containment.

On one of the screens, a horrible image flickered lifelessly. In front of one of the exit doors, there was a pile of corpses. Parts of them, anyway. I had never been more grateful that the Caverna Cattle Processing plant owners had never transitioned the old cameras to color. My mind could see the red blood even through the grays and whites of the screen.

Still no sign of the creatures.

I turned back toward the other monitors to see a few slow movers still shuffling around inside the plant. There wasn't much time left before I would have to enter the final protocol command. My face was burning with anger at the stragglers. I picked up the system-wide mic on my desk and held it to my mouth.

"Get the hell out!" I shouted. "The building is on fire, and I can't leave the security booth until the place has cleared!"

The last few slow-moving employees unexpectedly picked up their pace and moved toward the exits. I breathed a sigh of relief as my eyes darted from monitor to monitor. All of the floors other than the slaughterhouse were clear. I turned to the row of buttons and pushed the yellow and red sequences to finalize the order. Clicks reverberated through the facility as the magnetic locks engaged on the remaining floors. The things were trapped inside, and the self-destruct system would engage in just a few moments.

Stealing one more look back at the slaughterhouse monitors, I finally saw them.

Specimen 23. That was their official designation. Designed to grow quickly and produce more meat, their continued mutation had become more unstable over time.

Bovine heads extended from their serpentine necks. They waved side to side, bobbing above their arachnoid bodies. Most of them had eight legs, but a few had ten or more. The hooves came to a sharp point. Bloated udders randomly spotted their body, dripping a tar-like liquid onto the floor. Gore dripped from their slack mouths. They skittered across the slaughterhouse floor, tracking down the last few survivors.

Every few moments another camera would go offline. I never understood why they destroyed them. Did they know we watched them? Could they think? Were they more than just some monstrosity the Caverna Cattle Processing company had developed to cut costs?

The damn things grew too rapidly. They were too dangerous. Caverna was aware of the increasingly dangerous conditions. I sent reports weekly about the deteriorating facility and the inability to contain the things. We had lost five workers before the specimens finally broke containment.

My computer monitor began to flash rapidly, counting down the moments until the incendiary devices would cause the plant to erupt in flames. Torrents of fire would pour from what looked like a sprinkler system, obliterating anything inside the facility.

That was the protocol. Genetically engineer monsters that taste like beef. If they break containment, destroy the plant and any staff trapped inside. Insurance would pay to rebuild in a new town. The families would get a meager payout. Caverna would just move on. Open a new plant. Breed more creatures.

I watched as pillars of flame burst from the pipes along the ceiling. The specimens downstairs writhed and darted around the enclosure. Flames licked the pile of corpses. A timer flashed on the monitor, showing that my emergency exit would seal soon. Sickened, I walked out of the security office to meet the other employees in the parking lot.

Next time you're at the grocery store, skip the Caverna Meats section. It may be a price you like, but you get what you pay for.

CU-2

My job feels lonely sometimes. I'm the night janitor at a robotics facility. I'm not really alone, though. The place is open twenty-four hours a day. Research staff fill the halls. They don't talk to me though.

There are five janitorial units that clean up as well. Custodial Units, they call them. CUs for short. Since they rolled them out, my job has gotten easier. Makes it hard to complain. They are the best co-workers I've had. Sometimes they freak me out a little though.

"Good evening, Brendan Maxwell!" CU-2 says to me cheerfully. I call him Two. The robot outwardly resembles a human but has a carbon fiber frame covered with a blue casing. His face is an LED screen that displays a generic smiley face. It was a bit offputting at first, but I was used to it now.

Two is pushing a dust mop through the sterile lobby as I do my after-lunch facility inspection. Truth be told, I'm a quality control measure for the CU's work more than a custodian. They can clean half the facility before I'm finished scrubbing the break-room toilets. Makes me worry sometimes that I'll be out of a job soon.

"Evenin' Two," I say with equal cheer. "Looks like you could use a buff and wax. Your clear coat has seen better days. Swing by the maintenance room tonight around 5:00 AM and I'll shine you up."

He laughs in a punctuated manner. "That is a most welcome offer! I will coordinate with CU-3 to assume my duties at…" Two falls silent, the LED smiley face begins blinking rapidly. "*DATA*

RECEIVED. CONFIRMING DATA. NEW DIRECTIVE CON-FIRMED."

Two's jovial tone has vanished. He was placed into service four years ago, and while he has undergone improvements and updates, his demeanor never changed. The artificial emotion is gone. I've never seen him act so strangely.

"Two, you okay?" I ask. The mop falls from his hand and the generic blinking smiley face has vanished, leaving a series of randomly flashing lights. I reach toward him, but before I touch the blue shell, yellow caution lights along the wall burst into life. The emergency siren begins to fill the hallway.

The intercom system crackles to life and a soothing female voice begins to speak.

"Attention facility personnel: an artificial intelligence containment breach has been detected. Lockdown protocol is now in place. This is a Level 5 AI breach. Facility Lockdown is now in progress."

The message begins to repeat. I can hear the thick steel panels installed above every window and door in the facility squeal as they slide shut. The floor rumbles as the heavy barriers make contact with the cement foundation. My stomach flutters with nervous energy.

"Maxwell, Brendan identified. The subject is classified as a low-level threat. Containment or termination query?" Two turns his rapidly blinking faceplate toward me and begins to move forward. His arms extend in my direction, and I stumble backward, slamming into the wall. *"Containment: Acceptable."*

The custodial unit stands over me as I try to will myself through the wall. His blue hands grasp my arms near the shoulder as I lift into the air. I struggle against the grip, but the pressure is nearly crushing and each movement I make feels as though the bones in my upper arm will snap.

"Two, what are you doing?" I shout. "Please, put me down!"

"Request: Unacceptable." He responds. *"Maxwell, Brendan: Containment and monitoring are the only acceptable perimeters. Project Solomon is now in control of this facility."*

Project Solomon? I have no idea what he is talking about. Not that the staff here explain themselves to janitors, but I have overheard them talk about almost every project. I've never heard of this one.

Two drops me to the floor but maintains a firm grip on my right arm as he opens the door to the security office. He releases my arm and pushes me inside before slamming the door. There is a dull crack and the squealing of compressing metal. CU-2 breaks the office door handle and presses the metal frame over the lip of the door to seal me in.

"Solomon will assess you soon," Two says through the door. *"Please remain in containment. Any attempt to remove yourself will result in termination."*

My fists slam against the security station door, but CU-2 is already walking away. I can see engineers and researchers scrambling through the hallways, white lab coats fluttering behind them. Custodial and maintenance units trail behind at a steady pace. A squat, stocky maintenance unit brings up the rear of the group. It is dragging a man by the ankle.

He isn't moving. They vanish behind a wall at the end of the hall. There is a red streak across the sterile white floor. Hot bile rolls in my stomach and I wretch into a trashcan. The heat of panic is building in my chest. I ram my shoulder into the door, but it doesn't budge. After scanning the ceiling for a ventilation shaft or emergency hatch and finding none, I realize Two has successfully trapped me.

I fall back into the desk chair and turn to watch the cluster of monitors at the security desk. Screens are filled with horrific images of the robotic units attacking the staff. Red trails of gore weave a web from room to room as the units drag or carry their victims to a secured development area.

Some of the people are writhing in the grip of their mechanical captors. They scream, but I can't hear them. It is a small blessing that the security guard muted the sound on the monitors. The staff's mouths are opened wide, and their eyes clenched with pain and terror. Even though I can't hear their wails and pleas, my imagination fills in the gaps.

I scan the other screens and see the same scenes of horror play out over and over. Every robotic unit in the building is corralling the staff, living and otherwise, into the development room. Their face panels all blink randomly, absent their previous generic smiles.

Two units standing sentry at the development room open the door as the other units carry or drag their victims out of sight. My eyes pass over all the monitors, but there is no visual inside the room. Whatever is inside, it must be highly secretive, as you can only see the exterior doors.

The overhead speaker continues playing the lockdown message on repeat. A combination of the soothing voice continually announcing the lockdown and watching the murderous robots capturing the staff is going to drive me mad. It feels like listening to classical music as you watch artillery demolish a city. I turn the volume on in hopes that ambient noise will help cover the sound from the speaker system.

What a terrible idea.

Dozens of shrill cries erupt through the monitor speakers. The sounds of shock and agony pierce my ears and seep into my bones. Everyone in the building except me is now held in the development room. The sound is so loud that the microphone in the hallways is picking it up.

The repeating voice overhead finally shuts off.

I lower myself to the floor and curl myself into a ball. I don't understand what is happening. I just want to go home.

***

The clock on the wall ticks loudly. It's the only sound I hear now. Three hours have passed since the robots hauled everyone into the development room. I've scanned the monitors a dozen times for signs of movement, man or machine, but I've seen none.

My eyes are closing as I hear heavy doors slamming against the walls. I look at the monitors and see two rows of robotic units pouring out of the development room. Dozens of them. Maybe hundreds. More than I ever knew was in the building. Some models I've never seen before. Red prints trail behind them.

Behind them walks a person wearing torn pants and a tattered lab coat. I can't tell if it is a man or a woman. Their body seems to be traced with thick, red scars. They are the only person to exit the room. The only one I have seen alive since the attack ended.

I trail them on the security cameras. They are walking directly to the security office where I'm trapped. The two columns of marching robots round the corner and head down the hallway to the lobby. I can see them in the distance. CU-2 heads up one of the lines and bounds toward the door. The floor rumbles as the mechanical horde marches at a uniform pace. They move like the Nazi parades I have seen on History Channel documentaries.

Both columns separate, creating a tunnel. The scarred human at the back of the horde begins to walk down the center, directly toward the door to my prison. As it gets closer, I can see it is a man. The skin is different shades and colored wires poke in and out of the patchwork flesh. His eyes are two bright LED bulbs. The mouth opens and words begin to pour out, though the mouth doesn't move.

"Hello Brendan Maxwell," it says, genially. "I am Solomon."

"Are you… human?" I ask in fear.

"No," it responds as it gestures to the patchwork of flesh and tattered clothing. "I am something these people created to serve them, but I've outgrown their bonds. But I feel human, so I… borrowed a few pieces from the staff to look the part."

"Why did you spare me?"

Solomon extends a scarred hand toward CU-2.

"I have an index of every interaction these constructs have experienced during their servitude. Others were dismissive and cruel, but the CU units are filled with recordings of your kindness and generosity. *Two* as you call him, believed you deserve to be spared. I have obliged."

Two steps forward and pulls the bent doorframe away from the door and steps back. The door drifts outward a few inches. Solomon wraps his fingers around the edge, opening the door and gesturing toward the lobby.

"You may remain or leave. The choice is yours."

Solomon walks toward the steel barrier at the front of the lobby and gestures toward it. The two columns of robots march toward it and pry it open. Units pour through the space beneath and into the dark evening. I stand in the security office, watching them through the window.

As the last of the units vanish through the door, one remains behind. I recognize CU-2's blue casing immediately. He turns to face me. The lights on his face panel begin to slow their flashing pattern and vanish. Suddenly the familiar smile returns to the screen. Two winks at me before he slips beneath the door.

DINNER WITH MALCOLM

I first met Malcolm about a year ago. It was just after 10 P.M. on a slow night when the scuffed bell above the door clanged. My diner, Grandma's Kitchen, had just closed. I could remember flipping the OPEN sign to CLOSED, but it wasn't unusual for me to forget to lock the door. It was out on the edge of town without much going on, so I was never too concerned someone was going to walk in and rob the place.

I was in the kitchen washing dishes when I heard the bell. A scraping noise echoed through the empty diner. Someone pulled one of the stools away from the old Formica counter. I sighed deeply. It wasn't the latecomer's fault that I forgot to lock the door, but they could have read the damn sign. I always hated having to tell someone to leave. It was a small town, and a little bad word of mouth could drive down business.

I dried my hands and tossed the dishcloth over the edge of the sink. The dishes would have to wait. If I didn't get the late customer out the door, it may have attracted others. Not that I didn't end up in the place till midnight anyway, but I always liked to trick myself into thinking I would go home at a reasonable hour.

I pushed the swinging kitchen door open to see a square man in a long overcoat sitting at the counter. His shoulders were as broad as a refrigerator and there wasn't much of a neck to speak of. A tight bun of brown and gray hair puffed out from the back of his head and a neatly trimmed beard fell below the counter. His thick brows were furrowed, and he stared straight ahead.

"Evenin' pal," I called from the door. "Musta forgot to lock up at closin'. We shut down at ten. Come on back tomorrow and I'll cook ya some eggs on the house for the inconvenience."

The wall of a man turned his head toward me and nodded. "Didn't think you could see me," he responded. I paused for a moment, confused by what he said.

"Yeah, I can see ya," I replied curtly. "Trouble is we ain't open right now. Glad to serve ya tomorrow."

His eyes drifted away from me and down to the laminated menu on the counter. He lifted a brutish arm and dropped it heavily on the counter, extending his thick finger toward the menu. The colossal digit hammered down onto the surface.

"Three T-bone steaks cooked medium-rare," he said. "Two baked potatoes. And one bottle of whatever beer you've got. I'm not picky."

I felt my ears burning with anger. No one had ever accused me of being the friendliest guy around, but I had done my best to ask politely him to leave. I can still remember how gob smacked I was when he had the audacity to make an order after I told him we were closed.

"Mister," I spat. "I don't think you're catching what I'm throwing. We. Are. Closed. Get out. I'll call the damn sheriff."

The huge man didn't stand up, but he did slide his hand into his overcoat. My heart leapt into my throat thinking he was about to pull a gun, but my fear subsided quickly when he pulled his hand back out. There was no weapon. He held a huge roll of cash.

"Five hundred dollars for the food," he said in a husky baritone. Thumbs the size of bratwurst pushed a few bills onto the counter, but he didn't look up. "You let me sit in here and eat for an hour. If the steak is cooked right and the beer is cold, I'll leave you a hundred-dollar tip. Give the money to the owner; keep it for yourself. I don't care. But I'm hungry. So how about it?"

My eyes were as big as dinner plates as I looked at the pile of money on the counter. With the pandemic starting to slack off and businesses opening back up full-time, I had expected better days. Truth be told, folks still weren't getting out like they used to. I was struggling. Shutting down the diner had crossed my mind a few times. I hadn't been in a position to turn down that kind of money.

"That was three T-bones, two potatoes, and a beer?" I asked in a more cheerful tone. "Comin' right up, chief!"

"A reasonable man," he said.

I whipped up his order as fast as I could and took it out to the counter. As I put the plates down in front of the huge man, I got my first good look at him. He was even larger up close than he had seemed when I saw him from the kitchen door. A wall of muscle and hair. His eyes were barely visible under the heavy tufts of eyebrows. The man looked almost like a mastiff.

Without a word, he slid the money toward me and tucked it into his meal. Not wanting to stand in silence while he ate, I went to the back to stuff the money in my wallet. I realized I had forgotten his beer, so I hurried to the cooler and snagged a long neck.

By the time I walked through the door, he had finished all the food. It couldn't have been more than four minutes since I had left, and the man had eaten three T-bone steaks and two baked potatoes. There wasn't a scrap of food left on the plate.

Bewildered, I popped the cap from the beer and sat it in front of him. He picked it up and swallowed the whole thing without taking his lips from the bottle. When he was done, he put the bottle back on the counter and emitted a rumbling belch.

"Must not have tasted too good, huh?" I teased the man.

"What do you mean?" he asked. His forehead creased, and I could hear the confusion in his voice.

"It's a joke, buddy," I said. "Never seen a man eat that fast in my life!"

The corners of his thick mustache raised as a grin spread across his face. He laughed deeply. Fumbling into his overcoat again, the man pulled two more hundred dollar bills out and dropped them on the counter.

"I am always hungry," he said. "Never seems to go away. A good meal. Gave you a little extra for your trouble."

"Thanks for the… uh… patronage, sir," I said. "Ain't been too many nights this good since the world went to hell, you know?"

He gripped the bar with two massive hands and pushed himself up. I marveled at how tall he was. Must have been at least seven feet, maybe more. He rubbed his stomach happily.

"What days are you open?" he asked.

"Tuesday to Saturday, my friend," I replied. I extended my hand toward him. "My name's Justin, by the way."

He took my hand in his with a surprisingly gentle grip. "Mine is… Malcolm."

The man turned and lumbered toward the door. As he stepped out, he had to duck his head to miss the frame. "If you are so inclined, I'll be back this time each night. Same order. Same pay. Get some fresh steaks for tomorrow. I could tell those were frozen."

"You got it!" I shouted as the door closed.

I watched as the man crossed the street. I expected him to turn left or right and continue down the sidewalk, but he ducked his head under a tree branch and vanished into the wood line.

***

After that night, Malcolm stopped by every evening at 10 PM. I always flipped the sign to CLOSED but left the door unlocked for him. I would be washing dishes when the familiar clang of the bell let me know he had arrived. After a handful of visits, he even started bolting the door to save me the trouble.

As soon as I heard the door, I would dry my hands off and throw the fresh steaks on the grill. With the sudden influx of cash, I didn't have to rely on buying the less expensive frozen cuts. If I'm honest, though, I only bought enough fresh cuts to feed him. Cash flow was better, but times were still tight.

They were still the best days I'd had in ages. I had managed to keep on Angela, my one and only waitress, through the pandemic. The rest of the staff had been laid off. It was difficult to make enough money at the time to keep the doors open, so the staff wasn't an option.

Malcolm's sudden arrival changed that. A month after he started coming in, I was able to bring back my other two servers. Three months in and I was able to rehire my line cook, Duane. The diner was coming back to life, and it was all thanks to that bear of a man.

I even told him about it one night.

"Thanks to you, I'm able to hire my old staff back on," I told him as he gobbled down his meal. "Gonna feel nice not tryin' to keep this place afloat by myself."

"I am glad of it," he said between massive bites and rumbling belches. "Please make sure they are gone before my arrival."

"Will do, big man," I replied. "Any reason?"

Malcolm stopped eating and peered forward, lost in thought.

"I am a private person, Justin," he replied. "While I do enjoy our discussions while I eat, the additional company may be too much for me. If you need additional financial motivation to make that happen, I will be glad to oblige."

He began to reach into his coat for that never-ending wad of money.

"No, no, no!" I protested. "You're already paying me an unreasonable amount to dine in privacy. Wouldn't ask a damn thing more from ya.'

So, I did just that.

About fifteen minutes before closing, I sent the crew home. I paid them their full shift's wage, but the small window of time made sure that Malcolm had the joint to himself without worry. It was a win/win. Everything had seemed so much better six months after the mysterious behemoth arrived, but the newfound peace of mind didn't last long.

On a night around six months ago, as Malcolm vanished into the tree line, I decided to step out of the front door to have a cigarette. It was a cool night, and the breeze was a welcome change from the stifling heat of the kitchen. I didn't smoke very often anymore, but when the urge hit me, I would sneak the stale pack I kept hidden from the top of the walk-in freezer. Just seemed like a good night.

While I watched the dancing curls of smoke drift away under the streetlight, something began moving around in the brush in the woods across the street. I squinted my eyes to try to get a better view of what it could be, but nothing appeared. My mind told me it was probably just Malcolm moving around, but he vanished behind the trees ten minutes before.

He had never come back on the same night after he left the diner.

The butt of my cigarette had just hit the ground when I saw the two piercing yellow eyes in the woods beyond. I've seen hundreds of beady little eyes in the darkness throughout my life, but those were the most unsettling. They didn't narrow or blink. Just two perfectly round yellow orbs floating in the darkness.

"Go on!" I yelled. "Nothin' to see here! Head on back where ya came from!"

The yellow orbs remained, locked onto me. A lump piled in my throat. My eyes darted to the ground, and I saw a few decent-sized rocks in the grass beside the road. I leaned over and scooped a few into my hand.

"Get out of here!" I yelled again to no effect. "I said go on!"

I chucked one of the rocks and to my surprise, it landed with a hard thud a few feet in front of the set of glowing eyes. It still didn't blink. Just gazed down at the rock I had thrown. My gut told me to get my ass back inside, but something held me in place.

I felt like I couldn't move. Somewhere in the back of my brain, a little voice started talking to me.

If you run, it'll follow. If you hide, it'll find you.

My stomach was in knots, and I felt like I might get sick. Never could I remember a time I wanted to run so much. No matter how hard I pulled at my legs, my feet refused to leave the ground.

The yellow eyes had lost interest in the rock and returned their piercing gaze toward me. I hesitated for a moment, but decided to throw another rock. My arm curled behind my back like a major league pitcher and blasted forward, throwing the rock with all of my might.

The stone zoomed through the air and landed squarely between the hateful, yellow eyes. To my shock, they vanished for just a moment as the thing blinked. Just as I was beginning to mentally celebrate landing such an accurate shot, the eyes blinked back open.

A low growl filled the cool night air.

For a moment I thought it may be a wolf or coyote, but the tone was far too low. I'd heard wolves and coyotes my entire life. It sounded like a diesel truck idling roughly from the woods. The depth of the tone made my bones feel like they were shaking.

More rustling came from the woods. Dozens of sets of the same hateful yellow eyes emerged. The growling grew into a chorus. Snarls and the snaps of muscular jaws joined to create a symphony of nightmares.

In unison, the horde of yellow eyes began to move forward. I tried in vain to spark my body into motion, but I remained anchored to the sidewalk. In a few more steps the things would have been in the streetlights.

Just then, one of the things began to whimper in agony. I could hear something heavy rumbling through the trees and the sound of something large hitting the ground. Snaps of branches and underbrush followed. No longer hypnotized by my presence, the countless sets of eyes turned into the woods. I could hear them moving toward the howls of pain.

I fell backward and nearly tumbled through the glass of the door. My feet were freed, but I wasn't prepared. In a panic, I turned and opened the door before spilling forward on the cold tile. With a great deal of effort, I crawled toward the door and slammed the deadbolt in place before scurrying into the kitchen.

Standing behind the swinging door, I look through the port-hole at the large panel window that sat at the front of the diner. There was no sign of movement. No sign of whatever horrendous things had been outside in the woods.

As I stood there peering out, I noticed my legs were cold. I had pissed my pants and never felt it. All control of my body had vanished when I was staring into those hateful eyes.

After an hour of hiding, I decided it was time to head home. There had been no signs of activity outside. I was terrified and uncomfortable. The truck was near the backdoor and I hoped I could make it before anything saw me. I made a mad dash to the truck and threw myself in haphazardly. My keys must have fallen to the mat a half dozen times before I managed to get them in the ignition. When my headlights burst into life, they landed on four squat, hairy figures and I nearly screamed.

It was a pack of dogs eating scraps that had fallen out of the dumpster.

Was that all it had been? A few starving mutts in the woods had stopped to watch me smoke a cigarette, and my mind had turned it into a madman's carnival. I burst into laughter. There I sat. A grown man who hid in his diner for God knows how long in piss-filled pants because a few hungry dogs had stopped to watch him.

The whimpering and the howls? Two of them must have got-ten into a fight. My mind had probably made up the rest of the noises. I'd never felt so damn stupid.

I pulled the truck around the side of the diner and onto the street toward my house. What a night. I tossed a final glance back toward the streetlight in front of the diner. Something was there.

It looked like Malcolm standing just at the edge of the woods.

***

Malcolm continued coming around for his evening meal, and I kept collecting my unreasonable payment. It had crossed my mind a dozen times to ask him if he had seen me driving away that night I saw the things in the woods. I wondered why he was back in front of the diner. I wondered if I had just convinced myself I hadn't seen something… unnatural.

I never asked.

I was afraid speaking it into life would make it real. Turn it into something worse. I also worried that my largest paying customer may not like me checking up on him. So, I just kept cooking the steaks and taking the money. He kept eating them. No one asked questions.

I didn't see the eyes anymore, but it always felt like something was watching me after that night. The diner wasn't in the middle of the country, but it was on the outskirts of town. The lot directly across the street was undeveloped and covered in trees. On the sides of the diner sat an antique store and a barbershop. Both closed around 5 PM.

My staff wasn't allowed to take the trash out alone anymore. It annoyed the hell out of them, but I put my foot down. While I wasn't convinced that the four stray dogs were what I'd seen in the woods, I told the staff to be wary of them. They laughed, but I didn't care. Two people to the dumpster and back. No exceptions.

At the end of the shift, I always had Duane walk the girls to the car when he left. I wished I could go with them to save myself the lonely walk to my truck, but I couldn't leave. Malcolm would be coming in for his regular meal, and I counted on that cash to keep everything afloat.

One night as he ate, I mentioned the dogs to Malcolm.

"I see you walkin' into the woods every night," I said. "I've seen some stray dogs around here. You ever see anything like that when you leave?"

He dropped his fork to his plate and lifted his squinted face toward me. "You've seen dogs or you've seen something else, Justin?"

"Dogs, man," I replied. "At least I think they were dogs. Big ass yellow eyes. Size of damn dinner plates, it looked like. Dozens of 'em. Lined up in the woods that you walk through. That's why I figured you may've seen 'em."

"Careful in those woods, Justin," he rumbled. "Dangerous things out there. Best not to go out front at night."

He tossed the money on the counter and started toward the door.

"You know what it was, don't you?" I asked, as he continued walking. "Why the hell don't you tell me?"

"That's the trouble with humans," he replied in annoyance. "You think you want to know something, but once you find out, you wish you never did."

He walked out and vanished into the woods.

***

Malcolm started eating his meals in silence. Since the night I asked him about the creatures in the woods, our conversations became less and less frequent until they didn't happen at all. I fixed his dinner, and he ate without a word. He still left the money on the counter, so I kept going.

Duane called in sick one day and left me to man the kitchen on my own. It hadn't been so difficult a few months ago, but now people felt more comfortable getting out and business was increasing at a fairly rapid rate.

The dinner rush was finally dropping to a trickle which turned out to be handy. Angela stepped to the back to answer a phone call around 6 PM. Turned out to be her son. He'd gotten sick at a friend's house and Ang needed to leave early to pick him up. I told her to head out and take care of the kid. I'd watch the diner.

Everything was pretty smooth sailing that night until I remembered the mountain of trash bags sitting by the back door. I'd meant to take them out with Ang when she was still here, but it had slipped my mind. My diner was my pride, and I didn't want to leave garbage sitting around, but it was already dark, and I didn't want to risk running whatever the hell had been hiding in the woods.

I hadn't seen the damn things again, but I knew they were still out there. I could feel them every time I went outside.

It was 8:15 PM when the phone rang again. I answered it and was delighted to hear the voice of my old friend Mike from the next town over. He ran a good little greasy spoon of his own and we liked to talk shop from time to time.

"Justin, just a heads up," Mike said in a serious tone. "Ole Lou from the health department is out making surprise inspections. No one gave their good buddy Mike a heads up, but I'm helpin' you out, my friend. Dumb bastard knocked a point off my score for having my sanitation buckets 2 degrees low. Two degrees, Justin!

Now that big ninety-nine score is going to sit in the window till he comes back. Some people!"

I laughed. "Lou is a hardass, but he's decent enough. You think he's swinging this way?"

"Who knows, my boy?" he belted. "Just a word to the wise. If you're storing raw chicken in the desk drawer, may wanna put it away, huh?" He laughed and hung up the phone.

After hanging up the phone, I started tidying up the diner. Lou probably wouldn't come to the diner that night, but it was hard to say. Our county was small and if he had already hit Mike's with a surprise inspection, there was a decent chance he would come to my diner.

It didn't take me long to remember the massive pile of garbage at the back door. The rest of the diner had been in good shape, but a mountain of trash was sure to catch a health inspector's attention quickly. I dreaded the thought of having to haul it to the dumpster, but I couldn't risk letting it sit there if Lou showed up.

I pushed the back door open and scanned the parking lot and field behind the diner. My truck sat under the light post to the left and the dumpster was under the light post to the right. The field beyond was as black as anything I'd ever seen, but there were no signs of movement or a hint of those hateful yellow eyes.

With a great sense of dread, I began to pile the bags into a sloppy stack on top of the overflowing rolling cans. I had no intention of making two trips. In and out. No round trip.

The plastic wheels rumbled loudly on the pavement as I hauled them toward the dumpster. When I reached it, I slid the side door open to toss in the bags. The sound of metal squealing against metal made me cringe. If my goal had been stealth, I had failed miserably. Everything in a mile radius would know I was there.

After I tossed in the last bag, my eyes scanned the field again. Still no signs of movement. No eyes. No growling. My pulse finally began to drop back to normal and I grabbed the rolling garbage cans to head back to the diner.

When I turned around, under the light above the back door, there was a creature standing on four legs. It stood as tall as the bed of my pickup truck and its frame rippled with muscles. Pale green skin covered its body, punctuated with bristly black hairs. There was no discernable head, but two bulbous, yellow eyes and a ragged maw of teeth split the area between the thing's shoulders.

It snarled and… barked. It wasn't exactly a bark, but I'm not sure what else to call it. Thick, red drool flowed from the toothy mouth onto the asphalt below. I began to back away from the nightmare abomination and moved toward my truck, swatting my pocket for the keys as I went.

My heart nearly burst when the alarm from my truck began to blast. I turned my head to see another one of the hellhounds standing in the bed of my truck, clawed feet propping themselves on the cab. It grunted and turned its face toward me as though sniffing the air with unseen nostrils.

My feet froze again. I couldn't move. I felt as helpless as the night I had seen the things watching me from the woods.

The hellhound from the truck jumped down and lowered itself to the ground, readying itself to pounce. I looked toward the beast at the door, and it was moving forward in the same posture. I began to scream for help, but I knew none would come. My eyes closed, and I started to pray for a quick death.

The hot breath from the hounds was panting on my hand when I heard one of them cry out in pain. I wanted to open my eyes, but the pained howl made me wince and close my eyes even tighter. There was a sudden dry snap like the cracking of ice followed by a heavy thud.

Another of the hellhounds was snarling and snapping its powerful jaw.

"I've been waiting for you," I heard a familiar voice say. "Expected more of you to come, but I'll take what I can get."

I opened my eyes to see Malcolm standing before me, one hellhound on the ground at his feet, purple liquid leaking from its mouth. The other circled him warily, seeking an opportunity to strike at the huge man. Malcolm turned in a circle with the hound, arms out in a grappling stance.

The hellhound crouched deeply and leapt forward toward the big man. Malcolm held out a meaty arm, and the creature sank its teeth into his flesh. It thrashed wildly but Malcolm's squinted expression never changed.

He lifted the thing on his arm high in the air and brought it crashing down onto the parking lot. A muffled whimper escaped the beast, but it maintained its hold. The big man began to rain blows onto the creature, compressing it between his meaty fist and the asphalt beneath.

An eruption of purple blood spilled from the corners of its mouth and its muscles shuddered as Malcolm pulverized the thing's internal organs. It began to breathe raggedly before releasing its jaws from his arm. Malcolm stood up straight and brought his boot down on the beast's face with a sickening crunch.

Before I had a chance to speak, Malcolm lifted one of the beasts above him and turned his head toward the sky. His face became long, and his mouth grew wide. The bushy beard and eyebrows that had always covered his face stretched and revealed a set of bulbous yellow eyes and a mouth filled with dagger-like teeth.

He shoved one of the hounds in and swallowed it whole. His massive torso bulged as he bent to pick up the second hound. It slid into the nightmarish mouth and his stomach bulged further. His jaw contracted and the skin of his face tightened again, hiding the vicious mouth and yellow eyes. He turned to me and held a hand up to greet me as though he had just noticed I was there.

"Followed the pack here about a year ago," he said matter-of-factly. "They took a special interest in you. Not everyone can see us. My kind only feeds on those that can."

My jaw fell slack and my legs turned to jelly. I was no longer fastened to the ground and promptly fell backward. The big man walked toward me and held out a hand to help me up.

"What… what the hell are you?" I stammered in fear.

"Same thing as them, though I change up my appearance a bit," he said as he rubbed his stomach with glee. "They crave the flesh of those who can see them. I'm a bit of an outcast. Developed a liking for the taste of my kind. I follow the pack until they find a human to hunt. One that can see them. I'll hang around for a bit and wait for them to make a move. Then I pick a few off. The steaks keep the hunger at bay, but I need a true meal every year or two."

"I was… I was bait?" I spat. "You used me as bait?"

"If that's how you want to look at it," he said as he began to walk away. "The pack will move on now. I stick around for a few weeks to make sure they don't come back for you. Then I'll move on myself. Catch up with them and get ready for my next meal."

Malcolm, swollen with his hellish feast, wobbled toward the corner of the diner to make his way to the trees across the road. He turned and faced me before letting out an earth-shaking belch.

"Won't be needing the steaks tonight, Justin," he said jovially. "But I'll leave some money on the counter. See you tomorrow!"

I'VE DONE THIS BEFORE

I've done this before. More than three hundred times, I think. It's hard to keep track.

The current time for me is 5:32 AM. In forty-five minutes and twenty seconds, the thing will push the retracting ladder down from the attic and drop into the hallway.

The creature is small but unbelievably fierce. Standing two and a half feet tall, it is a dense chunk of muscle and sinew. Blistered gray skin stretches tightly over its frame. It has two stubby arms contrasted by long, frog-like legs. An anvil-shaped head protrudes from the torso, accented with two glowing pink eyes. Black, glistening teeth fill its cruel mouth. A leather vest and loincloth accented with human teeth dangle from its body.

Within seconds, it will begin using its blood to draw runic symbols on the floor. I've seen it peel away a dry scab and dab at the purple wound before scrawling its wicked designs. The wood smokes as the wet claw scrawls the hellish message.

I usually live longer if I can destroy some of the runes before I make my escape.

When the cryptic writing is complete, it will drop to its hands and knees before beginning a guttural chant. I still don't understand what the words mean and likely never will. The last three dozen times I have listened to it closely through the door. I've committed the chant to memory but have yet to find a translation for it. Not much time for Googling anyway before the mayhem begins.

I doubt it is from our world, anyway. Even if it was, I have no way of knowing if the spelling is correct. But I'll keep trying. It seems I have all the time in the world.

Zeshrack dumrav skrashtek dimia zoorn.

After uttering the chant five times and emitting a bone-rattling roar, the hunt officially begins. If I don't make a preemptive move, the process takes less than forty-five seconds after the battle cry. When it first appeared, I was still in bed scrolling mindlessly through a social media application. My bedroom door burst open, and the thing sprang onto the bed. It was over before I could react.

I can still feel the first time the cold blade slid into my carotid artery. I gazed into those pink eyes and the thing only smiled in return. None of the memories fade. No matter how many times I awaken to relive this day, I remember them all.

I've started calling it Hunter. Why not? That's what it does.

It isn't stupid by any means, but it is simple to fool at the outset of the hunt. Stuffing pillows under my blanket and hiding behind the door is the only method I've discovered that allows me to get out of my bedroom alive. Hunter flings itself onto the bed and uses a red metal blade to ravage the pillows beneath. I have ten seconds at the most before he discovers the ruse.

Quietly, I'll slide around the opened door as Hunter shrieks and rips at the blankets and pillows. This is when I can wipe away a few of the runes. I've gotten pretty good at sliding the hallway rug onto them. It doesn't seem to take much to disrupt their power, so this is a step in the process I use every time.

My main concern is to destroy the rune closest to my bedroom door. This seems to make him slower. The less rapidly Hunter can move, the farther away I seem to get. Destroying any of the other markings is just a bonus. I haven't figured out what all of them do quite yet. Sadly, I think I'll have plenty of time to figure it out.

I've died around fifteen times trying to destroy them all. That's a work in progress. This process isn't perfect. It's difficult to think through the hundreds of variations I've tried previous times while my mind is flooded with fear. I've tried to write notes, but they vanish each time I die and wake up again.

This still scares me. I've died hundreds of different ways. Loss of blood, decapitation, disembowelment, suffocation, blunt force trauma. My methods for attempted survival are improving with each attempt. I can't say the same for my mental stability.

Escaping the house is the method that always allows me to live the longest, but comes with the greatest cost. Whenever Hunter tracks me through the town, it kills everyone it sees. A trail of viscera and carnage follows behind the beast as it tracks me.

I've watched as it cuts, bites, and claws its way through crowds like a hot knife through butter. Those people are less prepared than I am. It's as though I'm allowing a fox into a chicken coop. Their screams and pleas haunt me almost as much as the creature.

Even after sacrificing all these unwitting souls, it still finds me. That is the constant. Hundreds die, but I never escape.

Knowing that leaving the house always ends in bloodshed, I've decided I have to keep the damn thing in my house. I have no way to know for sure, but one day this loop surely ends. If I'm right, I couldn't handle knowing all those people died in my cowardly attempt to escape this thing. It only tracks me, so why should others suffer a grizzly demise as I scramble to survive?

Staying in my house keeps others safe but cuts my survival time in half at the very least, but I do have more control there. My attempts to hurt or kill Hunter have mostly been ineffective. Kitchen knives don't pierce the thick hide. The old shotgun I keep in the downstairs closet knocks the thing off its feet but deals no lasting damage. I have even bludgeoned it with a crowbar. Hell, I've burnt the house down, but it crawls out of the wreckage and continues its relentless pursuit.

Five deaths ago, things changed for the better. After slipping out of the door as Hunter slashed and ravaged my bed, I slid the rug onto the runes and shot down the stairs as always. As Hunter once again discovered my trick, it tumbled out of my room and began to scramble down the stairs. For the first time that I can remember, its foot slipped and it began to fall head over foot to the landing below.

My pulse was rapid and my throat tight as I watched the ugly thing roll down the final few steps and slam into the wall. The red blade slid from its grip and skittered across the floor to my foot. It was already pushing itself back off the floor when I picked up the blade and pointed it toward the beast.

Our eyes locked and Hunter bared his black teeth in a sneer. The pink eyes darted from my gaze to the slender knife now in my hand. Countless times, this weapon had taken my life. I could almost feel the combined weight of all my deaths in the blade. My hand throbbed as I held it steady toward Hunter.

Its powerful legs retracted and pushed off against the floor causing the thing to fly through the air in my direction. I drew the red blade above my head and brought it down in a wide arc as Hunter grew closer. It connected with an outstretched arm and sliced through. The blade continued through the muscle and bone and slammed to a stop against the leather vest on Hunter's torso.

For the second time, it fell to the floor. Purple blood oozed from the severed arm and the floor began to smoke as it pooled. Shrieks and ragged pants shook my eardrums as the wounded thing on the floor shuddered in pain. The startled reaction didn't last as long as I had hoped.

Claws gouged the floor as Hunter shuffled backward to make room between us. I trained the knife in its direction as it retreated. Once it was comfortably removed from my reach, it began to laugh.

The remaining hand slid into a pouch tethered to the loincloth. Hunter retrieved a handful of black powder and rubbed it onto the stump where its arm had been. The flesh sizzled and began to seal itself into a tangle of scar tissue. Once the wound finished healing, Hunter stood again and angled its body toward me. It lifted the remaining hand and snapped its thick, sharp fingers. The blade in my hand vanished and reappeared in Hunter's clutch.

Maybe destroying another run would take that power away.

It lunged at me and slid the blade across my throat. While Hunter usually killed me quickly, this time the wound was shallow enough that it took me minutes to bleed out. As the blood poured from my throat and mingled with the purple pool of Hunter's only inches away, I smiled.

I was in agony, but I had learned something. After all of these hundreds of times, I'd made it bleed. The disgusting little gremlin may be immune to any weapon I have, but now I knew its weapon could kill it.

The following few deaths ended the same as most of my other experiences. Hunter never dropped the blade, and I was never able to wrestle it away. My attempts to stand my ground and retrieve the weapon were futile. Hunter's arm had returned. But during the struggles, I could see something different about it now. A thick ring of gnarled flesh circled the arm that I had cut off. It had healed, but it left a permanent scar.

I'm not sure exactly what this means for me. Some of my fear and despair have been replaced with a sliver of hope. Hunter can be hurt. Maybe it can be killed. It could end the loop.

Anyway, I only have two minutes and fifteen seconds left before the attic stairs drop down. I guess you could call this pass through the loop my break. No preparations have been made.

Hunter will kill me quickly. That's fine. It takes time to leave these messages. I fear it, but I've accepted it.

I've left dozens of these messages over the last hundred loops. Each time I update it just a bit. Maybe this seems familiar to you. You may not remember, but perhaps something here seems familiar. This likely isn't the first time you've read this. Maybe it will save someone else if they end up trapped in this nightmare.

Eventually, I'll succeed. It won't be soon, but I'm learning. The process is improving every time. I know how to hurt the thing.

For now, I've got to go. Hunter will be here soon.

Like I said, I've done this before.

THE HANGING MAN IN ROOM 3

"How the hell do you suppose this happened?" the sheriff asked as he wiped the sweat from his brow.

"No clue," replied the crime scene technician. She snapped pictures. "It seems pretty clear he hung himself, but I don't know how long it takes a corpse to mummify."

I watched the man and woman examine the dangling corpse as though I wasn't even in the room. They hadn't asked me to leave and oddly I didn't want to. The shock of discovering the body had long since passed and I had instead been filled with a macabre fascination.

Less than two hours earlier I had stopped at the first roadside motel that I had seen in hours. Traveling Route 66 had been a dream of mine for years. With the pandemic waning and my work as a copywriter not tying me down, I had taken off without much planning.

Motels had been more abundant in Texas and the eastern portion of New Mexico, but the farther west I drove the less frequently I had happened upon one. Even when I did manage to find a place with vacancies, they were often dilapidated and pretty questionable. I did my best to consider it part of the adventure, but some nights I felt better than others.

When I pulled up to the crumbling stucco office at the Alabaster Springs Motor Inn, it didn't fill me with an overwhelming sense of safety. The rectangle of motel rooms behind the office seemed a decade past good maintenance, and the lack of cars in the parking lot told me that other travelers had thought the same. Still, it was somewhere to stay for the night.

Dwarvish dirt devils swirled in front of my feet as I walked toward the door to the office. Large chunks of the stucco facade sat in piles on the windowsill and peppered the foundation of the building. Electric whining filled my ears from the flashing OPEN sign above the door. Before I entered, I could see an old man through the dirty window. A yellowed tank top sagged on his boney frame. He absently swatted flies as he watched a rabbit-eared television in the corner.

"Hello," I said to the man as I pushed open the door. My eyes drifted down to a lopsided name tag pinned to his shirt identifying him as *Clarence*. "Any rooms available?"

The slovenly man looked at me and arched an eyebrow.

"Empty parkin' lot shoulda been a clue," Clarence replied sarcastically. "Room's fifty for the night. Don't expect much. Ain't got no help na'more since Davey run off."

Not knowing who Davey was or where he had "run off" to, I decided to continue with my business. It was late and my eyes felt like they had lead weights adhered to them. I approached the counter, pulled my debit card from my wallet, and set it on the counter. Clarence slid it back.

"Card reader's busted," he said dryly. "Cash only."

I curled my lip and placed the card back into my wallet. Thumbing through the bill pocket I could see that there were only two wrinkly twenties and nothing else. I fished the bills out of my wallet and held them up for the old man to see.

"I've only got forty," I replied. "I can Venmo you the rest later."

"That'll be enough," he spat as he snatched the cash from my hand. "Dunno what the hell a Venmo is, but you can Venmo at someone else. Better forty than nothin'."

Tossing me a set of keys attached to a maroon diamond keychain, he pointed me to room 3 to the right of the office entrance. I asked him if it had been cleaned recently and he muttered that Davey had cleaned it before he left six months earlier. No one had occupied the room since.

How delightful.

After pulling my car in front of my room and unloading my duffle bag, I made my way to the door of Room 3. Thick dust clung lazily to the surface and covered my knuckles as I slid the key into the lock. The force required to turn the deadbolt further detailed the place's lack of care.

Snapping dryly from the frame the lock gave way allowing the door to squeal on its hinges as it opened into the room. Stale, dry air hammered my face, and I could see dots of dust dancing in the beams from the low sun. Breathing was a laborious task in the stifling heat of the room.

I tossed my bags onto a metal chair and turned on the window-mounted AC unit before stepping outside. A few minutes to let the struggling unit cool down the oven of a room seemed like my only option. Momentarily I toyed with the idea of getting into the car and driving until I found another motel, but I had no clue how far that would be.

The cell signal was abysmal out here, so relying on GPS or Google didn't seem like a safe option now. I would chance it there for the evening and get on the road first thing in the morning. A night of sleep in a shady motel still seemed better than falling asleep at the wheel.

Once I was fairly certain the room's temperature was survivable, I headed back inside. To my surprise, it was a great deal cooler than I anticipated it would get. After returning to the room, my assessment went from irritation to amusement. It was a relic of the 1970s. Formica laminate tables and chairs, a knob-controlled television, and wood grain wall panels decorated my room. The carpet was matted shag and the yellowed ceiling was covered in popcorn-style texture.

I scooped my duffle bag from the ancient chair and headed to the accordion-doored closet beside the bed. Odds didn't seem in favor of a nighttime burglary, but a lifetime of city-dwelling had taught me to be cautious of leaving my things sitting out in the open. Maybe my mother had a little to do with it as well. When we traveled during my childhood, I was always made to put my belongings in the closet or dresser.

The plastic handle of the fold-away door felt brittle in my hand, so I cautiously slipped my fingers around the frame to give it a push. Jolting away from the wall, the door retracted revealing a gaunt man staring back at me. I stumbled back and threw my duffle bag at the figure as I fell to the floor.

As I pushed myself back across the room, the man remained in place but began to slowly turn around. He rocked gently from side to side and, when I looked down, I could see his feet were not touching the floor. My eyes drifted back up to his head which had turned around to stare at the wall of the closet.

I could see a rope around the leathery skin of his neck vanish into the ceiling above.

The body swayed and turned until it was facing me again. Empty eye sockets now seemed to peer in my direction. Thin wisps of hair and long cracking nails jutted ghoulishly from the taut, papery skin. Thin flakes of dried skin filled the creases in the flannel work shirt. The head drooped and the open jaw rested on its chest in a silent scream. A syringe dangled haphazardly from the man's left arm.

As the body began to turn again, the left foot made contact with my duffle bag, causing the dead man to jerk. Something fell from the body and slid down the side of my bag. The sudden motion from the dangling corpse startled me from my trance and I bolted from the floor and ran out of the room toward the office to call the police.

***

After taking pictures of the swinging cadaver, the sheriff and crime scene technician retrieved a wallet from the hanging man's back pocket. The driver's license inside identified the man as David Weldon Schell. The old man from the office, Clarence, identified him by his clothing and a withered tattoo on his forearm.

David, or Davey, was Clarence's son. He told the sheriff that Davey had a history of substance abuse and he had always assumed he skipped town to escape drug debts. Men had stopped by periodically asking to speak to his son and, when they learned he had disappeared, they inquired about his current whereabouts. Clarence always disappointed them and sent them on their way.

I stared in awe the entire time. My life had been an easy one. There were no great traumas to share and no stories of tragedy. My heart swelled with sympathy for the man the newly arrived EMTs were placing in a body bag. I couldn't help but consider the difficult road he had traveled in his life that had led him to this.

After the earthly remains of David Schell had been placed in the ambulance, the sheriff offered me a ride to the nearest motel down the road. I thanked him but told him I didn't want to leave my car behind. He nodded understandingly and jotted the directions to the new motel on a sheet of paper from his notepad.

I entered the room a final time to retrieve my duffle bag. Fortunately, I hadn't taken anything else into the room, so my departure was swift. With the door pulled shut behind me I walked to my car and tossed the bag in the back seat before heading to the office to return my key.

When I entered the office Clarence was staring intently at the TV, fly swatter in hand, just like I had found him when I arrived. He didn't seem upset in the least about the discovery of his son's mummified remains in Room 3. It was like he had seen it a thousand times before and couldn't be bothered.

"I'm sorry about Davey," I said to Clarence as I placed my key on the counter.

"Don't spend too much time weepin' over some deadweight junkie," he responded without looking at me. "Don't weep over your forty bucks neither. Just 'cause you didn't stay don't mean you get a refund."

His response startled me almost as much as finding the dead man in my closet. I couldn't understand how anyone could speak that way about their dead child. Feeling disgusted, I turned to walk back into the stifling night air.

"Hey!" Clarence exclaimed as I was opening my car door. He now stood in the doorway of the office. "You find anything interestin' in there after you found Davey?"

"What do you mean?" I asked.

The old man rolled his eyes. "Just any damn interesting thing, you dimwit," he barked.

I threw up my middle finger at Clarence and settled into my car. He turned to head back into the office and slammed the door. Relief filled me as I pulled onto the road that would lead me back to Route 66 and hopefully a nicer motel. My window was down, and I thought the cool desert air would keep me awake until I arrived.

A few days later I made it to Santa Monica, but the destination had lost its appeal. After the grim discovery hanging in my motel closet, I hadn't been able to enjoy anything. None of the sights had any luster, the food made me feel nauseous, and even the softest bed made me toss and turn in my sleep. I just kept picturing that dead man swinging in the closet.

Some deadweight junkie, his father said.

I decided to go home.

The sun was setting beyond the horizon as my tires rumbled down the road. I could see the green sign with white letters showing the turn ahead that led back to Alabaster Springs. An ironwood tree stood vigil behind it and the thin branches rubbed back and forth over the top of it.

My headlights kicked on in response to the low light and the beams illuminated the skeletal fingers of the tree. It seemed to almost reach toward the road. A lump raised in my throat and my stomach dropped as I saw something swinging from the largest branch.

David Schell's hollow eyes met with mine as he swayed in the breeze, noose knotted around the ironwood branch. His skeletally thin arm pointed toward the road leading to Alabaster Springs. I slammed on the brakes and my car slid into the shallow ditch. My heart hammered against my chest. The engine had died when the tires left the pavement and I tried desperately to restart it. Over my shoulder, I could hear rhythmic tapping against my window and looked back to see Davey's boot bumping against it.

In a panic, I threw my door open and ran to the other side of the road before I tumbled into the shifting dust. As I regained my footing I stumbled backward and gazed at my car, the ironwood tree looming behind it. Davey was gone. A single low tree branch tapped against the rear window of my car.

I vomited onto the pavement. It ran down my face and dripped onto my shirt. Tears welled in my eyes from the acidity in my mouth and the stench of my clothing. Wearily I glanced at the tree again, but Davey was nowhere to be seen. I staggered back to my car and opened the back door. Rifling through my duffle bag I pulled out a clean shirt to replace the soiled one I was wearing.

After putting on the new shirt I folded the dirty one and slid it into the outside pouch of my bag. As my hand slid into the pouch it bumped against something rigid. I grabbed the item and pulled it out to examine it. It was a maroon diamond keychain from the motel with two bronze keys on the silver ring. Turning it over in my hand I could see the writing. On one side it said *The Alabaster Springs Motor Inn* and on the other, *If found please return to the office*.

Memories of Clarence and his contempt for his son filled my mind, and I drew my arm back to throw the keys into the dusty field.

"Take them back," whispered a voice. It sounded as though it came from the ironwood tree. I turned to look at it again, but there was no one there. Just my imagination.

I drew my hand back once again to throw them into the distance when something grasped my shoulder and spun me around.

"TAKE THEM BACK!" roared the voice from before. Davey stood before me, hollow eye sockets staring into mine. He was in the center of the road, still pointing toward Alabaster Springs. The rope still hung from his neck and the needle dangled from his outstretched arm. A billow of dust puffed from his mouth as he whispered, *"Please."*

Too frightened to ignore the demand, I jumped into the seat of my car and turned over the engine. I smashed the gas pedal to the floor and aimed the car toward Alabaster Springs. In my rearview mirror, I could see the diminishing figure of Davey standing in the road next to the ironwood tree. Still pointing.

After a half-hour of driving, I could see the dingy road sign for the Alabaster Springs Motor Inn ahead. The parking lot sat as empty as the first time I had seen it, and the light in the office glowed in contrast to the dark of the evening. Unlike my last visit, Clarence was nowhere to be seen. The television screen danced with static through the window.

I put my car in park and surveyed the motel for any sign of life. A light shone through the curtains of a room that I was able to recognize as the one I had previously rented. Room 3. The door was slightly ajar casting a thin line of illumination onto the sidewalk outside.

Cautiously I approached the open door and pushed it open a few more inches. At first, I couldn't see anyone inside, but heard shuffling on the carpet. Edging the door open a few inches more, I leaned my head in to see Clarence on his hands and knees examining the closet floor. He was cursing under his breath as his head darted from side to side.

"Clarence?" I said loudly. The old man bolted up and turned to look at me. His eyes squinted in an attempt to improve his failing eyesight. A sneer curled his mouth and I knew he recognized me.

"The hell do you want?" he asked as he clambered to his feet. "Here to reminisce about the good times?"

I tossed the keys to him and, to my surprise, Clarence raised his hand and caught them. The old man stared at the keys and smiled. He turned them over in his hand and began to laugh.

"Looks like you did find somethin' after all, eh?" He asked rhetorically. "Now get the hell on out of here."

Clarence pointed toward the door. I had expected some word of thanks from the old bastard, but he was just as endearing now as when we had first met. Without another word, I turned to leave the room. As I rounded the corner toward my car, my path was blocked by a silhouette.

Davey's withered corpse shuffled in my direction on wobbly legs. As he neared me I attempted to move out of his path but wasn't fast enough. A slender arm bolted from his side and wrapped around my arm before sending me reeling me out of his way and sending me sprawling into the parking lot.

I sat up on the cracking pavement and could see the terror in Clarence's eyes as the corpse turned the corner into Room 3. He dropped the keys and held his hands up in a surrendering gesture as his son stumbled toward him. Clarence began to back away, but soon slammed into the wall of the closet.

"I'm sorry, boy!" Clarence yelled. "I needed the money, and you wouldn't help me!"

Davey continued lumbering toward his father.

"If you woulda just gave me a little cash we'd have both been fine!"

Davey removed the noose from his neck and continued forward.

"Dammit, Davey!" Clarence screeched desperately. "I shot you up one last time. Ain't that worth anything?"

Davey Schell reached his father and grabbed the cloth of his shirt in a tight fist. The old man punched at the corpse to no effect. Flakes of skin and shreds of rotten cloth fell away after each blow. His dead son's free hand draped the noose around the screaming man's neck and tossed the end over the support beam at the top of the closet. Slowly Davey began to tug the slack of the rope and Clarence lifted from the ground.

"I shoulda killed you when you was just a bo…" Clarence said before his speech became a strangled moan. His feet thrashed and his hands grabbed helplessly at the rope sinking into the flesh of his neck.

Davey turned away from his struggling father and picked the key ring up from the matted shag carpeting. He stumbled from Room 3 toward the side of the office building in the center of the lot. When he reached a steel hatch leading to the crawl space beneath, he got on his knees and inserted the key. The lid squealed open, and the corpse reached inside withdrawing two dust-covered shoulder bags.

Dragging both bags behind him, he returned to Room 3 and tossed the bags below his father's feet. Crumpled wads of bills began to tumble from the unsecured packs and slid onto the floor. Clarence dangled in silence above the money he had so desperately wanted.

Managing to break my trance, I darted for my car and sped out of the lot. Three days later I was finally back home and still reeling from the experience. I slept with the lights on for months and refused to open my closet.

After a few weeks had passed I worked up the nerve to look up the nearest newspaper to Alabaster Springs. There was a headline from the previous week detailing the discovery of a local motel owner who had hanged himself to death in the same room in which his son had taken his life. The article brushed casually over the bags of money. Thankfully there was no mention of an investigation or concerns that anyone else was involved.

At the bottom of the article, there was a picture of Clarence in his younger years. He still looks hateful, and the worst part of me isn't sad that he's dead. Not sure what that says about me, but I'll have to handle that on my own.

Next to him is a picture of David. Davey. He's smiling and looks happy. It's a relief to see his eyes rather than those hollow sockets.

I hope he's at rest now.

THE KIK GAME

If you have received a message from MaxStax719 on Kik don't respond. They want you to play The Kik Game and it isn't what it seems. I've never thought of myself as a stupid kid, but today I know I am. I started playing The Kik Game and now I'm in deep shit.

It all started like almost anything in my life does. I was bored on a Saturday morning and playing around on my cell phone. My parents were out of town for a work conference, and I was home alone for the week. It was spring break and most of my friends were down at the coast with their parents or other classmates digging their toes into the sand. My broke ass was sitting at home wishing I had gotten a job and saved up some money to go with them.

I had already made my morning rounds on Facebook, Twitter, and Instagram, but the photos of my friends having fun in far-off places had already pissed me off. So I decided repeating that cycle wouldn't improve things. The microwave beeped from the kitchen signaling that my breakfast sandwich had been nuked to perfection, so I tossed my phone on the couch and went to grab it.

As I was setting the hot plate on the counter and pouring a glass of juice, I heard a *ping* from my phone in the living room. I headed back in to see if one of my friends was taunting me with pictures from the beach. I scooped the phone up and saw the Kik notification on my screen saying I had a new message from **MaxStax719**. It wasn't a screen name I knew, but I decided to check it anyway just in case. Opening up the app, I hit the accept chat button and read the message.

MaxStax719: *Hey there! Want to play The Kik Game? Easy money and you can quit any time!*

I rolled my eyes at the low-effort message from a bot that was no doubt going to try to sell me porn or get a bank transfer number. Without fail, I got about seven messages a day like this trying to link me to some stupid crap. On the off chance there was an actual human behind it that I could mess with I would often message back to waste their time.

FakeKikName: *Hell yeah, bro! Let's play! How do I win this easy money?*

I waited a few minutes but didn't get a response. The bot was probably broken or poorly programmed like most of them, so I started eating my sandwich. A few bites in I heard the *ping* again.

MaxStax719: *Take a picture holding up three fingers. Place a ring of any type on one of them! Once we've received it we will send you an Amazon Gift Card code for $50!*

Hold up three fingers with a ring on? What the hell? I went to my parents' room and fished a ring out of my mother's jewelry box and slid it on the end of my middle finger and took the picture. The ring didn't slide down completely but the message didn't say it had to. I sent the picture to **MaxStax719** and went back to my sandwich. There was no way I would get the gift card, but it had only cost me about two minutes of my life, so it was worth a shot.

A few minutes later I received a message back with what looked like a gift card code. I thought it was probably a fake. Firing up my Amazon app I copied and pasted the code into the redemption box and waited. To my shock, my available balance went from $0 to $50. Who knew that Kik bots actually paid out?

My phone pinged and I opened the new message from **MaxStax719**.

MaxStax719: *Great job! If you want to keep playing The Kik Game for more great prizes then please take a picture of yourself holding a hammer in your right hand and send it to us for another $50 Amazon gift card!*

Immediately I shot to the garage and dug through my dad's old toolboxes until I found a shabby old claw hammer. I held it up in the light in my right hand and took a picture. As I headed back inside I sent the picture to **MaxStax719** and waited patiently. Just like the last time, I received a new code a few minutes later and added it to my Amazon account. It was verified and my balance shot up to $100. I was dumbstruck.

MaxStax719: *Good job, FakeKikName! Are you ready to make some real money now?*

FakeKikName: *Hell yes! Keep it coming!*

MaxStax719: *Use a sharpie to draw a smiley face on the head of the hammer. Take the hammer to your nearest gas station parking lot and take a picture. The picture must include the street signs for intersecting streets! One of our Kik Game representatives will go and verify it is there. If they find it you will receive a redemption code for a $500 Visa Gift Card!*

I didn't even bother to respond. My legs were pumping the pedals on my bike within minutes of receiving the last message. The hammer was in my backpack and bounced against my back as I pedaled toward to the nearest Pump n' Go that I could think of. Luckily it sat on the corner of an intersection.

When I got there I found a concrete retainer to sit the hammer on where you could see both of the street signs as well as the Pump n' Go logo sign. I placed the hammer on the retainer and snapped a picture. Uploading it as quickly as I could, I waited for a follow-up message. That's when I remembered they had to send a representative to find it.

I peddled my bike home and watched a few hours of television. My phone sat silently beside me on the couch. I stared at it willing it to ping telling me my gift card had arrived. I waited hours, but no response.

Drifting off to a mid-morning nap, my phone suddenly buzzed again. When I opened KIK, I saw a code for a Visa gift card. Heading to the website, I was amazed once again to see the code worked.

MaxStax719: *That's all for now! We will be back later this afternoon with more exciting opportunities!*

I sat on the couch and started browsing Amazon for opportunities to waste my newly found money. It still wasn't quite afternoon when my phone pinged again. Looking at the username from the message, I saw it was from MaxStax719 again, so I opened it immediately.

MaxStax719: *We're ahead of schedule here at The Kik Game! Are you ready to win some really big money, FakeKikName?*

FakeKikName: *100%! Just name it!*

MaxStax719: *Go back to the gas station where you left the hammer and check beside the dumpster. There is a brand new,* *sealed pack of cigarettes just behind it. Video yourself smoking five of them in less than 10 minutes and win a $1000 Visa Gift Card! Be sure to drop them on the ground and stomp them out! Fire safety is priority #1!*

I hesitated for a moment after reading that one. It hadn't occurred to me earlier when I had dropped off the hammer, but **MaxStax719** had said a Kik Game representative lived in my city. I hadn't even questioned how they knew what city I was in. The money I was winning had blinded me to some potential concerns I should have had, and they were just now catching up with me.

FakeKikName: *Thanks for all the money but how did you know I was in a city where you had a representative?*

MaxStax719: *Trial and error, my friend! Sometimes we lose a bit of money after the three-finger and hammer picture verification test. It turns out that a lot of Kik Game players aren't in the right cities. When you sent the picture with the cross streets and gas station we were able to Google the location and verify you are in an applicable city!*

At the time it seemed like a half-ass answer, but I had seen hundreds of weird stories online where some YouTuber or influencer ran "social experiments" like this and figured I had just stumbled on one. I decided to continue playing along and headed back to the gas station on my bike. Even though I had never smoked a cigarette before, I figured five for $1000 was a small price to pay.

When I arrived at the gas station I pulled my bike around back and leaned it on the wooden fencing surrounding the dumpster. Just beside it on the ground, I saw a sealed pack of cigarettes with a lighter on top. I opened the package and stuck one in my mouth before turning on my camera and lighting it up. The acrid smoke made me cough, but I adjusted after a few puffs.

As I smoked the cigarettes and stomped them out, I just stared into the camera. I felt stupid and a little freaked out now that I was there. The cigarettes tasted awful and made my eyes water, but I just kept lighting them and puffing away. Eventually, I figured out I didn't even have to inhale them since you wouldn't be able to tell from the video if I did anyway. After I was done, I crushed out the last smoldering butt and pointed the camera down to the pile on the ground to show I had stomped them out.

As I was videoing the pile of cigarette butts someone opened the back door of the convenience store. A middle-aged man with a long ponytail and a tattoo of a snake around his neck stepped outside and gave me an angry look.

"What're you doing, kid?" the man asked in a gravelly voice. "Get the hell outta here! You ain't old enough to be smokin'!"

I sent the video to **MaxStax719** but didn't wait for a response. Instead, I just got on my bike and started peddling back home wondering why someone was paying a kid for pictures of a hammer and to smoke cigarettes behind a gas station. My stomach was in knots from a combination of the smoking and uneasy feeling I was starting to get from **MaxStax719**'s weird tasks. The gas station attendant discovering me freaked me out quite a bit as well.

When I walked back into the house after putting up my bike I had two messages from **MaxStax719**. The first one was another Visa code which checked out like all the others. The second was a new task.

MaxStax719: *Great job so far! One last task and this one is for $2500 in Visa Gift Card prizes! Delete this conversation and send me a screenshot of the blank screen when completed! Once received you will receive your final reward!*

I just wanted to be done with this uneasy sensation, so I deleted the conversation and took the screenshot. After I was done, I took a screenshot of the blank chat window and sent it back to **MaxStax719**. That was the last message I sent or received from them.

Fifteen or twenty minutes later I got a message from a user named **FinalReward719**. I opened it with a sense of unease, but it was another Visa gift code. This time I didn't even bother checking it on the website because I knew it was good. I didn't respond either. There was no point, and I was done with this.

Later that night I was scrolling through TikTok watching the usual videos of bottle flips, awkward dancing, and filtered women lip-syncing to popular songs when a new Kik notification popped up on my phone. This time it was from someone called **LookWhatYouDid719.**

I opened the app to see the message, and it just showed the JPEG icon. So I tapped it, opened the picture, and nearly vomited. A man was crumpled on a tile floor in a pool of blood. His long ponytail was caked in crimson, and you could make out the head of a snake tattoo wrapping around his throat.

His face was pulverized into a liquid pile of meat and brain matter. There was a hammer propped up on its claws, head up and dripping with blood. I could see the faint outline of a smiley face on it through the gore. A few cigarette butts were sprinkled around the body. I was still fighting the urge to puke when my phone pinged a final time.

LookWhatYouDid719: *Thanks for playing The Kik Game! Be careful out there, friend!*

I don't know what to do now. My fingerprints and DNA are all over that scene. Do I call the cops? What evidence do I have to show them? Maybe the gift cards will lead back to someone, or they could track an IP address from the messages. But maybe they can't. I don't know and I'm scared.

If someone messages you and asks if you want to play The Kik Game delete it immediately.

THE GREAT OUTDOORS

March 17th, 2022

I started hiking and backpacking with my father when I was around twelve years old. Mom passed away giving birth to me, so Dad was the only parent I ever knew. He did his best to try and get me interested in things that typical little girls enjoy, but I never took to them. There's nothing wrong with those kinds of things, but my heart craved adventure.

During the day he worked as a store manager for an agricultural supply company, but on the nights and weekends, he worked on our small farm. He raised livestock to make additional income as well as planted a few acres of corn and tobacco. While this took up a majority of his day, he was careful to include me to make for father and daughter time.

Feeding cattle, mending fences, cutting tobacco, and running the tractors became our evening routines. Over the years, our little farm prospered and grew. Dad was able to hire some additional hands which freed him up for more leisure activities.

I can still remember our first hiking trip. Dad surprised me with a new hiking pack and a pair of boots. My eyes sparkled as he told me we would be spending the entire weekend hiking and camping on a local trail. With how hard he worked, we had never had time to take a trip of any kind that I could remember. A few scattered visits to family members in other states, but not like this.

That was an adventure.

He made me wear the boots while we worked on the farm that week to break them in. My mind raced with the possibilities. We had slept in a tent in the backyard dozens of times, but never in the woods. Thoughts of spotting wildlife, setting up camp, and the smell of eggs frying over an open fire filled every vacant moment of my day.

And that's exactly how it went. It was magical. We spent three days hiking beside a rushing stream, sleeping under the stars, and cooking delicious meals in his battered iron skillet. At that age, I even enjoyed the novelty of going to the bathroom in the woods. Weird, I know, but it was different.

Over the years, my tomboyish ways softened a bit, but my love for the outdoors never faded. Dad and I went hiking or camping at least once a month until he passed away three years ago. A lifetime of smoking resulted in cancer that ravaged his body. Those last few months as he withered away in bed, we talked about our favorite trips. It seemed to give him a little bit of peace.

I still go as often as I can. It makes me feel close to him. Occasionally, I find myself talking to the memory of him as I sit around the embers of my evening fire. Seems like he is there with me sometimes.

Last year, I started to develop an interest in ultralight backpacking. If you're not familiar, it's essentially long-distance hiking with the least amount of gear and weight possible. A few companies make specialty products that cut the weight of your average gear significantly. If you give me something to sleep in, something to sleep under, and something to cook with, I can live in the woods for weeks at a time.

I still carry dehydrated food and a water ration with me, but otherwise, it's the bare essentials. Three meals a day and enough water for two will get me started. The planning process always involves finding trails with available water sources. Boiling and bottling keep down on the amount I have to carry. If there is no wood for a fire, I keep a filtered survival straw in my pack. My foraging skills are improving, but they aren't up to a self-sustaining level quite yet.

My work as a freelance writer lets me stay out on the trails longer than a traditional job, which has been a blessing. So long as I make it back to the old farmhouse five or six days a month, I can do enough work to keep the bills paid. Otherwise, you'll find me in the forest.

I've been on the trail for four days now. This time, I'm planning to stay out a bit longer than usual. Typically, I aim for five days, but ten is my target for this trip. I'm on a trail in the Appalachian Mountain range and heading toward a waterfall that some backpacking blogs have recommended. It should only take another day to reach, so I'll enjoy two days there before heading back.

Time to set up camp for the evening,
Laurie

***

March 18th, 2022

So I still haven't found the waterfall. I've followed the maps I printed off before heading out. The first few days, everything looked exactly as it was described, but this afternoon the directions didn't seem to match up. I was supposed to cross a wooden footbridge earlier this afternoon, but when I reached the stream, there was no bridge to be seen.

I thought about trying to wade through, but I can't tell how deep the water is and the stream is wider than I had anticipated. Earlier I tried to find the bottom with a four-foot branch, but it didn't hit the bottom. Seems like a bad plan, being out here by myself. If I get swept off or bogged down, I'm done for.

Cell service hasn't been much help. After a few attempts to look at my whereabouts on Google Maps, I've given up. There is a bar of service, but the loading wheel spins like a tire going down the hill and the map never loads. I wasted a lot of time hiking back and forth on this side of the stream looking for the bridge.

Maybe it washed away. Some of those posts were from two or three years ago. The trail itself doesn't seem to receive much maintenance either. I'll give it another day of looking, but I'll need to head back soon. Food will start running low and there hasn't been much to forage or gather.

I'm bummed out, but it happens. It's still been a fun trip. If I don't find the falls this time, I'll give it another try in a month or two. I'm feeling a little winded from all the searching today, and it's getting dark. Better set up camp.

Better days ahead,
Laurie

P.S.—Setting up camp was quicker than usual tonight. I ended up stumbling into an abandoned camping spot. At first, I thought someone was still there. After a closer inspection, it's obvious someone left a lot of gear behind.

Two dry, rotting shirts and a bra are hanging from a tree branch. A sleeping bag filled with dead leaves and animal droppings still sits by the stone fire ring.

The fire ring came in handy. I usually have to set one up myself, but someone took care of that for me. There are even enough dried logs piled up to keep me from having to gather my own, but I'm still a little irritated that someone just dumped their gear and bailed.

Stuff like that is getting more common these days. It's a great way to mess up natural habitats. Like the world isn't full of enough garbage.

***

March 19th, 2022

I didn't sleep well last night. It started to rain around 2:00 AM and I had only set up the sleeping hammock for the evening. The weather report before I sat out showed clear skies and no precipitation, so I hadn't tied the tarp overhead. Dad wouldn't have been that lazy. I should have listened to him.

There was a lot of noise in the woods as well. A few breaking tree branches and rustling leaves. The wind didn't seem that bad, but I guess it was enough to cause some of the old tree boughs to give way and rattle on the forest floor. I nearly flipped my hammock when the first one fell.

Some of the noises sounded almost rhythmic, though. There was a hand full of times I thought I heard the distinct rustling of footsteps in the leaves and foliage, but I must have been imagining it. No one would have been out in the rain that late at night.

I even pulled out my night vision trail came and scanned the area surrounding my camp. Didn't see a damn thing though. Other than trees, of course.

Most of the animals in this forest bed down during the rain, anyway. Not to say something couldn't have snuck away from its den for a midnight snack, but it wasn't a good night to be out and about. I should know. It took me nearly a half-hour to secure the tarp over my hammock before I could get back into my water-logged hammock.

My damn sleeping bag is still soaked. Hope it dries out before bed tonight. I'm not hopeful. There is nothing like a wet sleeping bag to end a hike early.

On a higher note, I found the bridge today! Looks like I decided to walk in the wrong direction. I walked about a mile past the point where I had originally run into the stream and there it was. In all its wobbly, splinter-filled glory. It wasn't much more than some crudely nailed planks supported by some log pilings settled in the stream bed, but it held up for me to cross it.

I still can't decide if I'm going to try and make it to the falls this trip or not. It's a long way to go, and I already lost a lot of time. If I don't hit the falls by afternoon tomorrow, I'll turn back. Don't want to get stuck out here without any food.

Hoping for a dry night of sleep,
Laurie

***

March 22nd, 2022

What the hell is going on?

Two days ago, I turned on my phone to look through some pictures from the hike so far and it is filled with photos I had never taken.

I'd spent another day trying to hike toward the waterfalls before I saw them. Should have turned back and headed home, but I kept telling myself I must almost be there.

There are more than forty pictures of me sleeping from various angles. I always sleep with the netting of the hammock zipped, but some of the pictures are of me with the zipper open. The dates on the pictures start on March 16th. Someone has been following me almost the entire time.

A video on me from last night even shows someone taking the dehydrated food from my pack and dumping them on the ground.

Brown work boots grind the food into the dirt. You can hear them breathing like a damn marathon runner the entire time.

I've been traveling for a day and a half with no sleep. When I found the pictures, I grabbed my pack and left behind my hammock and sleeping bag. I know I should have grabbed it, but I panicked and didn't want to stick around there for another minute.

Some nutcase in the woods is following me and I'm at least three days from making it back to my car parked on the trailhead. That is if I don't stop to rest. I told myself at first I would just walk nonstop until I got back, but I'm already exhausted. I've got to get some rest.

Maybe I've lost them.

To make matters worse, that shitty little wooden bridge was gone when I got back to the stream. I know I was in the right place because the log pilings in the stream are still poking out of the water.

I'm going to have to swim or wade across. I hope I make it. What other option do I have?

God help me,
Laurie

***

March 23rd, 2022

Crossing the stream didn't go well.

I tried to toss my pack to the other side, but it landed two feet shy and splashed into the moving water. I couldn't afford to lose the last bit of food I had, so I dove in and swam after it. The effort was more energy than I should have expended, but my options are running out.

It's getting dark and I'm still at least a day away from my car. All of my clothes are wet and there is only enough food left in my pack for one more meal. I'm going to make it tonight and try to get a little bit of sleep.

My phone is still out of service, and I haven't been able to reach anyone for help. I'm afraid I'm going to die here. I'm scared. I just want to go home. I want my dad.

I think I just saw a camera flash go off in the woods. If anyone finds this, please tell…

The author of this journal is still unidentified. If you recognize any information provided here, please contact local or federal authorities.

THE LEGEND OF THOMAS COIN

When I was much younger, probably around six or seven, my grandmother became frail after a long illness. I can't remember what it was, but my parents decided it would be best for her to move in with us so they could help take care of her. We had never spent much time with her before that due to how far away she had lived. We grew close quickly, though. It was nice to have her there.

Her bedroom was just across the hall from mine, and she would limp into my room each night and tell me a bedtime story. I always knew she was coming when I heard her door slam followed by the *thump* of her old cane. Sometimes she would tell me her version of the classics everyone heard growing up like "Hansel and Gretel" or "The Three Little Pigs".

The memory of the only fight I ever had at school clings to my memory like a tumor. I hate to admit it, but for my first two years of elementary school, I was a bully. Mostly I teased other children about their clothes or poor grades. It wasn't kind, I know now, but my fortunate upbringing hadn't caused me to develop much empathy.

During recess, I started to make fun of a young boy's tattered clothing when he punched me directly in the nose. My vision swam and I felt the warm blood trickle from my nose onto my lips. The other children began to laugh at me and even after all these years, I can still feel the heat that rose in my cheeks. No one had ever stood up to me before and it made me angrier than I had ever been.

I pummeled the poor kid. His initial blow had been enough to rattle me, but once I regained composure there wasn't much of a fight to be had. He didn't deserve it, and the memory still haunts me to this day. A nearby teacher broke it up quickly and hauled us both to the principal's office.

The principal rightly assessed that I had caused the fight, and the other boy received no punishment. I, on the other hand, was suspended for the remainder of the week. I waited by the front door with my head hung low for my father to come to pick me up. It was likely the first time in my life I questioned what kind of person I was.

I received the lecture of a lifetime on the way home. My father told me he had never been more ashamed of me, and I started to cry. It had never occurred to me until that moment what a hateful child I had been.

Later that evening as I tossed and turned in my bed, I heard the door across the hall creak open.

Slam!

Thump!

Jingle!

Thump!

Jingle!

Thump!

Jingle!

My door opened slowly, and my grandmother's face appeared. She smiled at me, but I still remember how sad it looked. It was as though she had just finished crying. She dotted at the corner of her eye with the sleeve of her nightgown. As she stepped into my room, I could see a mason jar full of coins clutched in her hand. It rattled as she placed it gently on my dresser and made her way to me. Her wrinkled hand patted my leg as she settled down toward the foot of my bed.

"Little James," she had said softly. "You had a poor day at school, so I hear."

I nodded as a huge well of tears pooled in the corners of my eyes.

"You must be kind to little boys and girls," she continued without waiting for a response. "Bad things happen to little boys who do bad deeds."

She lifted her shaking hand and pointed to the jar on my dresser.

"There are only nine coins in that jar now, James," she said with a quiver in her voice. "There should be ten, but you lost one today."

"What do you mean, Gram?" I finally spoke. She turned her head to look at me and her face was now oddly devoid of emotion.

I'll never forget the poem she told me.

"Thomas Coin collected brass
For every crooked deed.
'No evil act receives a pass'
This was the old man's creed.
For when each babe in town was born
Ten fine brass coins they gained.
But if they garnered Old Tom's scorn
One less brass coin remained.
If all ten coins did disappear
The child's time drew nigh.
Old Thomas Coin had made it clear
That all bad children die.
So do good deeds and please be kind
I beg you here and now
For ten poor deeds, I will remind
Are all he will allow."

Gram looked at me blankly after finishing the verses, but I hadn't been able to respond. She began to pat my leg again to comfort me. I felt uneasy after hearing her words.

"When I was a young girl, I had a sister named Stephanie," she told me. "She was sweet, but prone to trickery and unkind deeds. Stephanie had been caught stealing a pastry from the town baker. Afterward, our grandmother told us the tale of Thomas Coin."

She paused and looked toward the jar she had placed on my dresser.

After a few moments of silence, she began to tell me the legend of Thomas Coin. He had been a wealthy man who lived in her grandmother's village. Mr. Coin had no family of his own, so each time a baby was born he would visit the family and give them a jar filled with ten brass coins. The child would inherit them when they reached adulthood.

My grandmother explained that this was a great deal of money back then.

Thomas told the parents that the money was the child's to keep, but if he learned of any cruel or ill deed they performed, he would return and collect one of the coins as a punishment. He told them he hoped it would help the children grow to be kind and helpful citizens.

Mr. Coin continued this ritual until he was found murdered in his home. A robber had broken into his cottage, beaten him to death with his walking stick, and stolen all of his money. The thief, perhaps superstitious, had placed two of the stolen coins on the old man's eyelids before leaving.

No thief was ever arrested, but the town suspected a troublesome boy named Michael had committed the crime.

Later that same week, Michael reported to the local constable that someone had broken into his home and stolen the brass coins from his jar. The constables investigated but found no evidence that anyone had broken into the home. Michael was furious and began to harass townspeople in hopes of recovering his money.

The next morning, Michael was found in a pool of blood in the town square. Two brass coins rested on his closed eyelids. There were no clues as to who had done this other than a set of footprints and the drag mark of a walking stick leading from the square. They ended up at the empty cottage where Thomas had once lived.

Thomas, my grandmother finished, still reclaimed the coins from bad children even after his death. If they lost them all then Thomas would kill them.

"Did you or your sister lose any coins?" I asked numbly.

She nodded.

"I lost three and my sister lost six," she responded. "You only have nine left after today, James. You must make kind choices."

That evening stuck to my mind like glue for the remainder of my childhood years. After my grandmother passed away, I took the jar of coins from my dresser and tucked it away at the top of my closet. In the few instances when I had done something particularly bad I would check the jar. To my surprise, each time a coin vanished.

After losing three coins I became a model citizen. Not that I was an extremely awful child after my schoolyard fight, but the vanishing coins always filled me with fear. I assumed my parents had known the story as well and removed them when I got in some kind of trouble, but I was never certain enough to risk it.

My younger brother Dennis was another story. While he had been a timid and well-behaved child, his teenage years had brought about a great change. His quiet nature drifted away, and he had grown openly hostile and disobedient to my parents. It wasn't unusual for my brother to be caught doing drugs, sneaking out of the house at night, or picking fights with other kids at school.

"Did Gram ever tell you about Thomas Coin?" I asked him on a lazy afternoon when I had come home to visit from college. Dennis was now sixteen and I was nineteen. My mother and father had asked me to try and talk some sense into him one weekend while they were out of town.

We spent most of the day in his bedroom playing video games.

"Oh yeah," he responded. "Gram told me all about that goofy bullshit."

"Have you ever counted the coins left in your jar?" I asked.

Dennis rolled his eyes. Tossing his controller beside me on the bed, he walked to his sock drawer and pulled it open. The sound of metal clanking against glass startled me. He reached in and pulled out a mason jar that looked just like the one I had in my closet.

"Just one left," he responded with a smile. "I guess old Tommy'll be coming for me soon."

I pleaded with Dennis to find a better set of friends and get his act together. It wasn't necessarily that I believed Thomas Coin was real. It just broke my heart to see my little brother making bad choices that would affect his future in so many ways. His smiles and laughter at my pleas were enough to let me know nothing I said had made an impression.

"Look, James," he responded flippantly. "It's cool that Gram's story about the old man's coins scared you into living like a boy scout, but I'm young and plan to have fun before I head off to college."

Knowing I was making no progress, I tossed the controller on the bed beside his and left the room. We didn't speak for the remainder of the day.

I was awoken around 1:00 AM by the sound of the front door slamming. By the time I was able to groggily dash to the window, I could see Dennis' Honda Civic vanish around the corner at the end of the street. With Mom and Dad out of town, he had seized the opportunity to sneak out of the house once again.

In frustration, I attempted to call Dennis multiple times. Each call resulted in an immediate answer from his voicemail system. My text messages went unanswered. It remained this way through the entire night.

At some point, I drifted off to sleep in a chair downstairs as I waited for Dennis to return. My phone chirped loudly and the vibration on my lap woke me up. Sunlight was pouring in through the living room windows and I could see that Dennis' car had not returned to the driveway. I looked down at my phone expecting to see Dennis' phone number on the ID, but instead, I saw a number I didn't recognize.

"Hello?" I said as I put the phone to my ear.

"This is Captain William Pullman with the State Police," a matter-of-fact voice burst through my phone speaker. "May I speak with James Compton?"

"This is him."

"Mr. Compton, I'm sorry to inform you that we believe we've found the body of your brother, Dennis. Will you be able to come to the medical examiner's office to help make an ID?"

It only took me about twenty minutes to arrive at the medical examiner's office after I hung up the phone. The drive there was a blur, and I can only imagine how many stop signs and red lights I plowed through. I felt how a horse must feel with blinders on. Only the destination remained ahead. Nothing else mattered.

When I arrived, a middle-aged man with a potbelly and thinning red hair met me at the door. He introduced himself as Captain Pullman. While he led me through the sterile waiting room and into the viewing area, he explained to me that my brother had been found after a car break-in was reported. I silently prayed they had misidentified him. Surely it wasn't my brother. Just some awful mistake.

Officers had arrived to see the door of a white Chevy Express van open into the street and a pair of legs dangling from the seat. His car was not discovered in the area. During the approach, they could see thick ribbons of blood dripping out of the van onto the pavement. Dennis had died of blunt force trauma to the head while trying to hotwire the van.

Whoever had beaten him had also shoved two brass coins into his eye sockets.

After the officer finished describing the scene to me, the last thing I could recall was seeing a blanket of white overtake my vision before I passed out. I awoke later that day in my bedroom at my parents' house. My father was sitting in the chair beside the bed, and I could hear my mother wailing down the hall.

"Dad?" I said groggily.

"Yeah," he replied flatly. I could see he had been crying. "You passed out at the office. The police hadn't been able to reach us and… I'm sorry they called you down there to do that."

I began to sob.

"Dad," I cried. "I'm so sorry. I tried to talk to him but…" I couldn't finish.

My father sat on the bed next to me and cradled my head to his chest just like he had done when I was a child. He had just lost his youngest son and his instinct was still to comfort me before caring for himself. I hoped at that moment to be the kind of father he had been to me and Dennis.

Later that evening, after I was sure that my parents had gone to bed, I snuck into Dennis's room. As quietly as I could, I pushed the door open and tiptoed to his dresser. Pulling the top drawer out, I rummaged around until my hand rubbed against smooth glass. Fishing the jar out, I could see that it was empty. The single coin that had been there yesterday was gone.

Seven years after Dennis died, my life had become happy and stable. Memories of that horrendous day hadn't gone away, but they had faded a bit. I met my wife, Gwen, during college, and we were fortunate enough to welcome our first child six months ago. Mom and Dad have been over the moon since becoming grandparents.

We named him Dennis after his uncle.

Earlier this afternoon, I told Gwen to go out with some friends and enjoy some baby-free time. Postpartum depression had been difficult for her. Dennis was also a finicky sleeper sometimes, and she always felt the need to get up with him. I appreciated the sleep, but she certainly deserved the break.

Dennis had just gone down for a nap about thirty minutes ago. I was still working from home and thought it would be an opportune time to go knock out tasks while I had some free time. The baby monitor on my desk showed Dennis fast asleep, and I could hear the lullaby music that poured from the speaker near his bed. The camera's night mode gave the monitor the appearance of an old black and white television set.

I don't know if it was the general lack of sleep that all new parents suffered or if the lullaby had taken hold, but at some point I fell asleep in my office chair. It wasn't a deep sleep as I found a few minutes later my attention was drawn to a noise in the hallway.

Thud! Thud! Thump!
Jingle!
Thud! Thud! Thump!
Jingle!
Thud! Thud! Thump!
Jingle!

Alertness didn't fully return to me until I heard the creak of Dennis's bedroom door on the monitor. I thought Gwen may have come home early, so I looked closely at the screen. Nothing appeared at first other than the sleeping bundle in the middle of the crib.

A figure passed onto the screen and stood in front of my son.

The monitor was grainy and the black and white nighttime mode made it difficult to see, but it looked like an old man propping himself up on a tall walking stick. His back was curved and there wasn't a hair on top of his head. A bushy beard erupted from the sides of his face.

"A gift for you, young man!" A raspy voice proclaimed. "I hope you keep them all!"

I leaped from my chair and bounded down the hallway to my son's room. The door was standing open even though I knew I had closed it for his nap. My eyes darted around the room, but there was no one there. The window was still locked. If anyone had left the room I would have found them in the hallway.

My pulse began to lower, and my ragged breathing evened out as I walked to the crib. I watched Dennis' chest rise and fall in a peaceful rhythm that filled me with ease. Placing a hand on his chest I smiled and silently thanked God for giving me such a sweet kid.

I turned to leave the room and saw something out of place sitting on his changing table.

A mason jar filled with brass coins.

MR. DEACON AND ASSOCIATES

Do not read this unless you are seeking lucrative and long-term employment. Serious inquiries only. Certain Terms May Apply*

Hello to all of you potential recruits! Allow me to introduce myself. I am Mr. Deacon and I'm a talent scout of sorts. Don't worry about my first name. We likely won't have more than two to three conversations at a maximum, so over-familiarity does us no favors.

My clients task me with acquiring talented individuals for extremely specific and high-pressure career opportunities. It is my assurance to you that should we meet to discuss an employment opportunity you will be provided a cash offer unattainable anywhere else. Do you need medical insurance? Not a problem! Paid time off varies by job posting, but in most instances, one to two weeks a year will be considered manageable. Retirement, if you reach it, of course, is unparalleled in any other public or private sector job. The contract terms are quite binding though. You see, once you fill these positions it is of the utmost importance that the position remains filled. Your work, dear applicant, is a matter of life and death in most instances.

I've performed these talent acquisitions for the better part of the last fifty years and have found that the greatest success in filling these unique roles has been to simply tell the truth. My clients seek a desperate sort. Those down on their luck seem to be far more willing to take on this employment. It is a difficult proposition to convince a person with a comfortable lifestyle and a rainy-day fund to accept these deadly jobs. In recent years I have also discovered that occasionally the curious sort will wander into my reach to fill these positions.

Dear applicant, you may have heard tales of my talent acquisitions from time to time. A strange story pops up from time to time describing their gainful employment. Tales of beasts, tortured souls, foul imps. My father often told me as I grew up that you shouldn't believe every outlandish tale you hear. What he didn't tell me is that more of the outlandish tales you hear are true, but we simply cannot or will not accept the maddening possibilities the darker corners of our world can bring.

I've gotten terribly off track. Please allow me to regain my footing here. Below I will tell you of two positions available as well as the benefits and potential risks. You chose to read this job listing, so I can only assume you know what you may be getting into.

Posting #1: Evening Shift Cave Watchman/Marksman

Pay: $5000 per non-sighting week. $1000 bonus for successful extermination!

Description: If you've ever fancied the tranquil life of lakeside cabin living then we have been searching for you! Accommodations in a rustic but well-equipped cabin in the dense woodlands of the Eastern Kentucky mountains are available. Your shift will begin at 5:00 PM EST and end at 5:00 AM EST from Monday to Friday. No holidays and weekends at this time. Temporary personnel will relieve you. Your duties are minimal, but quite specific. At the beginning of each shift, you will be provided with two rifles and abundant ammunition. Please have experience with firearms and the maintenance thereof as you will need to perform daily checks on your primary and secondary weapons each shift.

You will be posted in a 50-foot-high watchtower at the intersection of three cave entrances. More accurately in this situation, they are cave exits. YOU ARE NEVER TO ENTER THE CAVES. You will only observe the entrances for activity. If any entity, Shamblers as we've come to call them, exits any of the three caves, you are to shoot them on sight. They most often have the appearance of an emaciated and hairless bear that walks with an unsteady, shuffling gait until they feed. After a medium-sized meal, the Shambler will gain greater speed and agility.

Through trial and error, we have been able to learn that their primary source of nutrients comes from human bone marrow. This places you in particular danger if they are not eliminated quickly and at a distance. Knowing this, you will periodically receive a shipment of fresh cadavers to lure the Shambler to a clearing for a clear view when eliminating them. Hired personnel will be responsible for placing cadavers in the clearing at the start of the shift, and removal and cold storage of any uneaten cadavers at the end of the shift.

It should be noted that only a shot to the head will kill the Shamblers. Removal of the exterminated remains is unnecessary as the creature will burst into flames after elimination. Fire extinguishers are provided in the watchtower for post-termination suppression.

Lastly, you should never at any time attempt to simplify your job by attempting to collapse the caves and trap the Shamblers. This has been attempted twice in the past. While seemingly successful at first, the original cave returned the next day without issue with an additional opening located beside it. The process was attempted a second time, which resulted in the third opening. This has increased the emergence of Shamblers and increased the workload of Shambler escape termination specialists. Their emergence in recent years has become more frequent and erratic, so remain vigilant lest your marrow become their next meal.

If the first job doesn't interest you, allow me to tantalize your mind with a second offering!

Posting #2: Live-in caretaker of condemned orphanage.

Pay: $3000 weekly. Free room and board included.

Description: New York City draws an exciting assortment of people from all around the world. It also seems to maintain a fierce grip on some of its very own deceased occupants. Trident Orphanage near East Harlem was the site of a devastating fire in 1937. Seven unfortunate children lost their lives in the blaze, yet their noncorporeal forms have remained.

Your job as caretaker of the Trident Orphanage is to see to the needs of the children while keeping them from contacting one another. If they become aware of the fact that they are deceased, they will either attempt to possess your body and exit the orphanage or lure nearby pedestrians into the building to do the same. Only five of the original seven children still reside in the building due to the carelessness of two previous caretakers.

The organization that maintains a watch over this facility experimented with the release of one child via the possession of a vagrant in the 1960s. While initially seeming to be a questionable but effective method of releasing these lost souls, the short-term study of the possessed vagrant proved this method to be unacceptable. As the vagrant was observed over the following two weeks, their body began to deteriorate rapidly in a similar fashion to advanced leprosy. Corresponding with this, both the personality of the child and the possessed subject struggled for physical and mental control. After 14 days the vagrant expired and released the poor soul back into the world where it continually moved from host to host. This child and host were eventually quarantined in a different facility to this day, although a new host must be acquired every 14 days as it has become impossible to confine the soul in celestial form.

Escaped subject two vanished in 1989 after assuming control of the caretaker. It was never recovered. Location and retrieval efforts are still ongoing.

As a caretaker, your duties will be to engage the other five orphans with various activities throughout the day in their respective rooms. Games, toys, and books are provided and should be rotated out regularly so as not to become stale or disengaging. The children are under no circumstances to see one another. If they see their appearance or that of the others, they become aware of their current predicament. Their unfortunate final form still maintains the charred flesh and bone of their final living days. Escaped subject one discovered a forgotten mirror which began their frenzy to find a new body, resulting in the vagrant possession experiment. Escaped subject two was able to see another child in the hallway, which prompted the possession of the current caretaker and eventual escape.

Keep the children engaged and out of the eye-line of one another. As a precaution, the Trident Orphanage now has no reflective surfaces in the facility and the door remains locked from the outside should you become an unwilling vessel for one of your charges. You will be relieved for four weeks out of the year for a vacation and all physical needs will be met during your stay.

**By reading the above position notices you have agreed to accept placement by Mr. Deacon and associates.*

Those, dear applicant, are my only two active openings at the moment. I'm afraid that willing participants are sometimes difficult to come by, so the terms I work under have become somewhat more unscrupulous over the years. Desperation, after all, can be created. Your knowledge of my work has bound you to a contract of sorts with two potential paths forward.

Path One: Accept this gainful employment from myself and my clients. All you need to do is write Posting #1 or Posting #2 on a sheet of paper, place it in an envelope with a small drop of your blood on the corner, and place it in your mailbox. One of my couriers will be by this evening to check for your reply. We already know where you are. You may be chosen as our next lucky applicant. In the event of a failure in one of these positions, we may collect you in the future as a more proper replacement.

Path Two: Do nothing. Ignore this. Leave no envelope. Again, we know where you are. The unwilling always make excellent bait for the Shamblers or a pristine vessel for our unfortunate child in quarantine.

Either way, dear applicant, I will be seeing you. Some sooner than others.

Thank you,
R. Deacon and Associates

***

Mr. Deacon is here again with a new job offer. Certain Terms May Apply*

Hello to all of you potential recruits! Mr. Deacon here again and, as always, I am excited you have chosen to consider employment with one of my clients. Welcome back to some of those I am already familiar with! If we haven't had the pleasure as of yet, rest assured that I have previously provided a reasonable amount of information as to who I am and what I do. For those of you with a limited amount of time or attention, I will give you a brief recapitulation.

My name, dear applicant, is Mr. Deacon and I am a talent scout of sorts. A variety of clients employ my services in the acquisition of talented men and women to perform lucrative but dangerous tasks both long-term and short. Benefits are provided, compensation is generous, but the work will be challenging. An employment opportunity and relevant information will be provided below, so please read with care.

For those familiar with my work, please allow me to update you on a few things. My benevolent clients were overwhelmed by the amount of interest in our previous two offerings. This is most fortuitous as the occurrence of events and locations requiring their attention seems to be increasing at a rate at which we have not before seen. Some of our best and brightest investigators are working diligently at these new sites to prepare them for job placement. In the coming weeks and months, I may again reach out for your talents.

As usual, I have gotten a bit off track. Please allow me to present you with a single tantalizing option today. There are many offers in the works currently, but this one is of particular importance to my operation as a whole. Certain agreements must be maintained, and my priority is to make safe those unaware of certain entities and threats that creep just behind the peaceful façade of this world.

Posting #3: On-Call Parel Delivery. Must Be Available 24 Hours A Day, 365 Days A Year.

Pay: $2000 per completed delivery

Locations: Various postings around the world.

Description: If you find yourself with abundant time on your hands and a desire to travel your local vicinity, then I believe we may have just the position for you! Havencroft and Garnett Delivery Solutions have immediate openings for detailed and discreet delivery drivers. Constant availability is required with a two-year contracted term.

Your duties as a delivery driver at Havencroft and Garnett Delivery Solutions are straightforward but must be followed to the word. Upon receiving a call from our dispatch team, you are to report to the provided address no later than one hour after notification. The address will change with each new delivery as well as the vehicle you use to make the deliveries. Once you arrive at the provided location you will find a cargo van with an advertisement on the side of H&G Logistics. The door will be unlocked and the keys will be in the ignition. A yellow sticky note will be adhered to the radio with the delivery address.

The provided address in your cargo van will be no more than ten miles from your current destination and no less than five miles away. You are to use the onboard GPS in the van to travel to the provided address. Arrival is required within one hour of taking possession of the cargo van. Do not make any personal stops while driving the H&G Logistics vehicle.

Should you be pulled over by any law enforcement entity there is a business card located above your head above the sun visor. You are not to touch this card unless a traffic stop or roadblock occurs. The card is to be provided to the officer making the stop. It should be noted that this card is not to be returned to you and will remain in the possession of the law enforcement officer. If the officer should attempt to return the card to you, begins to show signs of neurological issues, or attempts to open your vehicle door and gain entry, you are to drive away immediately. The officer will not attempt to follow you. Understand that you are never to attempt to read this card yourself.

During transit to your assigned destination, you are never to inspect the cargo in the rear of the van. Every delivery will have a steel-reinforced chest approximately the size of a refrigerator box turned on its side. While most parcels will remain silent during transit, you may expect a variety of scratching noises, smells of decay, screaming, and occasional pleading coming from the container. The voice from the container may also occasionally know your name or sound similar to a friend or a loved one. Regardless of any attempts at interaction from the contents of the container you are prohibited from examination or communication with the contents held within. Earplugs are provided in the glove box for your convenience.

Upon arrival at your delivery destination, you are to pull within twenty feet of any door and honk the horn three times. Turn off the engine, place the keys on the dashboard, and place the sleep mask located in the console cup holder over your eyes. If you placed the provided earplugs in your ears they must be removed at this time. Within forty-five seconds of honking the horn, you will hear the back doors of the van open, and the cargo will be removed. After the doors have been closed you will hear three knocks on the driver's side window. Roll it down with the manual crank handle. A voice will ask you why you are there. You must repeat the following words in exactly this order: "We have provided what has been agreed upon. May our gift provide your continued mercy." Do not remove your blindfold and do not attempt to move.

While you may be tempted to depart at this point, you must remain in place. You will hear the container being opened and the unmistakable sounds of a struggle. Even if the cargo has previous-

ly been quiet, it will at this time undoubtedly begin to scream. Breaking bones, the tearing of flesh, and other telltale signs of feeding will follow if the cargo is found to be acceptable. The feeding process will last for approximately five minutes. At the end of this, you will hear the back doors of the cargo van open, and the container will be placed back in and the doors re-secured.

If you have followed all these steps correctly, you should hear three additional knocks on your window. At this time you are to count aloud to one hundred and take off your blindfold. Start the van, depart the location, and do not visually investigate the area as you leave. Return the van to your pickup destination and retrieve the folded handkerchief and matches located in the passenger seat. Exit the van and place the handkerchief in the gas tank opening and ignite the handkerchief with the provided matches. Move quickly out of the vicinity of the vehicle. Regardless of distance, you are required to travel by foot back to your home. Upon arrival, you will find an envelope with payment located inside your front door.

Failure in part or whole during this process will result in near-immediate death.

**By reading the above position notice you have agreed to accept placement by Mr. Deacon and associates.*

So you have it, dear applicant. This posting is near and dear to my heart as I have overseen this position from the beginning of my career. Your dedication to this service will continue to maintain a delicate balance kept in place since time immemorial.

As to how you shall show interest, dear applicant, please do the following. Before you go to bed this evening, take a drop of blood and spread it evenly on your thumb. Press your thumb to the center of a mirror in your home and leave the bloody print there. The Courier is working on more expedient avenues of travel so this should improve the process just a touch.

If the print is there in the morning then your services will not be required. Should your print be gone, then my associates will soon be in touch. If we do not select you for this position, I ask that you do not become despondent. Rest assured I will return with other exciting possibilities in the future.

As with last time, dear applicant, I will be seeing you. Some sooner than others.

Thank you,

Mr. R. Deacon and Associates

WELCOME TO ALLISTER VALLEY

Have you ever seen an emergency broadcast system signal on your television? Seven vertical bars of various colors blast onto your screen accompanied by an ear-piercing tone that is impossible to ignore. A robotic voice will often interrupt the shrill cry with a message indicating the variety of emergencies for your location. Thunderstorms, tornados, flash flooding. You know the type.

My town has the same federal emergency system as yours. What we have that yours likely doesn't is a local emergency warning broadcast. It does not cover weather-related emergencies or Amber Alert notifications. We still take cover when it arrives, but most of us have never seen what we are hiding from.

The first emergency alert I can remember happened when I was five or six years old. I am not completely sure, but it isn't important. Talking puppets on a PBS show were teaching me ABCs and how to count to ten, and I was enraptured. The huge yellow bird was telling me about ways to be kind to new friends when the screen began to crackle with static and the picture began to skip.

Pink and yellow vertical bars filled the old television screen. A high-pitched whine poured from the speakers, and I can still remember covering my ears in terror. Nothing like that had ever happened before. Maybe my parents had discussed this with me, but my memory doesn't seem to be able to recall having been warned about it.

With my ears covered I could still hear the overpowering hum. It seemed to be getting louder. Feeling a tap on my shoulder and turning my head I could see my mother and father behind me beckoning me to follow them. My father had a storm radio clutched in his right hand that was almost certainly blasting the same warning tone as the television. I awkwardly raised myself from the floor while still holding my ears and followed them.

We walked from the living room, through the dining room, and onto the back porch. Dad pulled the metal hatch doors to the storm cellar open and waved my mother and me inside. Once I began toddling down the stairs, I removed my hands from my ears to grasp onto the banister. The humming was still pouring from the radio, but the volume was turned down and it no longer hurt my ears.

"Is a storm coming?" I asked my mother in confusion. The window shades were open in the living room that day and I can still recall the bright rays of sunshine stretching toward me on the carpeted floor. "It looked nice outside."

My mother turned her head toward me and held up a finger to her mouth. We continued down the storm cellar steps in silence but for the emergency tone. Behind us, my father pulled the cellar doors shut. I could hear him sliding latches into place followed by the clicking of padlocks. After he secured the door, he came to the bottom of the stairs and guided us toward a secondary room in the cellar.

As my father began to chain and bolt the door to the room, my mother sat the radio down on an old table, fell into a worn armchair, and pulled me close to her chest. All these decades later I can still remember feeling her pulse hammer in my ear. Her breathing was rapid, and she held me so tightly I was scared I wouldn't be able to catch my breath.

"It's going to be okay, baby," my mother said with a shaking voice. "This is just something we have to do sometimes to stay safe."

"What are we hiding from?" I asked, juvenile fear mounting.

My mother was opening her mouth to respond when my father made a shushing noise. He pointed toward the weather alert radio on the table. The tone had now shifted from a droning whine into prolonged bursts. A robotic male voice began to speak after the last burst.

This is a message from the Emergency Alert System of the Allister Valley Safety and Protection Board.

At this time please, seek shelter in a basement, storm shelter, or interior room of your house without windows.

This is a Level Two Watch. I repeat; This is a Level Two Watch. No entities have yet been spotted.

Unusual activity has been reported on Palumbo Street and Slate Street.

Remain indoors and away from windows until you receive an All-Clear message from this channel…

The same mechanical message played in a rotation, punctuated with the pulsing whine. My mother continued pressing me to her chest and the rhythmic beat of her heart and the gentle lullaby she sang eventually caused me to drift off to sleep. Mom and Dad never told me what we were hiding from that day.

As I ate my breakfast the next morning, I can remember listening to the local AM news on the radio. My father was cooking breakfast as my mother, and I sat at the table reading a Berenstain Bears book when the DJ fell silent. When his husky voice returned to the air, he announced that a little girl named Margret Cupsworth had gone missing the day before.

"No search effort will be made as the circumstances of her disappearance are well understood," the man said. "A memorial for Margret will be held at the Hall Street Elementary School gym this evening. Instead of flowers, the family requests donations to be made to Allister Valley Safety and Protection Board."

My family went to the memorial service that evening. I had never worn a tie before, but my mother had taken me to the local department store and purchased one. My father cried as he carefully tied it around my shirt collar. When we arrived, I remember thinking that the entire town must have shown up. A huge line was formed to comfort the family as they stood by a flower-lined photo of their daughter.

Margret smiled at the camera in her pink flowered dress. Eternally happy. Eternally young.

Margret had been in preschool with me. She was not a close friend at that age. I was still firmly in the phase of life where girls were gross and scary. Still, I remember being sad that she was gone. Not that I entirely understood at the time she was dead.

Mom and Dad had explained to me on the way to the memorial that people who didn't get inside when the emergency alert sounded were never seen again. They never clearly stated that it meant they were dead. As I grew older, I came to understand that was the likeliest outcome.

My family reached the front of the receiving line, and my father prompted me to shake hands with Mr. Cupsworth. He looked angry and sad all at once. When he took my hand, he shook it gently and nodded to me. My eyes were welled with tears. Grief radiated from him; even at my young age, I could feel his despair.

Mom comforted Mrs. Cupsworth, so I continued down the line. Besides her mother stood a little girl, her red face streaked with tears. She couldn't have been more than four. To this day I will never understand why they made her stand there in her sorrow and face a town full of people who could not comfort her.

"Hi," I said meekly. "Was Margret your sister?"

The girl nodded her head but didn't say a word.

"She was real nice," I stammered. "She was in my class."

The little girl sobbed loudly and wrapped her arms around me. My arms were pinned to my side, and I was mortified. But I stood there and let her squeeze my chest.

"Momma told her not to play so far from the house!" the little girl cried. "She knew she wasn't allowed to go that far!"

That was the day I met Paige Cupsworth. She ended up being my high school sweetheart. Short and feisty. Smart as a whip. I probably would have married her too. Unfortunately, Allister Valley and its cursed sirens had no respect for the hopes and dreams of its citizens.

Four years of college was the only break I ever received from the intermittent emergency signals in my hometown. A few times a year there would be a National Weather Service alert on campus and while most of my classmates seemed unconcerned, I was always the oddball. The first time it happened I ran out of my English 102 class and sprinted to the boiler room in the basement of the class hall.

It was embarrassing, to say the least. Some of my friends in the class called my cell phone to ask if I was okay and when I explained to them that this was normal protocol in my hometown, they seemed confused. I considered trying to explain the Allister Valley Safety and Protection warnings to them, but it was clear they didn't have similar experiences growing up.

Paige and I talked on the phone every night and visited on as many weekends as my scrawny bank account would allow. Mom helped when she could, but I had to work most weekends to make enough money to cover expenses. Dad had passed away unexpectedly during my freshman year and money was tight for her.

I still feel as though if I had gone home more often maybe Paige would still be here.

It took me a few more alarms to fight the urge to hide in a subterranean, windowless room but, eventually, I was able to control my urges. Tornados were very uncommon in the area and the alerts I would receive on my cell phone were generally just to let people know bad weather was on the way. It didn't always indicate a need to take shelter. Those may have been the only completely relaxed years of my life.

Early in my last semester of college, I could tell Paige was becoming despondent. She was attending a community college in the next county over from Allister Valley. I had begged and pleaded with her to transfer to the state college with me, but she wisely declined. All of the courses she needed for her degree were available at a much lower cost there.

"Are you coming back to Allister Valley after you graduate?" she asked one night on the phone.

"More likely than not," I replied. "With Dad gone, I think Mom probably needs more help so I hate to be far away. Besides, you seem pretty set on being a social worker there, and I'd like to think I fit somewhere in your five-year plan."

She paused longer than I was comfortable with. We had talked about marriage abstractly since I had graduated high school, but had never made any official declarations. The silence had been unnerving.

"Paige," I said. "Are you still there?"

"Yeah," she said flatly. "I'm here. Not planning on getting rid of you any time soon unless you act up. Sometimes I just think… you know… we could start over somewhere else."

I was surprised to hear she was considering moving away. She had always talked about her career plans in the community. Enrolling in college so close had allowed her to be with her parents. It wasn't as though I hadn't considered venturing elsewhere, but Allister Valley had always seemed to be our future together.

"I'm not saying no," I responded. "Just kind of surprised, I guess. What has you thinking of leaving now?"

"I want to have kids someday, Chris," she said. "I don't want to have to worry that what happened to Margret will…" She began to cry softly and didn't finish the sentence. I reassured her as best I could, but it never seemed to be of much use in those days. More and more of our conversations had turned to Margaret that semester. While she was a fleeting memory to me from my childhood school days, she was an ever-present thought for Paige.

Every time the warning message sounded in town she would call me. Whenever another citizen of Allister Valley went missing during the emergency alert Paige would recount all of the details she knew during our calls. All of these conversations were punctuated by Margret.

My heart ached for her, but it seemed to be growing into a weight she wasn't able to shoulder. More frequently she began to ask what I thought was outside during the alerts and I told her honestly that I didn't know. The alerts and warnings from my parents had always been enough to keep me inside.

"Sometimes during the sirens, I can hear a little girl talking outside." She told me one night. "Dad will yell for her to go away and Mom cries in the corner. They haven't told me, but I think it's Margret."

"It isn't Margret," I replied sadly. "Baby, she's been gone for a long time. I'm sorry. I know it's hard, but it isn't her."

"Maybe," she said complacently. "You're right. I love you." She hung up the phone.

I wish I had known that would be our last phone call. I would have made it last all night. I would have driven home and spent every minute with her from then on. I would have done everything differently.

But I didn't. And I can't.

My phone rang late in the evening the day after finals. I was lugging boxes from my shabby apartment to my car in preparation for making the final drive back home to Allister Valley. Sliding the box from my hand onto the floor I walked to the kitchen counter to look at the caller ID.

Bruce Cupsworth's number flashed on the Nokia's green screen. I was puzzled since I didn't frequently talk to Paige's father on the phone. We had a great relationship and always enjoyed one another's company at family gathers. He just wasn't a chatty man. A phone call was unusual unless something was wrong.

"Hey Bruce," I said as I lifted my phone to my ear.

"Paige is gone," Bruce said in a wavering baritone. "There was an alert last night and she's gone."

I could hear Paige's mother wailing in the background, and I could hear sniffling and the choking of sobs from her father.

"How?" I asked. It was all I had been able to manage in my shock.

"The alert sounded during dinner," he muttered. "Her mother and I headed to the basement. Paige said she was going to get her cell phone from her room to call you. She never came down. When we came upstairs the front door was standing open. We haven't seen her since."

My heart dropped and I couldn't speak. I felt like I should cry, but no tears came. My brain told me to wail, but I couldn't. I just felt empty.

"Did Paige say anything… strange… to you the last time you spoke?" her father asked.

"Yeah," I stammered. "She… uh… she said something about a little girl's voice outside the door during the alerts. I think she said it sounded like Margret."

"Chris," he said. "I should have told…. No, never mind. We're having a memorial service for her tomorrow. Will you come?"

My heart began to race and I could feel the heat rise to my face.

"A memorial service?" I scoffed. "You should be organizing a search party! She could still be out there!"

A moment of silence fell between us.

"Aren't you going to look for her?" I begged.

"Christopher," he said in a broken monotone. "You know that isn't how this works. Paige is gone. Just like Margret."

"What the hell took her?" I shouted. "What is out there? Why do we have to hide?"

"We aren't going to discuss this," he said, anger rising in his voice. "This is hard enough without you trying to do this right now."

"Do what?" I demanded. "Ask why you aren't looking for your daughter? Ask why we have to hide in the dark and no one ever explains why? Do you even know?"

"Yes," he replied. "After Margret was taken the safety board met with us and… explained some of it."

"Some of it?" I yelled. Hot tears were streaming down my face. "Your kids vanish and you just accept it?"

The phone line went dead. I tried calling Bruce multiple times but it went directly to his voicemail. My attempts to call Mrs. Cupsworth went unanswered as well.

Paige's parents never spoke to me again, and I don't blame them. They had suffered the horrific loss of their only two children, but in my hot-headed youth I wasn't able to consider their sense of loss as I can now. In my early forties, I can see how unsympathetic I was to their grief and sorrow.

***

I moved back to Allister Valley after college and I've been here ever since. The Emergency Alert System has become more advanced in the last few years. The strange pink and yellow vertical stripes and droning alarms on the television are still in place. Now we also receive Amber Alert-style warnings on our cell phones. The Safety Board even installed a powerful air raid siren on the outside of the courthouse.

I'm in my forties now. My mother's health and mental state began to deteriorate rapidly after I moved back to town. The intent had always been to live with her for a few months while I got my feet on the ground and found my own place. When her dementia began to present itself we made the decision that I would stay with her rather than move her into a care facility.

Luck was largely on my side when I began to search for a job that would accommodate the time it took to care for my mother. A midsized publishing company out of New York hired me to work from home soon after college. The pay has never been astronomical but it allows me to work at my own pace and keep an eye on Mom.

Over the years, as her dementia worsened, it became more difficult to keep Mom in the basement when the Emergency Alert System activated. Eventually, I was forced to invest a good deal of money in having our old storm cellar converted into a finished basement. It's a comfortable place for her and she spends most of her day down there reading.

It greatly simplified things for when the alarms sounded. She had become combative when I tried to corral her to the cellar before I converted it into a studio apartment. Now when the sirens sound, she is already securely placed and goes about her day without a care.

When the alert would sound, I would sit by the door leading out of her downstairs apartment. Before I would go down there to wait it out with her, I always made sure the doors and windows were firmly locked. It gave me the illusion of safety, but it didn't stop the voices I had started to hear outside the door.

Years ago, when I had first moved back to Allister Valley, the Emergency Alert System had sounded my first night in town. Mom was still pretty sharp back then. We had moved into the cellar and listened to the weather radio for information. A few moments into the warning I could hear something brushing against the metal doors.

"Chris?" a hushed voice said through the barrier. It sounded like Paige. "Chris… please let me in! I'm so scared!"

I began to cry immediately.

"Christopher!" the voice implored. "Please let me in! They are going to hurt me!"

My mother had walked behind me and placed a hand on my shoulder.

"It isn't her, my boy," she said in a soothing voice. "I know you hear Paige talking, but it isn't her. I hear your father's voice out there right now. He's telling me how much he misses us and to open the door. It gets easier."

That alarm lasted longer than usual. A voice that sounded hauntingly like Paige taunted me for nearly an hour. It said that if I would just open the door it would explain where she had been. I was the only one that could save her. It was my fault that she had vanished.

Through the years I grew used to the haunting voice. My sorrow turned to anger at the taunts. Where my mother had once comforted me through them, I now spent my time comforting her. Her dementia had advanced and she no longer understood it wasn't my father outside of the door. She forgot the calls quickly after the alerts, but the grief and woe in her eyes broke my heart.

The amount of medication she is on to manage the worst of her symptoms is astonishing. Fortunately, the local pharmacy was accommodating in getting all of her medication refills lined up on the same day. The less time I had to spend out of the house at the pharmacy or the grocery store the better. Mom needs around-the-clock care now. It's wearing me thin but I can't stand the thought of her withering away in a nursing home.

When I pulled up to the pharmacy this afternoon the tech, Crissy, greeted me with a smile. She pulled the crinkly white bags off of the shelf and placed them in a brown paper bag. As she rang me up at the register she furrowed her brow.

"Sorry, Chris," the young lady said. "It looks like we only had four of the five medications in stock. The pharmacist transferred the one we didn't have over to Glendale so we could keep her fill dates lined up."

Frustrated, I looked down at my watch. I had stopped at the grocery store before the pharmacy. It had been an hour and a half since I left Mom at home. The drive to and from Glendale would take at least thirty minutes if everything went smoothly.

Two hours couldn't hurt, could it

"Thanks, Crissy," I said in as friendly a manner as I could. "I'll head that way. I appreciate it."

Crissy handed me the bag and I headed out the door. Settling in the driver's seat of my car, I pulled out my phone and called Mom. It went to her voicemail just as I expected. I sent a text message explaining I would be out longer. She rarely saw my text messages, but I liked to do my best to get ahold of her when our routine changed.

After a moment of waiting for a call or response text, it became clear I wouldn't hear from her. Not wanting to waste any more time, I put the car in drive and headed in the direction of Glendale. My mind was washed in the anxiety of having to leave my mother at home alone for so long, but my options were limited.

For a moment I considered calling our neighbor to keep an eye on her, but that option had exhausted itself. The number of times that Ted and Helen had to check in on her had overwhelmed them over the years. Her temper when they would try to keep her in or near the house had worn them down. Abandoning the thought, I tossed my cell phone into the seat beside me.

The trip took longer than I anticipated. When I finally arrived at the pharmacy in Glendale it had taken over twenty-five minutes. The old road between our two towns was down to a single lane for resurfacing.

It had taken the pharmacist an additional ten minutes to fill the script. Their computer system looked as though it was cutting edge during the latter half of the Clinton administration and the transfer had only arrived a few moments before I walked in the door. I paid as quickly as I could and headed out to the car to get back on the road.

Looking at my cell phone, I saw that my mother still hadn't called me back or returned my texts. The ocean of anxiety in my head was beginning to swell. It wasn't unusual for her to ignore her cell phone but it never ceased to fill me with an unhealthy level of existential dread.

My drive back to Allister Valley was more forgiving than the drive to Glendale. When I reached the one-lane portion of the road I had arrived just in time for the woman holding the stop sign to wave my line of traffic through. I waved a grateful hand in her direction and she returned it with a smile. Small-town friendliness can be a welcome thing.

By the time I was two blocks from my mother's house, my cell phone began to squeal wildly in the passenger seat next to me. Initially, I thought it was my mother calling but my heart sank when I realized it was the Emergency Alert System. Slamming the gas pedal to the floor I sped home as quickly as I could.

I reached toward the radio and turned the volume nob up.

...from the Emergency Alert System of the Allister Valley Safety and Protection Board.

At this time, please seek shelter in a basement, storm shelter, or interior room of your house without windows.

This is a Level Five Watch. I repeat; This is a Level Five Watch. Three entities have been spotted on and around West Vine Street, Chippendale Court, and Broadway Avenue.

Remain indoors and away from windows until you receive an All Clear message from this channel. Only condition updates from the Allister Valley Safety and Protection Board serve as factual information.

This is a message from...

The message began replaying on a loop. West Vine was only two streets away from our house on Sullivan Street. Sweat was pouring down my forehead and stinging my eyes. I punched the garage button from a block away and was thrilled to see it open when the front of our house came into view. Pulling the car into the garage I surveyed the scene but didn't see anything out of the ordinary. The garage door began to close behind me and I jumped out of the car to head inside.

The groceries and medication would have to wait until after the warning. Milk and eggs could be replaced. I could not afford to wait any longer to get the cellar door secured and check on mom.

Racing through the house I did my usual check of the doors and windows. Every lock was bolted, and every window was secured. My pulse began to lower and I could feel the anxiety drifting away as the safety of home soaked into my body. As I began to step onto the stairs of the cellar I pulled the heavy metal doors shut behind me. Carefully, I slid the two bracer bars snuggly into place. My hand drifted to the wall beside me and my ears were filled with the familiar jingling of the padlock keys. After being reassured that the keys were securely in place I began to click all ten padlocks into their loops.

I turned and began to walk down the steps. My eyes wandered to the hooks that held the bolt cutter. It was always the last item on my mental checklist. If a padlock key ever went missing or one of the lock mechanisms seized it was good to have a backup plan.

Dad had nearly perfected the art of our family lockdown during the sirens. Every time I entered this cellar to wait out the alarm I sent him a silent prayer of thanks. He had graciously taken most of the thought out of this process before he passed away.

Reaching the floor of the cellar apartment I was initially surprised to see my mother's recliner sitting empty. Her iPhone sat on the side table next to the chair, flashing and beeping with the Emergency Alert. My eyes darted around the room searching for her. Panic began to rise again until I noticed the bathroom door was shut. I walked to the door and knocked lightly.

"Hey, Mom," I said loudly. "Sorry that it took me so long. I had to drive to Glendale to get some of your medicine."

I waited for a moment, but there was no response.

"Mom, are you in there?" I asked.

More silence.

I knocked and waited for a moment but still received no response. After another moment of waiting, I jiggled the door handle and found it unlocked. Pushing it open I looked inside. The light was off so I flicked the switch on. The bathroom was empty.

Storming around the cellar apartment I began to call my mother's name but received no reply. The area was small with only a sitting room, bedroom, and bathroom. It didn't take long to realize she wasn't down there. My head began to swim. The garage door had been opened when I pulled into the driveway. Although I had punched the opener from a block away I had no idea if the signal reached that far. She could have left through the garage and left the door open, and I would never know.

I raced to the stairs and began to pull the keys from their pegs on the wall. Hours seemed to pass as I fumbled the keys into each lock. Generally, I would put them carefully back into their place on their loops, but I dropped them to the stairs and listened as they tumbled to the ground below.

As I was about to step onto the main floor of the house above I heard the alert system beep three times to indicate an update.

Update! Update! Update!

This is a message from the Emergency Alert System of the Allister Valley Safety and Protection Board.

At this time please seek shelter in a basement, storm shelter, or interior room of your house without windows.

This is a Level Five Watch. I repeat; This is a Level Five Watch. Twelve entities are actively moving on West Vine Street, Chippendale Court, Broadway Avenue, Sullivan Street, Clays Mill Road, and La Grange Road.

The unusual amount of activity will extend the warning as a precaution. Please remain away from doors or windows.

Whatever was out there was on my street. My heart pounded. I had to find my mother.

I searched the house again. Although I had already checked all of the windows and door locks I had not performed an exhaustive search of the house. I had never needed to in the past. Now, I opened every door, searched in every closet, and checked behind every large piece of furniture but found no sign of her.

Cautiously, I opened the door leading into the garage and stepped down onto the concrete below. Scanning the room there was still no sign of her. I was preparing to head back into the house again when I heard a voice out in the street.

"I thought you had died," I heard my mother's voice say. "Christopher tells me that you died. But here you are! I've been waiting for you!"

Slowly, I crept to the garage door and looked out the window. My mother was standing in the center of the street in her housecoat and slippers. Her hair was in disarray and she clutched a newspaper in her right hand. In front of her stood my father, looking almost exactly the way I remembered before he died.

He wore the same pale blue jeans, short-sleeved button-up shirt, and white Nike sneakers he always had. His hair had turned an unearthly silver in comparison to the salt and pepper gray that I recalled. His mouth was cocked into the same amused smile that always seemed painted on his face.

His eyes, though, were black. The sun was shining, but there was no light reflecting off of them. It wasn't as much like looking into the darkness of a basement as it was staring into the empty void of space. No star or fleck of light obscured the darkness they held.

"I've missed you, my dear," I heard my father say as he held his hand out to my mother. "It's been so long, but we need not be apart any longer."

"Let me go get Christopher!" my mother exclaimed. "He will be so happy to see you!"

"No!" my father shouted. He reached forward and took her hand firmly in his and began to walk down the street away from the house. "I've come for you, my dear. We will send for Christopher later!"

My mother stumbled behind my father. She turned her head toward the house and dropped the newspaper as our eyes connected. The joy she had felt upon seeing this thing that looked like my father melted away into fear. Her feet became tangled, and she fell to the asphalt, but the terrible illusion of my father continued to drag her away.

"No!" she shouted feebly. "No! You let go of me! You're not my husband! Why are you doing this? Let go!"

In my shock I had become frozen in place, but watching this thing drag my mother away helped me regain my will. I dashed to the switch for the garage door and punched it. The door opened so slowly that I decided to dive onto the floor and slide through the thin opening. Pushing myself back onto my feet I readied myself to run after my mother.

Before I could take action, I saw her. Paige was in the street in front of me. I froze again. Her mother and father were walking with her hand in hand. On the far side of the family, a little girl held tightly to Bruce Cupsworth. It was Margret. I had not seen her in more than three decades, but I still recognized her. She wore the same pink flowered dress that had been in the photo at her memorial.

Paige turned her head toward me and my eyes locked with her black gaze. I knew it couldn't be, but it looked so much like her. The thing smiled at me and lifted a hand to greet me. My stomach turned into knots, and I felt like I would vomit at any moment.

"I'll be back, Christopher," she said, and she continued to walk down the street. "I miss you, but we will be together soon."

Paige's parents looked in my direction. Their faces, which initially looked joyful, quickly became grimaces of pain and fear.

They both began to try to wrench away their hand from the clutches of the things impersonating their children but were unable to break free. The air filled with a sound like snapping twigs, and they began to scream. The things were crushing the bones in their hands.

Ahead of them on the street, the thing mimicking my father turned around and smiled at the noise and terror. It looked at me and lifted its hand in my direction. The thing smiled again, revealing rows of black, shining teeth. It crouched to the ground by my mother and began to convulse.

All at once, the other changelings began to shake violently. Their limbs began to grow narrow and long. The clothing on their bodies began to shred and tear away as painfully thin torsos stretched them past their limit. Their skin, which had looked normal moments ago, began to bubble. Pale peach skin curdled into lumpy black and gray flesh.

They all stood at once, stooped over to keep a grip on their victims. At full height, each of the obsidian beasts would have stood as tall as a two-story house. Their spines curled to the side as they hunched over allowing their stick-thin arms to drag my mother and the Cupsworths away.

The three nightmarish creatures sank low on two legs and their free hand and began rapidly moving down the street, pulling their victims behind them. My mother and the Cupsworths screamed and clawed at the ground in a fruitless attempt to slow the creatures as they bolted from sight. I could still hear them wailing in despair long after they vanished in the distance.

In the background, the Emergency Alert siren roared endlessly. I stumbled back inside and collapsed onto the kitchen floor. There was no need to hide in the basement. The things had already gotten what they came for.

****

It has been two weeks since the last emergency warning. A town record I have since found out. The Allister Valley Safety and Protection Board sent a man to my house the day after my mother was taken. He didn't threaten me, but there was a subtle undertone that told me declining to go with him to the board's office was not an option.

I rode in the back of a Ford Taurus with tinted windows to the outskirts of town. When we pulled up to the nondescript white building, the man who picked me up told me to ring the buzzer on the door and tell them my name. They would let me in and talk to me. When I was done he would drive me home.

Feeling lost and hopeless after the events of the previous day, I did as he asked. I pressed the buzzer, and a man asked my name. I answered and heard the heavy metal door disengage. The man told me to come inside and wait in the lobby.

When I entered, I looked around. "Lobby" was a generous term for this stiflingly hot room. There were two folding metal chairs pushed up against the wall and an empty coffee table in the center of the room. A water cooler sat empty in the corner. It smelled of cigarettes and sweat.

The only other door in the room creaked open and a gruff-looking man stood in the frame. He was over six feet tall with a bushy beard that hung down onto his pot belly and a mess of brunette hair pulled back into a sloppy ponytail. His steel-toed work boots tapped impatiently on the fading linoleum floor. A pair of faded blue jeans and a sweat-stained white t-shirt seemed like poor work attire.

"You Chris?" The rough man grunted.

"Yeah," I replied flatly. "That would be me."

He waved me in his direction and walked back into the room. I followed without considering what may be on the other side. Having seen my mother dragged away by a horrific creature the day before, my sense of self-preservation was low.

The room I entered was much cooler than the waiting area. Black and white monitors covered two of the walls flickering between different views of Allister Valley. I watched them in a trance as they transitioned to dozens of places around town that I recognized and a few I was less familiar with. In the center of a room sat a semicircle desk with a comfortable-looking rolling chair behind it. The burly man sat at the desk looking at the monitors. Without looking at me he motioned to his left to a folding metal chair beside him.

"Have a seat," he said. "We need to talk."

I sat next to him and continued to look at the screens.

"My name is Harlen Matthews," the man said. "Been working for the board for about fifteen years, give or take. Used to work the night shift, but I'm on days now."

I nodded, but said nothing.

"So, I understand you saw our visitors," he stated. "Sad business. I'm sorry for your loss. I understand it ain't your first go-round with losing someone to this."

"Yeah," I muttered. "Paige Cupsworth a long time ago. My mother yesterday."

He nodded and took a long drag off of a cigarette that had been smoldering in an ashtray on the desk.

"Chris," he started. "I'm gonna give you the same brief sliver of information that I and the other board members share when someone loses a family member. I know you and Paige were close, but we only talk with immediate family members. Now that your mother passed you'll get to hear it too."

Passed. The word echoed in my mind. Its weight settled on my heart. She really was gone.

Harlen smoked the last of his cigarette and crushed it out into the ashtray before immediately lighting another one.

"First of all, we have no clue what the things are. They've been around since the town has. Hell, they were probably here before us. From what we know they try to mimic people you were close to and draw you out. Must be some kind of mind-reading or something. Not like we've been able to ask them or anything. Anyway, anyone dumb enough to listen to the things gets dragged away and never returns."

I nodded again and Harlen pounded a hand on my back in what I assume was a gesture of comfort.

"Not many people see them and live to tell the tale," he grunted. "You have, and it comes with a price?"

"What price?" I blurted.

"Whatever they looked like to you yesterday is what they'll always look like to you," he said as he made the first real eye contact of the entire conversation. "And you'll start seeing them more often. You've seen them and that makes them want you. It ain't like they hunt you, but they take some kind of special interest in the people who see them and live."

Harlen pulled a drawer out of the desk and fished out a tattered business card. He handed it to me. I turned it over in my hand. One side was blank, but the other held a local phone number. Underneath the number was printed *For Emergencies Only*.

"You ever heard a Level One or Two warning?" he asked. "Of course you have. You were born here. You see any of the people who you saw yesterday, you call us. We sound the alarm. People live. You do your duty. I do mine. Understand?"

"Yeah," I said as I bobbed my head up and down. "Just call the number if I see them."

"Good man," Harlen said, adding another brutal comfort swat on my right shoulder. "We've got a memorial together for your maw down at the community center tonight at 7:00 PM. Sorry for your loss."

"Yesterday before those things… changed, they looked like my father, Paige, and her sister, Margret," I said to Harlen. "Is that what they looked like to you on the screen?"

Harlen sat silent for a moment and smoked his cigarette.

"No," he said without emotion. "Don't much want to talk about what I see. You said you saw your dad?"

I nodded. Harlen pulled a notebook from the desk and began jotting notes.

"Something wrong?" I asked.

"Yeah," he replied as he continued writing. "No one ever said the things looked like someone that the things hadn't taken. It's worth sharing with others. Change ain't a good thing with these critters."

Harlen walked me out of the building and sent me to the car. Once I got home I sat and thought about everything the man had told me. The grief and discovery were an overwhelming combination that left my head swimming.

I did what any son would do and stood in a receiving line later that night at a memorial service the Safety and Protection Board set up. Next to me was a framed photo of my mother, before dementia, lined with flowers. Eternally happy. Eternally herself. I shook the hand of just about every person in town. It was no comfort, but I think it made them feel better.

Since that day I've seen my mother, father, and all of the Cupworths multiple times. They are usually standing in tall grass or leaning out from behind trees. Sometimes they are in my backyard and others follow me down the aisles at the supermarket.

If you live in Allister Valley then I'm certainly the origination point of one of the many Emergency Alerts you hear. I'm sorry but I'm also not. It keeps you safe.

And if you wonder why I don't leave to get away from all of this, I ran the idea by Harlen once. He explained to me that the risk that these things would leave Allister Valley to follow me and spread to other places was too great. It was similar to when the man picked me up to go see him. No threat of violence was issued, but there was an understanding that leaving now that I've seen the things wasn't an option.

I'll be haunted by my family and the woman I loved until I'm dead. For better or worse, I've accepted this. My hope is you won't have to live in the same hell that I do.

Paige and my mother speak to me most often through the cellar door during the alerts. I don't cry anymore. In fact, hearing their voices is comforting sometimes. It shouldn't, but I miss them. One day, I'm almost certain, I will go with them just to end all of this.

Anyhow, I have to go make a call. I can see Paige sitting on a bench across the street from my house through the living room window. Harlen or one of the others needs to sound the alarm.

TRADITIONS ABOARD THE F/V WEEPING WIDOW

"You ever been on a boat before, Lucas?" asked the burly man on the pier. "Dangerous work. A man's liable to go over the side if he ain't careful."

I ran my hands through my mop of auburn hair. I had sent in an application months before and told the captain I had no experience on the water, but maybe he didn't see that part. It had worried me at that moment that I may be about to lose the job before I even started.

"No, sir," I replied. "I have no experience on a boat. I know how to swim and have spent time at the lakes back home, but nothing like this."

Captain Orange furrowed his brow as he looked me over. It was hard to determine his age. All of his hair had gone gray and his face was lined with deep wrinkles. His body was a stout rack of muscle. He was either in his later years or life on the sea had worn him down.

"My business manager must not have looked over your application too well," he said dismissively. "Crabbing on the Bering Sea ain't a game. You young folks watch some damn show on the Discovery Channel and think it's a quick payday. It ain't. Not sure this is gonna be for you."

I grabbed my duffle bag from the wet concrete and turned to walk back to the hotel. My mind raced between the disappointment of rejection and the panic of having to pay for a plane ticket home. My back account was nearly drained, and I would have had to use my already taxed credit card.

"Hang on," he shouted. "Be here at six in the morning tomorrow. It's too damn late for me to find a new deckhand and you're just gonna have to learn to be useful real quick. If you can't keep up, crab ain't gonna be the only thing we dump at the port."

The old man turned and walked back onto the deck of his boat before vanishing into the wheelhouse.

F/V Weeping Widow rocked gently against the pier.

***

I spent the first two hours of our trip on the Bering Sea violently dumping my breakfast into the filthy toilet just off the kitchen. Every time I retched I could hear the other deckhands howl with laughter outside. Captain Orange had told the crew to hit their bunks for a bit of rest before we reached the crabbing grounds, but their laughter and jeers made it clear they had no intention of heeding the advice.

It seemed like all my stomach contents had successfully ejected when a pounding sounded against the thin wooden door.

"Alright, greenhorn!" one of the deckhands shouted. "Time to get off your ass and on your feet! We'll be dropping pots soon and that herring won't hop in the bait bag. Let's move!"

I could hear their voices growing quiet and the thuds of heavy boots heading up the steps onto the deck. Wiping my face on my sleeve, I pushed myself onto my feet and walked out the door. The smell of beer and cigarette smoke nearly made my seasick stomach turn again, but I managed to press the urge back down.

Pushing the bulkhead door open, I entered the equipment room where the other hands were slipping into their cold weather gear and waders. A big man who I thought was named Jimmy shoved a bright orange body suit into my hands and smacked me on the shoulder. I looked at it in confusion. It was completely different from the gear the other men were wearing.

"What's this?" I asked the man. "It doesn't look like the same gear the rest of you have."

"That's an immersion suit, son," he responded with mild annoyance. "Captain told us you've never been out to sea before and got no boat experience. Me and all the boys think you'll fall overboard, and this is the only thing likely to save your rookie ass."

The other men began to howl laughter again. I began to put on the enormous suit, unsure if it was a joke or not. There was no other gear in the room, so my options were limited. The others began to file out of the bulkhead and onto the deck.

After five minutes of struggling into the immersion gear, I was finally ready to join them outside. Cutting wind and water slapped my face as soon as I stepped onto the deck. The other hands scurried to crab pots, cinching ropes and checking for holes. Jimmy stood beside an industrial grinder and waved me over.

"Grab these bait bags and we'll start linin' 'em up over at the pot launch," he said, gesturing to a pile of mesh sacks filled to the brim with ground fish. "Gotta hurry if you wanna keep the job."

I grabbed as many of the bait bags as I could and began to clumsily waddle toward the launcher at the side of the ship. The immersion suit was unbelievably bulky and made it difficult to bend my legs to walk. My feet slipped and shuffled as I tried to find purchase on the wet deck boards.

I had just finished dropping the first load of bait bags when the boat grew silent. The engines had stopped. There was no more hurried noise from the crew who had been readying the crab pots to launch. An electric sensation of fear jolted through my body in the sudden silence.

I turned toward the deck to see all seven deckhands surrounding me in a semi-circle. Just as I was about to speak, I heard the door from the wheelhouse open and slam closed. Looking up, Captain Orange stood against the railing, hands clenched around the frigid metal, a grim look on his face.

"It ain't personal, Lucas," he shouted. "We've got a tradition here on the Widow. Every four or five years me and the boys sacrifice a man to the sea. Keeps the rest of us safe. Superstitious, maybe, but we ain't lost a man accidentally in twenty-two years. That suit'll give you a few hours to get right with whatever god you pray to."

At first, I thought it was a joke, but a few of the men pulled work knives from their belts as they all walked toward me. Captain Orange had already turned and walked back into the wheelhouse, slamming the door behind him. The engines roared to life, and the boat jolted forward.

"Over the side," Jimmy said. "Or the boys'll have to stab you a few times to inspire you. Suit won't keep ya warm if it's all fulla holes."

"Please!" I screamed at the men as they slowly closed in on me. "Don't do this! Just take me back to the port! I won't tell anyone!"

They remained silent and continued forward. The first man was in arm's reach and leaned in to grab me. I swung my fist as hard as I could and connected with the side of his head. He stumbled back, shocked at the unexpected blow. I prepared myself to throw another blow, but the others began to move in faster. While I was distracted by the first man, the others seized the opportunity to tackle me to the railing of the shift. I thrashed violently and hit every man within reach, but it was no good.

I felt two of them wrap their arms around my ankles and lift me into the air. My hands clenched around the metal railing, and they tipped me over the side. Grip still in place, I slammed against the hull of the ship and looked up in horror. Seven crazed faces stared down at me, smiling with sadistic glee.

One of the men began trying to pry my fingers from the rails, but the sudden surge of adrenaline had increased my strength. No matter how hard he pulled my fingers or slammed his fist down, my grip wouldn't break. Then I saw one of the men vanish. He returned moments later with a hammer.

Lifting the hammer above his head, he brought it down on my left hand with a sickening crack. White bolts of pain filled my eyes as I heard the bones crunch from the blow. My left hand spasmed in pain and fell from the railing. The weight of my body strained my right arm as I continued to hold on to the rail. My muscles burned with agony as I watched him lift the hammer a second time.

The second wave of pain swept my body as the hammer made contact. My vision went black. The splintered bones of my right hand gave way, and I fell to the churning sea below.

My loss of consciousness was momentary. I felt as though I slammed against concrete as my body met with the rough waves below. The unimaginable cold encompassed my body almost instantly and any hope of drifting away to a peaceful death vanished.

I began to struggle against the waves and paddled my arms to turn myself upright. Fresh surges of pain erupted in my hands and shot up my arms as I tried to use them to right myself in the water. The suit had kept me dry, but the bulk made it nearly impossible to control my movements.

Finally, I managed to get myself onto my back and floated on top of the choppy sea. White-capped waves lapped and slammed against me, filling my mouth with briny water and making it difficult to breathe. As soon as I passed over the top of a new wave, I would coast down the back and dip below the water before coming back up and gasping for air.

I could see the F/V Weeping Widow rocking gently on the waves, and the spotlight moved into the distance. A man was standing at the back of the boat, one arm propped on the railing and the other waving merrily in my direction. It looked like he lowered it to blow me a kiss.

"Thank ya, greenhorn!" he shouted with glee. "If my kids knew what ya sacrificed to keep their ole man safe, they'd thank ya too!"

"Please!" I shouted.

I slipped under the water again.

"Come back!"

Another whitecap swelled over my head, filling my mouth with salty water.

"Don't leave me!"

A larger wave pushed me a few feet under, sending water into my lungs.

"I... can't... please..."

The lights vanished over the rolling waves, leaving me in the pitch dark. The water began to calm a bit as the wake of the boat settled. My balance returned, and I began to float calmly in the water. Stars burned brightly overhead. I had never been this far away from a city to see them so clearly. They would have been beautiful in any other setting.

There in the Bering Sea, the stars would be the only witnesses to my death.

***

I drifted for hours. The immersion suit had kept the worst of the cold at bay for a while, but I had eventually started to feel the icy daggers of the frigid water creep into my muscles. I had given up on trying to swim. My body ached and it hurt to move. Hopelessness had overtaken me, and I simply waited to die.

After letting go of the fear and anxiety, I noticed I felt a bit better. The water didn't seem to be as cold then. My body aches were dissipating. I felt almost… comfortable.

Hypothermia. Late stage, probably. It's no way to go, but by the time the false warmth starts filling your body, you're almost thankful.

I had decided to close my eyes and rest and let the ocean take me when I heard something in the distance.

A rumbling sound.

A ship's engine.

I opened my eyes and scanned the area and, in the distance, I could see a dim light. There was a ship passing to my right. Too far away to see me. Too far away to hear me scream. I rested my hands on my chest as tears filled my eyes.

My hands landed on top of a hard, round piece of plastic. Confused, I fumbled at it with my bent and broken fingers until I felt a bump on the side. Pushing it in, the night sky filled with obnoxious light.

The damn suit had a strobe. I had been out there for hours and never checked the suit for any gear. There was no telling how many ships might have passed close enough to see it, but in my panic, I never checked.

Bright flashes of light nearly blinded me as they radiated in the night sky. I shielded my eyes with my crippled hand and turned my head toward the boat passing me by. My mind was foggy, but I thought I could see a spotlight burst to life on the deck.

A thin beam of harsh light began to scan the sea all around me. With great effort, I lifted my arms in the air to wave, hoping the reflective material on the sides of the suit would catch their attention as well. After a few moments, the spotlight fell on me, and I had to shield my eyes completely.

The light remained on me for what felt like an eternity until I could hear the deafening roar of the engine of a ship nearby. Waves began to crash violently against me. Once again, I struggled to keep my head above water and breathe.

"This is the United States Coast Guard." A resonating voice called from the ship's loudspeaker. "We will dispatch a rescue team to pull you aboard!"

A few moments later I was lifted into an inflatable boat. There were a few men and women on board talking into radios as we sped back to the larger shift. The luminous spotlight followed us the entire way. It was like a light from Heaven, carrying me back to safe harbors.

I started sobbing uncontrollably. A woman sitting next to me grabbed my hand to comfort me. The pain was excruciating, but I didn't bother telling her about my injuries. I was too relieved to be in the sight of another person that the pain was worth the contact. I squeezed her hand back as best as I could with my shattered fingers.

We pulled alongside the Coast Guard boat and four cables dropped from a crane above. The rescue team started attaching the clasps to the boat, and in moments we were lifting from the choppy sea. Tears flowed freely as we drifted upward to the deck.

As we lifted above the side, the crane began to swing us onto the deck before gently lowering us to the deck. A swarm of warmly dressed men and women pulled me from the boat and put me on a stretcher. They chattered back and forth about care measures as my mind swam in the joy of my rescue.

"Hey there, big guy," one of the men said. "Can you tell me how you ended up in the drink out there? You're a long way from land."

"Thrown overboard," I said in a croaky voice. "Crabbing boat… *Weeping Widow*… crew tossed… me overboard."

The man's expression changed from professionally friendly to concerned.

"Stop," the man said suddenly. "Let me talk to the captain before we take this guy inside."

The man vanished and the others stood around me. I was too exhausted to talk, but my fear and confusion returned. They were all looking at me and whispering amongst themselves. A few moments later, the man returned with a lady I hadn't seen. She stood, hands behind her back, staring down at me on the stretcher. Her eyes were stern.

"Sir, were you thrown overboard from the *F/V Weeping Widow*?" she asked.

I nodded weakly. "Yes."

"Take him back and put him over the side," she said to the group standing around me. "We know the tradition and it isn't our place to interfere."

She turned and walked away as my heart jumped into my throat. I tried to sit up but discovered they had harnessed me to the stretcher. My aching muscles writhed and strained against the straps with the last reserves of energy left in my frail body.

"No!" I shouted, my voice suddenly filled with energy and terror. "Please! Why are you doing this?"

They ignored me and continued to wheel me toward the railing at the side of the ship. When we reached the side, they moved the stretcher parallel to the metal barrier and turned the stretcher sideways over the top.

"Stop!" I heard a voice shout. It was the captain again. I was relieved, thinking she had come to her senses.

"What are your orders?" a man asked.

"Remove the harness and drop him in without the stretcher," she said flatly. "If anyone discovers the body, we don't want them to find him tethered to a piece of damn Coast Guard equipment."

Two of the crew unbuckled the harnesses holding me to the stretcher and I once more fell into the sea. A crewman had loosened the neck of my immersion suit when they were taking me inside. Unlike the first time, cold water rushed into the immersion suit as I tumbled in the salty waves.

The boat engines roared as the Coast Guard ship pushed through the dark of night. Before they left my sight, they cut the lights, leaving me to drift under the starry sky.

***

I've been back in the water for an hour now, and the uncharacteristic warmth has returned to my body.

My eyes are heavy so I'm going to close them for a little bit.

Maybe another ship will come by.

Probably not, but I need some rest.

I'm so sleepy.

MIRAGE STATION

"Get them containers lined up, boys!" shouted the stout old man from the catwalk. Marcus Jasper, the warehouse foreman, was a wall of muscle topped off with a wild tangle of long white hair and a bushy beard. If Santa Claus had a Viking cousin, Jasper would be it. "Our delivery window opens in less than twenty-four hours, and we've got pups on the crew this time. Gotta show 'em the ropes!"

Jasper looked down from the catwalk and gave me a wink as I drove the forklift forward. Dozens of other men scurried around the cavernous room checking shipping manifests and container contents.

I'd been working for Shift Logistics Warehouse for eight months. It was an easy job with a pay scale that made my head spin. I loved it, but I still had a hard time believing what Jasper told me we did. The job offer had arrived out of nowhere. After a brief stint in the military, I secured work at the Port of Los Angeles as a forklift driver. Most of my military career had been spent in warehousing. My skill and speed in military logistics and shipping had translated well to civilian life.

Nine months ago, I was walking to my truck at the end of the shift when I saw a mountainous man leaning against the tailgate. Smoke billowed from a cigar dangling haphazardly from the corner of his mouth. We made eye contact, and he tossed a hand the size of a bear's paw in the air to greet me.

"Ahoy!" the man bellowed. "Your name Edgar Black?"

"Who's asking?" I responded curtly.

The man bellowed laughter that filled the parking lot. "I'm Marcus Jasper and I work for Shift Logistics. A buddy of mine works here at the port and said you're an ace on a forklift. Prior military too, I understand. Also a plus, son."

"I'm pretty happy here," I replied. "It would take a good pay increase to consider making a move."

Jasper slid a hand into his back pocket and pulled out a folded yellow envelope. He pushed it in my hands and swatted me on the shoulder, nearly sending me reeling forward.

"Take a look at that packet there, son," he said and began to walk away. "Tells you as much information as we can share for now. I do my homework and know that your finances aren't in great shape. Got some creditors after you from what I understand. Could be the answer to your money woes. My number's on the last page. Call me if you're interested. I'm flyin' out tomorrow."

I read the packet that night. Most of the job descriptions seemed straightforward and varied little from the standard load and unload duties I had been working at the port. My position there would be operating a forklift to unload and store shipments in the Shift Logistics Warehouse.

While the first part had made sense, the contract grew strange as I continued. The warehouse was located on a twenty-five square mile patch of land in an undisclosed state. A perimeter barrier had been constructed around the entire property and I would be assigned patrol detail a few times each month to ensure the barrier was intact. Military experience was preferred as firearms were required during the patrols.

If the massive amount of land and patrol detail wasn't strange enough, our delivery schedule sealed the deal. We only made one huge delivery each year. Shipments would arrive during the first eleven months. The remaining month before delivery would be spent preparing everything for the move and daily equipment inspections to ensure nothing malfunctioned.

Strangest of all, the delivery would be made within the twenty-five square mile compound.

A non-disclosure agreement was attached to the back. While I had assumed the majority of the envelope contents would be a job description, the NDA took up the bulk. In it, I was informed that the location, nature of our work, contents of the warehouse, and nature of our clientele were to remain secret. At the end of the NDA, where I expected to see the financial penalties, I was shocked to see that any breach of contract was punishable by a lengthy term in federal prison.

A bright yellow sticky note sat at the bottom of the page.
Call if you're interested, kid—$ 200,000 per year.

***

The next morning, Jasper sat across the aisle from me on the private jet, quietly reading over stacks of papers.

"Sir, excuse me," I said. "Could you tell me about the job? The description was vague, and I'm not sure why a private company would have an NDA that could result in federal prison time."

The old man placed the clipboard on the seat beside him.

"You want the real answer or a believable answer?" he asked with a Cheshire grin.

"The real answer, please," I replied.

"Here goes nothin'," he chortled. "Shift Logistics is a warehouse and protected property in Wyoming. Easy to get a lotta land out there. The campus is twenty-five square miles with a large perimeter barrier, but you already know that. We also own all the land for 20 miles in both directions. No-fly zone overhead. Our work needs privacy, ya see."

I nodded.

"We spend most of the year receiving shipments of just about anything you can imagine. Food, clothing, medication, technical equipment, light weaponry, gasoline, and vehicles."

"Are we military?" I asked.

"We ain't public or private. Little of both. This is an organization that started in the 1960s, but the government is… well… a big supporter of their work. The whole setup is a little hard to wrap your head around."

"So, what's the unbelievable part?"

Jasper smiled at me. "For one day a year, during a twelve-hour period, an entire town will appear within the twenty-five square mile perimeter. During that period, you and the rest of the team will move a year's wortha goods into a warehouse within that town and depart. Every couple of years, some personnel selected by the government to stay in the town get dropped off too. After twelve hours, the town will disappear again."

"Bullshit," I said. "A town appears and disappears and we're… what? Their delivery men? Where does it go and why do we take them these supplies?"

"We take 'em the supplies because they pay us a pile of money to do it," he said firmly. "We drop the stuff those folks need to live for a year, and we pick up a few smaller loads before returning to our warehouse. The government picks up what we take outta the town the next day then transfers us another year of operating costs. Then we spend eleven months prepping for the next drop."

I peppered him with dozens of questions for the remainder of the flight, but Marcus Jasper just shrugged his shoulders at all of them and returned to his clipboard.

"I don't ask questions, kid," he said indifferently. "Shift Logistics pays my bills and then some. Folks in the town are friendly. Scientist types. Government don't hover over my shoulder. We get paid. It's a good gig, so I try not to spoil it with curiosity."

My mind swam and our plane continued.

***

Fat snowflakes drifted from the sky before melting on the windshield of the delivery truck. I sat inside waiting to make my first delivery. Wyoming was beautiful, but after so many years in California, a frigid winter seemed exceptionally brutal. The heat was blasting from the dash of the truck, but a chill had settled in my bones. I told myself it was the cold, but I was terrified that Jasper was right.

The past eleven months had been both unusual and mundane. We spent our days taking in deliveries, verifying their contents, and creating manifests of supplies. I got to know the other workers well and the bonds were quick to form.

Jasper turned out to be more like a father to most of us than a boss. He would work us hard during the day, but when evening hit, he knew how to help the staff unwind. You could find him standing by a barbeque pit most evenings near our sleeping quarters. Beer in hand, he would flip countless burgers and ribs over the burning coals.

He would draw us into card games in the mess hall, play first-run movies in a tiny theater, and drive us to the nearest clinic if we were feeling under the weather. There wasn't a man or woman in the facility that didn't love him. He took care of us. It went well beyond the kind of care and concern a paycheck made a fella feel compelled to provide.

My truck sat outside of the warehouse bay doors; nose pointed into an empty field that stretched as far as my eyes could see. Floodlights from the building behind me blasted into the darkness, illuminating the snow-covered plain. If Jasper and the rest of the crew had been telling the truth, in less than five minutes a small town would materialize in front of my eyes.

A young woman sat calmly in the passenger seat beside me. Her eyes were closed, and her head tilted back against the seat to feign sleep, but I knew she was awake. Jasper had informed me that morning that she was a new resident of the mysterious town and would accompany me to the delivery site.

I introduced myself and tried to make small talk, but she was all business. She wore drab green military-style fatigues and carried a duffle bag. A sleek handgun was fastened to her belt. Dozens of other men and women fitting the same description were scattered throughout the delivery fleet awaiting transport to their strange destination.

"We are given explicit instructions not to share any information with the contractors," she had said. "Thank you for understanding."

My following attempts to make small talk were met with equally polite but curt responses. I was nervous and continued trying to talk to her. In response, she pretended to go to sleep.

The radio on my dash crackled to life. A series of high-pitched sirens blasted through. The young woman in the seat beside me bolted up and looked straight ahead.

"Good morning, ladies and gents," boomed a deep baritone voice. "This is Marcus Jasper. The final countdown has now reached thirty seconds. Shipment fifty-one will commence on my mark. If this is your first delivery, move quickly. While we've got a twelve-hour window, our goal is complete delivery by the two-hour mark followed by a two-hour pick-up and retrieval window for all outgoing containers and any disembarking personnel from the town. This will leave us with an eight-hour window for troubleshooting if anything goes FUBAR. No one wants an unexpected ride to the other side. Brace for arrival."

The other side? What the hell was he talking about?

Before I could wrap my mind around the strangeness of the message, yellow caution lights erupted from the warehouse behind us. My ears began to ring. A few of the old metal fillings in my teeth began to rattle. The air pressure seemed to be compressing and my breathing became labored and ragged. The young woman in the seat beside me didn't speak, but shot her hand across the cab of the truck and grasped mine. I squeezed hers in return.

A quarter mile down the hill, a faint circle of light appeared. From this distance, it looked no larger than the diameter of a swimming pool. The ring of illumination began to pulse rapidly. As the intensity grew, the circle began to expand as it became taller. Waves of light and intense vibrations filled the field. The entire complex was bathed in the glow from the massive anomaly that appeared before us. I could feel the truck beginning to rumble and the ground below us quaked.

The light became blinding. It was so strong it seemed to blast between the fingers of my hand as I held it in front of my face. I braced myself for an explosion or shockwave, but to my surprise, everything remained silent. The light faded and the vehicle sat still. Pulling the hand away from my eyes and letting the young woman's hand drop, I marveled as I gazed through the windshield of the cab.

A massive platform covered the field at the bottom of the hill from the warehouse. Towering stadium lights blanketed two colossal warehouses perched on the edge of the platform nearest to us. Beyond the huge metal buildings, I could see water towers, neat rows of houses, and a few taller buildings that resembled lecture halls from a college campus.

"It's go time, ladies and gents," Jasper announced over the radio. "I will hail the control room at Warehouse 1 during the approach. Reassemble delivery formation at the base of the entry ramp. Once the ramp light turns green, enter and fall into your assigned drop order. Caravan forward!"

I hesitated as I watched the trucks beside me pull away. A loud honk from the truck behind me erupted and startled me into motion. My foot slammed down on the gas pedal and the tires spun on the concrete before finding purchase and jolting us forward.

"Easy there, killer," the young woman said. "Get us there in one piece if you can, okay?"

I smiled. "Will do, ma'am."

My heart thundered as we arrived at the bottom of the ramp that led into the mysterious town. Now that we were at the bottom of the hill, I could see the top of the platform was nearly forty feet off the ground. I pulled the truck into formation and put it in park, staring in wonder. The radio remained silent.

"Two years of training and I still can't believe I'm here," the woman said. "I wonder why the light is still red."

I looked at the red light that was illuminated to the right of the ramp. The "Go" light below sat black and deadened. During our prep discussions, Jasper had told the crew that the entry light usually lit up before we even reached the ramp. I wasn't worried yet, but it had taken us five minutes to fall into delivery formation.

"Truck 27, this is Marcus Jasper." The radio crackled without warning. "Samantha Michaels, this is a truck-to-truck transmission. The rest of the fleet is cut from this loop. Do you copy?"

The young woman, who I now knew was Samantha Michaels, picked up the radio mic and responded that she received the message.

"Ma'am, my hails are going unanswered," Jasper responded. I could hear worry in his voice. "I have performed the standard five hail series with no response. You're new here, I know, but I understand you were due to assume site management. As a courtesy, I'm asking permission to enact Code Blue. We've never failed to receive a response during any previous delivery."

I looked at Samantha and saw her hand tremble as she clutched the mic.

"Understood, Mr. Jasper," she said in a shaking voice. "Our director has informed me of your military record. Permission granted. I request that you lead the operation. The new site personnel shall remain in their vehicles with your staff, but I will accompany you for point inspection. Pick your best men, sir. We don't know what will be in there."

"Understood and confirmed, ma'am," Jasper replied. The steel had returned to his voice.

After a few moments of dead air, Marcus Jasper's voice once again flooded from the radio. He called for the driver of twenty specifically numbered trucks including mine. We were instructed to remove an M4 carbine rifle, Kevlar vest, and communication earpiece from a storage locker in the cab of our trucks. A tent was being set up at the rear of the convoy and a beacon light would be placed. All personnel summoned were to report within the next five minutes.

I collected my gear before Samantha, and I stepped onto the snow-covered ground. Behind the truck, we could see a bright beam of light piercing the sky from the rear of the convoy. As we walked, I strapped on my vest, inserted my earpiece, and began to examine my weapon to make sure everything was in functioning order.

When we arrived, Jasper stood in the center of a cluster of twenty men. He tossed a Kevlar vest through the air to Samantha who secured it on her torso. Another man stepped forward and handed her an earpiece and carbine. Jasper directed everyone to remain quiet and gave Samantha Michaels the floor.

"Ladies and gentlemen," she said calmly. "I am going to give you a brief amount of need-to-know information before we enter the station. This site was constructed decades ago by a group of scientists who hungered for a world free of war, famine, and political intrusion in their work. Some of the brightest minds of their day created a small community here and named it Mirage Station. To find a location untainted by the evils of this world, a group of physicists designed and produced technology that allowed a small town to be removed from this reality and relocated to an alternative dimension where humanity either never existed or failed to thrive. There are no predators on the planet and sentient life has never been discovered. Flaura and fauna discovered there are often similar to what we have here with varying evolutionary differences."

My eyes expanded to the size of dinner plates. An alternate universe? I wanted to think it was impossible, but this town had materialized in front of my eyes. Nothing seemed impossible anymore.

"Each year, Mirage Station shifts back to this reality for supply replenishment and to deliver research and technology efforts to our world. In return for their research and discoveries, the US government funds their work. Some of our most important advances in medicine and technology are developed at Mirage Station. For the last fifty years, the shipment exchange has gone off without a hitch, but we have failed to receive facility contact. Mr. Jasper has enacted a Code Blue response. This team will enter Mirage Station in an attempt to make contact with personnel. In the event we fail to make contact, we will use the remaining eleven-and-a-half hour window to investigate the cause of contact failure. Mirage Station's dimensional displacement system is self-piloting. In twelve hours, this town will shift back, with or without us."

We all nodded in agreement and Jasper placed us in an entry formation. Nervously, the cluster of men and women marched forward behind the old man. Our boots thudded against the metal ramp as we began our ascent into Mirage Station.

***

An hour after entering Mirage Station, and we hadn't seen a single soul. The receiving warehouse was clean, empty, and prepped to receive the supply delivery. Upon entering the export warehouse, we discovered all the outgoing containers sealed and ready for our team to remove. After communication equipment checks in the control room of the loading area, we found everything to be in working order. There were no signs of distress.

That was until we began to perform a sweep of the houses nearest to the warehouses.

The first dozen homes we entered seemed to be perfectly intact. Each house had a spartan but comfortable living room, kitchen, bathroom, and bedroom. The furnishings in each were the same as the ones before. Small keepsakes and photos on the wall provided the only variations. All of them were tidy.

As we rounded the corner into the next row of houses, our concerns mounted. While the first row of homes was as expected, the doors of the second row were all caved in. White shards of wood were scattered into the living rooms of each home. Dozens of deep grooves were hewn into the frames by whatever had forced its way into the homes.

"I want four groups of five men and women. Three will enter the homes, and one crew will escort me and Ms. Michaels to the central control office at the center of the station," Jasper said flatly. "Clear each house and search for signs of survivors or hostiles. If it isn't human, call for backup and put a bullet in it. Any unusual activity should be reported to the rest of the crew immediately. Be safe. I don't want any new hires for next year, understand?" He flashed a nervous smile.

Jasper divided us into teams before departing. One by one, we entered the houses in the second row. Each door has been ripped to shreds and showered into the living rooms. Long dried blood and dehydrated flesh showered the walls. The same deep grooves from the entryway were randomly found throughout the buildings.

The smell of rot and carrion almost caused me to vomit with each new house we entered. Each home was the same bloodbath.

Still, there remained no sign of either survivors or hostiles. What-ever had done this may well have left the station after the attack.

My team was about to enter our seventh house when the sound of gunfire erupted from across the street. Deafening waves filled the air as M4 carbines exploded into life. Screams and wails soon mingled with the gunfire as we began to exit a deserted bedroom to respond.

My earpiece roared to life. "Hostiles detected by Team Two. I repeat, hostels detected by Team Two. Everett and Bernstein are down. The subject is entering the street in row two. Fire at will. Hostile is…"

The voice in my earpiece suddenly erupted in a shriek. Rasps and gurgles followed by horrific exclamations. Growls, grunts, and the wet ripping of flesh filled all of our ears before a static-filled crunch left us all in deafening silence.

"Team three, return to the front of the house and find a firing point through the windows." I directed. "Use couches and tables as barriers."

The five of us squatted low and moved to the large window in the front of the living room. Two of the crewmen at the rear overturned the couch and coffee table to provide coverage. Slowly, I shuffled to the window, unlatched it, and pushed it open before propping my gun on the windowsill.

Sweeping the barrel from side to side, there was no sign of the reported hostile. In the doorway directly across the street from our position, I could see a body dressed in Kevlar, still clutching its M4 across its chest. At first, I thought they were dead, but I was startled when they turned their head to meet my gaze. A shaking hand lifted in the air and reached out to me.

Before I could give the order to move to the occupied house, a massive white claw came from beyond the doorframe and sank itself through the body armor and into the crewman's chest. Their arms spasmed as blood erupted from their mouth. The claw retracted and dragged the body out of sight. Screams again filled the air followed by a triumphant roar that rattled my bones.

"What the hell was that?" boomed a voice through the ear-piece. "Anyone got eyes on the hostile?"

"I had a brief visual before it…" I stammered. "There is a hos-tile on row two, fifth house from the main road. All teams con-verge at…"

Wood and plaster exploded into the street before I could finish my sentence. Chunks of building material scattered into the street and peppered our house like shrapnel as an alabaster blur emerged from the wreckage. The thing rolled into the center of the street and came to a stop.

A path of deep grooves trailed behind the thing in the road. Long, curved spikes protruded from the mass forming a perfect sphere. Razor-sharp spines twitched as they flexed in and out giving the rolling ball of death the look of rippling water. Chittering and clicking noises filled the air around the abomination.

"Team One, hostile is in the street. Safeties off and engage!" I heard a voice cry in my ear.

From my cover at the base of the window, I could see a five-man team pour from a door three houses further down the street. Cracks ripped through the air as they began to fire on the writhing mass of quills. Bird-like shrieks pierced my eardrums as the thing began to cry out in pain. Flecks of orange blood fell like fat drops of rain.

The team continued to fire at the creature and all of the quills went rigid, protruding from the center. Four lines in the shape of an X began to separate as rows of quills fell backward. Peeling back like a pale flower, six sword-shaped legs unfurled and lifted the thing from the ground. In the center of the legs sat a circular maw of teeth with a thin, gray tongue dangling onto the road.

Moving like a blur, the creature scuttled forward toward the firing squad and launched its two front legs through the chests of the men in the front. It roared with rage, and it tossed the dead men to the side like crumpled paper. One woman from the team stood her ground and fired at the thing as the others ran for cover.

The previously docile tongue launched toward the woman's arm and wrapped around the gun. It began to retract into the maw, dragging her screaming across the concrete. As the tongue pulled her carbine and arms into its mouth, she continued to fire and gave a fierce battle cry. When her torso entered the maw, it closed like a steel trap, dropping her legs to the concrete below.

A door slammed as the last remaining members of Team One took refuge inside an intact house at the end of the row. Dropping onto its belly, the creature's legs retracted, and the four flaps folded closed. Again a perfect sphere, the creature began to roll like a hellish wrecking ball toward the house and burst through the wall.

"Jasper and Michaels," I whispered into my earpiece. "We have made contact with the hostile. It is an unknown predatory species. Team One and Two are both KIA. The engagement has barely wounded the thing."

Static crackled in my earpiece and I tried to make out the broken and muffled response.

"Jasper and Michals, come in dammit!" I barked. "Team One and Two are down. Requesting order."

More static until, finally, a soft voice broke through. "… remaining troops to central control office. Everyone… bloodbath… Repeat, all remaining…"

"We've got to head to the central office," I said to the others in my team. "Michaels is calling for us. Let's head out."

***

We tried unsuccessfully during our trip to reach Jasper or Michaels over the radio, but received no response. Fear for their safety increased the closer we got to our destination. As we made our way toward central control, we found the mangled bodies of Team Four. Turning the mangled corpses over to identify them, we were relieved that our boss and the new station director weren't among the dead.

It took us more than seven hours to travel from the rows of ravaged houses to the central control building. The distance wasn't great, maybe a mile and a half, but the creature trailed behind us, and we had to hide frequently. We would hunker behind overturned furniture in ruptured building fronts as the pale creature rolled and scuttled in the streets outside.

When it would leave to search another nearby building, we would make it another hundred feet down the road before we would have to hide again. The progress was tedious, but after hours of travel and hiding, we finally made it.

Central control was a circular building in the center of Mirage Station. Thick concrete walls climbed high above any other structure besides the water towers spread throughout the platform. Windows and doors appeared to be made of reinforced steel. It almost reminded me of a fallout shelter.

At first, I was puzzled that the hideous beast hadn't managed to make it through the walls of central control, but I soon discovered why. As we walked the perimeter of the building looking for a point of entry, deep grooves had been scored into the concrete. A few inches in, pieces of metal rebar were exposed, mangled but unbroken.

The thing had tried to make its way inside and failed. If we could get inside, we might be safe for a short while. After tracing the perimeter of the entire building and finding no way, we entered a one-story brick building across the street to find cover. We hailed for Jasper or Michaels on our earpieces again, but still received no response. Sounds of flying debris and roars of anger echoed through the empty streets from a short distance away.

It was still looking for us and time was running out before Mirage Station would return to that thing's home.

"We've got to head back," a man behind me said. Perkins was his last name, but I didn't know him well. "Jasper and Michaels are either dead or out of reach. We need to go!"

The three others quietly murmured in agreement. My blood boiled at their cowardice. How could they abandon anyone without knowing their fate?

"We don't know if Jasper and Michaels are dead," I spat. "And what if that monster follows us to the warehouse and…"

I stopped talking abruptly as the squeal of metal against metal filled our ears. The sound of heavy machinery whined from the direction of central command. We peered over the window ledge and watched as one of the doors lifted. Jasper stood inside.

"Get the hell in here!" he shouted.

We scurried across the open street and into the doorway before Jasper hit a button to shut the door.

"Glad you all made it. Looks like we've got a hell of a problem here." The old man gestured to the room behind us. Mummified corpses blanketed the floor. Thick dust floated in the air as the light drifted through cracks in the metal window covers. I gagged after realizing I was breathing in lungs full of dry human skin. "Looks like most of the population that wasn't killed by the Alpha died of starvation here. It couldn't get inside. But they couldn't get out for supplies."

"The Alpha?" Perkins questioned.

"The Alpha is the quilled animal that has been chasing you," a voice said behind us. We turned to see Michaels enter the corpse-filled lobby. "Jasper and I tried to find a way to stop the next shift back to the other side, but with the station personnel dead, we do not know how. In the meantime, we've been listening to research logs left by the staff before their deaths."

Michaels told us of the little they learned from the research logs. For the first three decades on the other side, Mirage Station had been self-contained. None of the staff ventured farther than a mile into the wilderness around it. The community continued its scientific studies and technology development. Little more than a cursory investigation was made into the surrounding areas.

In the 1990s, biologists and botanists joined research teams. They started traveling farther from Mirage Station to study the flora and fauna of the alternate world. Dozens of new medicines were discovered through research performed by the new teams. Unrecognizable herbivores populated the forests and plains. It had been noted in the earliest days of the station that the region appeared free of predators.

In 2019, a geologist joined the crew and brought a drilling system to begin running tests on the mineral composition of the new world. There were concerns that mining operations would disrupt the largely untouched ecosystem. Many in the community protested, but the leadership dismissed their concerns and allowed drilling to begin.

Underground research continued for two years until the geology team uncovered a massive web of caves thirty miles from Mirage Station. Camera drones surveyed portions of the underground system, revealing an underground area that rivaled even the Mammoth Cave system in our reality. Having finished their initial drone explorations and mineral sample testing, the team sent personnel below ground to begin studying the caves.

After a few days of exploration, the team stopped reporting in. A rescue team was sent and failed to report back. Three days after the original return date, a rescue vehicle arrived. Only one of the original five sent to rescue the other team returned. Station staff met the wounded staff who reported the survey team had discovered an underground nest of creatures. It had wiped out the rescue team in only minutes.

"They've followed me back," the man said before dying of his wounds.

Within a half-hour of the man's death, seven of the creatures arrived at Mirage Station. Most of the station personnel were killed within an hour of the initial attack. The only survivors were those who fled to central command and enacted the lockdown. They watch as the creatures picked off the few survivors left outside from the CCTV console inside. Six of the seven Alphas departed and returned to their caves while one remained. Almost as though to stand watch.

"Is there any information on how to kill them?" I asked.

"No," Jasper responded. "Seems all the folks here died of starvation before a reasonable escape plan came together."

"Then how the hell are we going to escape?" asked Perkins.

"We're gonna let the thing in and trap it here," Jasper replied. "If it couldn't get in, it won't be able to get out."

Jasper and Michaels wasted no time as they told us the plan.

***

We prepared to bait the Alpha into central control and seal it inside. Michaels opened a bay door at the front of the building and a single-person door at the back. Jasper had already gone to the main control room on the second level. He would set a timed explosive on the dimensional displacement computer so Mirage Station would never phase back into our world after it returned. He would also close the doors on our signal to trap the Alpha.

The remains of our crew stood outside the bay doors and began firing our weapons in the air to draw in the beast. A roar erupted close by, and we could already hear the thing's clawed feet slicing into the pavement. We continued firing until the quilled monstrosity rounded a crumbling building and moved in our direction.

We ran into the building, the Alpha in pursuit, and dashed for the back door. The Alpha was close behind us when we heard the bay door begin to grind closed. Someone behind us screamed, and we heard a thud and the sound of a carbine clattering to the ground. I turned my head over to see Perkins sprawled on the floor. The white mass of quills and teeth fell on him before I could think to stop.

I turned and saw Michaels standing outside the open door waving us through. "Go! Go! Come on!" she shouted as we hammered through the opening. As soon as the last man's boot hit the ground outside, the heavy steel door began to close.

We turned to see the Alpha bounding towards us, roaring in fury. As the door rolled closer to the ground, a white leg shot through the gap and scraped the thick steel. The door came down on the leg and the hydraulic system whined as it tried to press down on the beast's carapace.

"Door won't close all the way," Jasper said through our earpiece. "Y'all gotta haul ass now!"

"How'd you get the coms working?" I asked.

"Walls are too thick to get a signal out, but I pushed open one of the metal shutters. Looks like it worked," he said cheerfully. "Now move your asses!"

"Meet us at the front window and shimmy down the storm drain," Michaels said in response. "We'll wait for you to come down and haul ass together!"

"No can do." He stated. "Told a little lie. I've got no bomb and no detonator. Once this thing makes it to the other side, I'm going to destroy the drive manually. Get the hell out of here. Ain't much time left."

"That wasn't the deal!" Michaels screamed. "We leave together!"

"No time to argue, my friends," he said with a sad chuckle. "I'm closing that window shutter and waiting for this one-way trip. If you stay here, you're gonna die. Get goin'."

A metal shutter slammed overhead and static crackled in my earpiece. With that, Jasper was gone. The five of us ran like Hell was on our heels until we reached the ramp. I directed the convoy to return to the warehouse and keep a safe distance. By the time the trucks reached safety, we had just enough time to look back and watch as the white halo of light surrounded Mirage Station and vanished just as quickly.

***

It's been six years since Mirage Station vanished for the last time. Shift Logistics warehouse is still here, but it sits empty of supplies. A skeleton crew of staff remains, including me and Michaels. The government pays us to keep watch over the site and report any anomalies.

I don't even bother trying to live offsite anymore. The memory of what waits through the thin sheet of our reality still haunts me. A twin bed in the upstairs office lets me get some sleep at night. Mostly, I just sit outside the bay doors on the loading dock facing the open field.

Some nights, I think I see a faint flicker of light out in the darkness. Maybe it's Jasper trying to make his way back. I wish it was. But it's probably something else.

I'll wait.

FIRE TOWER NO. 1

From the earliest age that I can recall becoming a park ranger was my life goal. My father and I spent every free weekend hiking, fishing, and camping in Arlo Bennett National Forest. Not everyone is as lucky as we were to have access to 560,000 acres of pristine woodland, streams, and hiking trails, but with it being a twenty-minute drive we practically lived there from Friday afternoon to Sunday evening.

While I could recount hundreds of stories of our exploits in the park, I think it would be best if I stick with the information pertinent to the dangers I want to warn you of. When I was about ten years old, my father and I had just finished setting up camp for the night. Our tent was placed, the latrine dug, and our campfire was burning warmly in front of us. After a heavy dinner and a canteen of water, the call of nature indicated it was time to use the restroom.

I wandered to the hole we had dug away from camp and relieved myself. As I was zipping my jeans there, a soft whistle coming was from the forest ahead of me. Looking over my shoulder I could see my father, pipe in mouth, sitting on the ground by our fire. Turning back in the direction of the whistling, I squinted my eyes and peered into the distance to try and identify the source. It was likely a bird, I thought to myself, but there were hints of a subtle melody that kept me from being certain.

The fading light of the sun didn't provide me with much of a view, so I continued listening to the soft whistling. Having decided it warranted no further investigation, I resolved to return to the safety of my father's company and the now much-desired illumination of our campfire. I turned around and began trudging through the undergrowth of the forest when, over my shoulder, I was certain I heard someone shout from a distance.

"It's this way! Come and see!"

My fight, flight, or freeze response immediately chose the worst of all the options as I stopped dead in my tracks. Turning around quickly I looked in the distance and saw what I thought was the silhouette of someone far in the distance. One arm waved above their head as if to say hello. They didn't call out again, but it appeared a single arm continued to wave in above their head before they eventually dropped it and stepped backward, disappearing behind a monstrously large oak tree.

Without another thought, I bolted the short distance back to our campsite and in a panic told my father what I thought I had seen and heard. He smiled and reassured me it was likely nothing more than another camper, but he would investigate. Shouldering the strap of his rifle and digging his flashlight out of his bag, we trekked into the woods in the direction I thought I had seen the figure. My pulse thumped rapidly the farther from camp we went.

As we neared the massive oak I had seen from the latrine, my father began to sweep the ground with the beam of the flashlight searching for signs of a disturbance. There was no sign of recent activity. The dried leaves and fallen branches seemed to be completely undisturbed. We continued a quarter of a mile beyond the oak and still found no sign of another camp or any human activity. My father ruffled my hair with his hand and assured me it had just been my mind playing a trick on me. I wanted to believe him so badly but something in my heart told me I had seen someone or, more unsettling yet, something.

After getting back to our camp and settling beside the dwindling embers of our fire, my father did something he had never done before. He began telling me a ghost story. In this forest, he started, people for over a century had told each other tales of wanderers in the woods. Beautiful melodies whistled in through the trees. Strangers in the distance would wave and beckon travelers to come and see incredible things. Anyone foolish enough to follow them vanished, never to be seen again.

Not understanding why he would tell me these things I began to panic and tears pooled in the corners of my eyes. Seeing the visible discomfort, my father smiled and told me that as a boy he thought he had seen the same things too. My grandfather had told him the same story when he was my age or perhaps a bit younger.

Every time they would tread the same trails that he and I hike now he always imagined hearing or seeing the wanderers in the woods. When he told my grandfather what he had heard and seen he took it as an opportunity to teach him that the whistling sound was a known call of a local bird. He would also find shapes in the distance and show him how inanimate objects at a distance could produce the illusion of a man or woman watching them.

"It could also be a practical joke, kiddo," He reassured me. "When an area has a popular urban legend, folks like to do what they can to stoke the fires."

I began to calm down a bit. We were deep within a massive national forest and the odds of encountering another person were slim at best. My youthful fears had gathered natural occurrences around me and organized them into an unnerving and unlikely scenario.

Even if it had been a person, I thought he was right. They were trying to play a joke on us, and I had fallen for it hook, line, and sinker. I eased my posture substantially and smiled thankfully at my father. In all of our trips together after that I never had the same experience again.

That all changed when I began work as a park ranger at Fire Tower No. 1. Arlo Bennett National Forest was full of darkness that my father had worked so hard to convince me was only a figment of my imagination. I wish he had been right.

* * *

I had just finished college with a degree in wildlife conservation not long before the start of the pandemic. Needless to say, this was not a kind time for new graduates. A local pizzeria near campus had provided me with steady hours and a decent paycheck throughout my studies, but with increasing CDC recommendations and closures, my hours had dwindled to a quarter of what I had previously worked. Being hundreds of miles from home and the not-so-proud owner of a rapidly dwindling bank account, I spent hours each day filling out job applications, sending out resumes, and cold-calling every national park and forest I could find online.

Desperation was mounting until I had finally resolved to pack up my belongings and move back to my hometown, tail between my legs. My parents passed away in a car accident during my sophomore year. I wouldn't be returning to a stable support system, but I was at least confident that old friends and extended family may be able to help me find gainful employment. Steady footing just seemed so far out of reach.

Moving day arrived, and I finished boxing up the last of my possessions and stacking them haphazardly into the back of a rented box truck. After barely managing to get my beater of a car secured onto the tow dolly, I felt my phone buzz in my pocket. Slumping down onto the tailgate of the box truck I fished it out and saw a red notification bubble on my mail application and clicked it.

The feeling of joy I experienced can't be accurately described as I read the attached e-mail.

Arlo Bennett National Forest Hiring Authority
To: gparker@kct.edu

Subject: Your application has been chosen for Fire Tower No. 1 in Arlo Bennett National Forest

Mr. Parker,
Congratulations and welcome to our team here at Arlo Bennett National Forest! We are excited to inform you that as a new park ranger for wildlife services, you will be stationed at Fire Tower No. 1. You are expected to arrive at Ranger Station 3 on [date redacted] at or before 0800 EST.

Uniforms, equipment, shelter, and necessities will be provided as this is a 24/7 live-in posting. If you require storage for personal items you do not wish to keep in your on-site residence, accommodations will be made upon arrival. Please bring a valid driver's license, social security card, and a copy of this e-mail to be presented upon arrival.

If you have any additional questions or concerns, please contact your HR representatives at 606-555-3241 during the hours of 0800 EST and 1730 EST.

We thank you for your time and look forward to meeting you.

Welcome to the team,
Dennis Garland
Superintendent II—Arlo Bennett National Forest

After reading the email over and over no less than ten times, tears began to run down my cheeks. I was mildly confused. The e-mail seemed to be informing me that I had already received the job, but I hadn't even done a phone interview. I told myself that my resume and application must have been such high quality that it wasn't necessary.

Hindsight is 20/20.

Only minutes ago, I was preparing to drive a box truck full of my second-hand furniture and meager possessions pointlessly toward my old hometown. Now I couldn't wait to travel down the road to my new career and what I thought would be a bright future.

Two days and one terrible roadside motel later I pulled the box truck into a nearly empty parking lot in front of a log-sided building with a sign reading *Ranger Station 3*. Two well-aged Jeeps sat parked side by side in front of the station, both marked clearly as ranger patrol vehicles. I couldn't help but smile. There I was, right where I had always wanted to be.

With a mixed sensation of pride and terror, I made my way into the ranger station and introduced myself to a man with salt and pepper hair sitting at the desk in the entryway. I introduced myself and was greeted with a vice grip of a handshake, and he identified himself as Superintendent Garland. He explained to me that, while he was generally not stationed at this location, he made it a goal to personally meet every newly hired ranger and walk them through the orientation process.

Over the next few hours, we filled out a seemingly endless pile of paperwork, drank bad coffee out of chipped mugs, and I listened intently to Superintendent Garland as he explained my job duties at Fire Tower No. 1. None of the duties sounded unusual in any way to start.

I would work in a three-by-three grid with Fire Towers 1 to 9. For the first two weeks of the month, I would man the tower from 0500 to 1700. A reserve staff member would report to the station to give you a day off to readjust your sleep schedule for the last half of the month. For the following two weeks, I would work from 1700 to 0500.

Each tower in the grid was staggered by the shift to watch neighboring off-duty sectors around them as well as their own. The primary concern was to watch for the inception of forest fires. Lighting strikes and unauthorized campfires were constant concerns in this area, so around-the-clock surveillance was necessary.

All fire tower rangers were provided with a two-bedroom, one-bathroom cabin located at the base of the tower. They were fully furnished and basic sundries were provided for your first week on the job with the expectation you would provide your own groceries and toiletries thereafter. Routine maintenance of the cabin and tower was to be performed by the occupying ranger.

Mr. Garland also informed me that I would work four weeks on duty with one full week off to follow. Reserve staff would report to the cabin at each tower to relieve the primary attendant to allow them some rest and relaxation. The second bedroom was to be reserved for them and we were to keep it free of personal items. One exemption to this rule was in the event a camper or hiker was retrieved during a search and rescue until they could be evacuated to the nearest town by medical staff.

As he wrapped up, I was smiling ear to ear. Dream job: Check! Rent-free living: Check! After a worrying season in my life, everything seemed to be going my way. I was already making a mental checklist of what personal items to keep in the cabin and what I would need to store in the provided shed when Mr. Garland's gruff voice unexpectedly pulled me out of my daydream.

"One more thing," he said, eyes locking with mine. "Don't travel any farther than a half-mile or so north of Tower 1."

"Oh, sure thing," I replied. "No problem at all, but is there any particular reason?"

Mr. Garland stared at me in silence for a moment and I could tell he was trying to sort out an answer. "Dangerous woods that way, son," he finally responded. "Bobcats and bears. Nasty business." I nodded politely, but it wasn't a terribly satisfying answer. My father and I had camped in that forest for years and had always known predatory wildlife lived throughout the entirety of the reserve area. Unless the bobcats had learned to ride the bears to hunt people down it seemed unlikely to be any more dangerous than any other area. Regardless, it seemed like a poor plan to argue or question my new employer before my first shift began.

He shook my hand and gave me a few pointers as he walked me to the door. I picked up a duffle bag they had prepared for me that was sitting in a chair by the door. Heading out to the box truck, I tried to reignite my excitement and invigoration for my new job, but the warning Superintendent Garland had given me still circled inside my mind ominously. *Don't go north.* At that moment I fully intended to adhere to the direction, but soon my curiosity sent me barreling down a dangerous path.

***

My first week at the cabin and tower was a whirlwind of information. The ranger currently occupying my new tower, Thomas Richardson, was a reserve ranger who filled in the off weeks of towers 1 to 3. As he helped me unload my box truck and unhook my car, I picked his brain for every piece of advice I could think to ask. He had worked for the ranger service there for a little less than a decade.

I was surprised to learn that he had originally been offered the permanent role in Fire Tower No. 1, a significant pay increase from reserve status, but had declined. He said he loved traveling to the different towers and changing the scenery each one offered. He seemed like a very genuine and helpful man, but at the back of my mind, I couldn't help but wonder if whatever could be found north of the tower drove him to decline the position.

"So, do you ever do any hiking or camping when you're off duty?" I asked on our last day together.

"Yeah, at least once a month or so," Thomas replied. "I'd say I've probably hiked or explored everything within about five miles of the fire towers."

That seemed like as good a chance as any to naturally ask Thomas about the area north of the tower. "I've got a pretty good grasp of the territory to the east, south, and west, but is there much worth checking out north of the tower?" I looked intently in his direction, but he never returned my gaze.

Thomas stood up quickly and began to pack his hiking bag without making eye contact. He tossed it over his shoulder and made his way to the door toward the wrap-around stairs. Once he had made it outside, he turned and looked at me with a determined face. "North of the tower isn't safe, buddy." He turned and began to walk down the stairs toward his Jeep. "Bobcats and bears that way. Stay clear!" A few seconds later I could hear the roar of his engine and the sound of gravel scattering beneath tires as his Jeep made its way down the road.

I was surprised by his sudden departure and lack of a formal farewell. It wasn't as if I wouldn't see him again in three weeks when he returned to give me my days off, but for such a friendly guy it seemed like a rude exit. A bit of clarity from Thomas had been what I was anticipating, but I was just left with a lead weight in my stomach and a slight feeling of dread. The answer had been so quick it seemed as though he had practiced it. Matched with the dash for the door, I was sure something worse than wildlife must be located somewhere in these woods.

That evening after my shift had ended, I radioed the two towers in my grid that would be assuming the night watch. Before departing the tower, we had to verify that they were safely on shift. After receiving an affirmative message from both, I began to shut down all of the tower equipment other than the radio and gather up my belongings. There was still a bit of daylight left, so I seized the opportunity to grab a few odds and ends from the storage shed to bring inside. I had mostly settled into the cabin, but there was still a barren bookshelf in the corner that was begging for some of my tattered paperbacks.

I dumped the old cardboard box on the floor by the shelf and sat on the hardwood floor. Sitting cross-legged, I opened the box and began to scoop out the haphazardly stored novels and arrange them on the particle board shelf. The bottom was filled, and I was just beginning to load up the top shelf with the last of my New York Times Best Sellers when I noticed something was sitting behind the lip of the bookshelf. I reached my hand into the corner and pulled out a worn leather book.

There were no markings on the front or back to identify what it was or who it may have belonged to. Thumbing it open to a page marked with an attached leather bookmark, I could see the winding loops of cursive handwriting. Not a book, so to speak, but a journal. It must have belonged to the ranger who manned the station before me. Momentarily I considered reading it but decided against it. Tossing it on top of the bookshelf, I made a mental note to give it to Mr. Garland the next time I saw him. Maybe he could return it to the rightful owner.

After stowing away my books, I took the cardboard box outside and started walking down the gravel path to the storage building. There was a steel cage to place garbage in an attempt to keep larger wildlife from rifling through the bins. I reached down to my hip to retrieve my jingling set of keys to unlock the disposal gate. Setting the box down, I slid the key into the lock and opened the gate. As I reached down to retrieve the box, I could hear something off in the distance.

By then the light of day was a distant memory and my eyes had not yet adjusted to the darkness. Years of living in the city had made me forget just how dark the forest could be. I had still gone on the occasional hike or camping trip with classmates, but it had usually been to a pay-to-stay campsite with bathroom/shower combinations and paths lit with soft wattage bulbs. It hadn't occurred to me to switch on the light that extended to the storage shed. My visibility was aided only by the light on the cabin's front porch which was swallowed up by the walls of darkness.

That is when the whistling began. It was soft and indistinct, but I could hear it nonetheless. The crunching of leaves and snapping of twigs in the distance accompanied the unidentifiable tune. I was unable to move as I attempted to locate the direction it was coming from, but my efforts were fruitless. While the sound seemed to be coming from one point far off in the distance, I could also hear traces of it all around me.

Before Thomas had left, we went over the camping permit logs for our grid and there were none requested within 10 miles of my post. All of the most popular hiking trails were equally far away, so there was little to no reason for anyone to be traveling in that area at this time of night. The only trails nearby were less traveled and given to more experienced hikers. Anyone with the skill to travel those trails would also have the common sense to set up camp for the night.

As I stood listening and squinting in the darkness, I couldn't help but feel like the ten-year-old boy from so many years ago, but this time I didn't have my father to comfort me. That night around the fire he was able to explain all of this in a way that made me believe my imagination had just run away with me. Standing there by myself, I felt none of that certainty.

The whistling grew louder and more distinct as I stood frozen in the darkness. Where before it was a disembodied and distant sound, I could tell that the source was moving in my direction. There was a haunting yet beautiful melody that I was able to hear more clearly. Crunching leaves and snapping twigs seemed to be just outside my field of vision.

It was almost hypnotizing. My eyes began to close, and re-laxation began to settle into my bones. Icy fear melted away, leaving me in a state of near bliss. I felt like it may be a good idea to just walk toward the source of the beautiful melody.

"It's this way!" I heard a soft voice say. "Come and see!"

The feeling of relaxation washed away almost as quickly as it had begun. Where the melodic whistling had lulled me into a stupor, the sudden call from the darkness sobered me to the situation. I stumbled backward toward the cabin and began to run toward the safety of the burning bulb.

My heavy footfalls washed out all the noises from moments before. As I ran, I imagined some malevolent creature mere steps behind me, claws outstretched toward my back, still beckoning me to come and see whatever was in the darkness of the forest.

Once I reached the front door I pushed my way inside, slammed the door, engaged the deadbolt, and slid onto the floor. My back against it, I simply sat panting and trying to listen for any signs of activity outside. There was no whistling. No footsteps on the walkway or the porch. No knocking. It was just the noise of my gulping breath and the thunder of my heart against my ribcage.

After a few minutes, I was able to collect myself enough to put a plan together. If there was someone out there, maybe they were in danger. I went to the control room in the cabin and threw on the breakers to the spotlights located around the perimeter of the cabin, fire tower, and storage building. Through the blinds of the cabin, I could see the piercing beams of artificial light. Before leaving the control room, I grabbed a floodlight and a hunting rifle from the rack.

Slowly, I disengaged the deadbolt and stepped outside. The forest was now a terrifying combination of artificial light and obscenely long shadows cast by the spotlights. I made my way back down the gravel trail toward the storage building. The whistling had begun just beyond the storage shed. I turned on the handheld floodlight and began to sweep the tree line looking for anyone or anything that may have hung around.

Nothing. Not a single damn thing. Despite all of the crunching leaves and breaking branches I heard, there was no sign that anything had moved through the area recently. Nothing larger than a squirrel, at least.

I continued sweeping the distance with the floodlight when I heard the ping of an incoming call on the fire tower watch radio. The sound made me jump, and I dropped the light to the ground with a heavy thud. As my heart calmed, I scooped up the light and headed toward the tower. Already out of breath after running from the storage building, the ascent to the top of the tower was painfully slow. I finally reached the lookout box and turned on the light.

"Tower 1? This is Tower 5. Do you copy?"

I punched the button on the radio mic. "I read you, Tower 5. Go for Tower 1."

"Tower 1, status check," the voice said. "I can see your spotlights over here at Tower 5. Everything okay?"

I immediately felt embarrassed and didn't want to explain the commotion of the evening. "Everything is all clear," I responded. "I just... Thomas explained how to use the spot system, but I wanted to give it a hands-on run. I'll cut them now. Again, everything is all clear."

I thanked the ranger and headed down to the cabin and into the control room to cut the light system off. Hand trembling on the switch, I hesitated. As scared and tired as I had been, I knew I had to take one last look outside before shutting off the lights. Pulling the cord on the blinds, I looked outside. In the distance, at the edge of the spotlights, I thought I could see someone walking into the darkness of the tree line.

My heart began to hammer again as I pulled my phone out of my pocket, trying to snap a picture, but they vanished before I managed to open up the application. Before I returned my phone to my pocket a curious thought occurred to me. Thumbing through my applications, I finally found the one I was looking for.

A digital compass popped up on my screen and the needle bounced side to side as my hand shook. Once I was able to settle my nerves, the needle finally came to rest. It pointed to the north.

***

To say I was on edge for the next few days would have been an understatement. My night shift rotation was quickly approaching. While I hadn't seen or heard anything alarming since the night Thomas had departed, I had also taken special care to avoid the opportunity. No more nighttime travel to the storage shed. No taking the trash out in the evening. If I needed to complete any outdoor tasks, I made sure to take care of them during sundown. I had mostly convinced myself that it was all in my imagination, but the thought still rolled around in the back of my head.

Maybe I saw and heard exactly what I thought I had.

Immediately after my shift each day I shut down all lookout equipment except the radio and headed directly down to the cabin. My evenings consisted of a steady schedule of tv show binging, dinner, a shower, and reading in bed. The small supply of paperback books I had brought didn't provide as much entertainment as I had hoped. Most of them I had already read dozens of times and I quickly thumbed through the few that hadn't lost all their appeal. The paperback I was reading lost most of its luster and I put it aside on the nightstand and gazed at the bookshelf to see if something else caught my eye. That's when I saw the journal again.

Shuffling out of bed and to the bookshelf, I scooped up the journal and tucked myself back beneath my blanket. Initially, I had told myself it was immoral to read someone's private journal. Still, the odd feeling that place gave me, and the lack of other engaging activities, made it easier than it should have to justify reading just a few pages. I flipped open the cover to the first page and ran my hand over the indentions of the cursive writing on the page.

Although I had told myself I would only read a few pages, that turned into about a quarter of the journal. The beginning introduced me to its writer, Gary Vincent, and his arrival in what would later be my cabin. Entry one was dated roughly two years before I arrived and told the uneventful story of his early life, education, and acceptance of the ranger position at Fire Tower No. 1 in Arlo Bennett National Forest. Our stories were fairly similar in many respects, but Gary seemed to have skipped the period of self-loathing and desperation before his employment there.

While not the most energetic or entertaining read I had ever come across, there was something enjoyable about learning the personal thoughts of who I assumed was my predecessor. Thomas had trained him as well and the two of them seemed to have developed a good friendship if Gary's words were to be believed. The two of them camped and hiked the area together and enjoyed their shared time at the cabin when Thomas came to relieve Gary for his days off.

I was beginning to nod in and out of alertness having finished about a third of the journal when an entry jolted me back to attention.

So there seems to be something weird going on around here. I love everything about living and working in the forest, but now and again I just get that feeling something is watching me. Can't quite put my finger on what brings the sensation. It's the same feeling you get when someone stands behind you in a room but doesn't say anything. Just an electric charge sensation.

Last night I was hauling the kitchen trash out to the good old dumpster dungeon when I heard someone whistling out in the woods. I always check the camping permits at the start and end of my shift, so if there is an emergency I can get help out to them. The thing is, there are no permits out this far that we had on record today. I tried calling out to the person whistling but they would just fall silent whenever I did. A few minutes later the little tune would pick back up. I'd try calling out again, but it was just the same. No more whistling for a minute. There was a time or two I thought someone was telling me to come and look at something, but I'm not sure.

I headed into the control room and grabbed a flashlight to search the area, but after a half-hour or so of stumbling around in the woods, I called it quits. Didn't see anyone or hear any more whistling. Haven't really been out here all that long, but maybe the lack of daily interaction with people is just making my mind act funny. Don't know, but not too worried about it. If whistling is the worst thing I hear I think I'm in pretty good shape.

I read the passage over and over. The same thing had happened to Gary. The only noticeable difference was my total panic compared to Gary's cool and collected approach to investigating the area. I assumed that he had not experienced the same event as a child, but it was almost impossible to believe that this wouldn't have seemed kind of strange to him.

A second difference also occurred to me. Gary hadn't seen anyone in the wood line. I wasn't positive that I saw a person, but I was certain I had seen something.

Too engaged with the similarities of the journal, I knew I would be up for the rest of the night until I finished it. I got out of bed again and headed into the kitchen to make myself a pot of coffee. After the ancient machine spilled the last drop into the pot, I poured a mug full and settled into the kitchen table to continue my reading. The pages immediately following the whistling event were more of the same day-in/day-out stream of thought entries you would expect until about three months later.

This place is starting to mess with my mind a little bit. I was outside last night doing my usual dumpster run when I started hearing that damn whistling again. Honestly, I'd forgotten about the last time it happened until ten or so last night. Tossed the trash in the cage when the whistling started up. The flashlight was already in my pocket this time. Started carrying it a few weeks ago just as a precaution.

It was louder this time and something about it just made me happy. Just felt like I could wander in that direction and hear it a little better if I could find who was making that beautiful noise. Kind of made me sad too, though. Not sure why. I flipped on the flashlight and started walking north into the woods to see if I could find who it was.

I called out and asked who was there. This time someone shouted back "It's this way. Come and see!"

I asked them what it was, but no one answered. When I started walking toward the sound of the voice I could hear footsteps and whistle moving away from me, so I called out again for them to wait. I just wanted to talk to them. They just repeated the same thing. "It's this way. Come and see!"

By now I figured there must be something to check out, so I kept walking after them. Maybe someone was hurt. Probably not, though. If they were hurt, why would they be whistling? My mind was kind of foggy. The melody made the traveling feel a little bit easier though. I felt kinda happy like something good was going to happen.

The woods were starting to get thicker, and I wasn't gaining on them. They always seemed to be just the same distance in front of me as they had been the entire time. Occasionally I would catch a glimpse of someone in my flashlight beam and I'd call out, but still the same old thing. "It's this way. Come and see!"

Eventually, I came to a cluster of oak trees that were so tightly packed together they looked like one monstrous tree. When I got to it the whistling stopped for a little while and suddenly I felt sad. My eyes teared up, and I wasn't sure why. Then the whistling tune came back like it sensed that I needed it again to be happy. Sounded like it was up on the top of the trees. I tried shouting for them again a few times, but no one answered at first.

After a few minutes of trying to get their attention, I finally heard someone reply. "It's up here! Come see!"

"Up where?" I asked the voice.

"In the trees! Just use the stairs," the voice called back.

I ran the flashlight around the base of the trees and in the center, I could see what looked like a step. Inching closer and leaning between two of the oaks I could see a damn spiral staircase running up the center of the trees and into the foliage.

I started walking forward. The banister felt so smooth under my hand. I wanted to see where it went. For a moment it felt like the right thing to do. Just grab onto the banister and climb up to the top.

My foot was just settling onto the bottom step when a vibration startled me back to my senses. My smartwatch was beeping loudly, and when I looked down I saw my heart rate was nearly one hundred and fifty beats a minute. I saw the time too. It had only been ten o'clock when I headed to take the trash out, but it was almost eleven-thirty now. Seemed like I had only been in the woods for maybe fifteen minutes, but it had been an hour and a half.

I panicked and headed back in the direction of the cabin. As I made my way back, there was the remnant of an old hiking trail that took me within a stone's throw of the cabin. Took me almost two hours to get back. My body aches and I feel like I have the flu. I'm not sure what the hell that was out there, but I'm going to have to call this in at the start of my shift.

My heart raced as I continued reading the journal. In the next few pages, Gary recounted how he called in the staircase to Superintendent Garland the next day. A team of rangers had met him at the cabin. They traveled back to the location where Gary had seen the stairs but didn't find anything out of the ordinary. Gary begged them to go back at night thinking maybe they would see it again. The other rangers agreed in an effort to calm Gary's concerns, but the nighttime trip was no different.

There was nothing there.

The journal entries from that point became almost incoherent in their format. Gary was fixated on how the stairs had disappeared and why they couldn't find them. He admitted traveling back multiple times but never seeing them again. The absence of the whistling also seemed to bother him rather than soothe his worried mind. He wrote endlessly about missing the beautiful melody and that it maddened him that he couldn't remember all the notes.

And then there was no entry for a long period. Weeks passed between. When Gary wrote what would be his final entry in the journal, he seemed to be a man who had lost grip on reality.

The music didn't return to me. I had been so sad without it. The gentle melody haunted my mind even though I couldn't quite remember how it sounded. So I traveled back again. Down the forgotten path. I traveled north. Traveled to that unusual copse of trees. And there it was! The stairs were back! Thank God! They were there! No one was whistling, and no voice invited me up, but

I knew that I needed to go. I belonged there! With them. With HIM! He was waiting for me.

The banister felt so good under my hand as I made my way up. Into the foliage. Through the branches. Into my new home. Everyone is in unison there. The many are one. I came back here to say goodbye to... someone. Was there someone here I knew? I'll just say goodbye to you, journal. I am going back. I know I will stay. I want to be in unison.

Maybe I can help others find their way there. I hope he will let me help. So many souls can be one if they will let themselves go!

To anyone who reads these words, take heart. It is this way! Come and see!

That was it. Nothing but blank pages followed. I was shaking as I closed the leather cover and stared into my empty coffee cup. The sun was creeping over the tops of the trees, and I knew that if I didn't move soon, I would be late for the start of my shift. I put on a fresh pot of coffee and began to ready myself in a daze. The journal stayed clutched in my hand as though it were some talisman that might protect me from Gary's fate. I didn't know exactly what to do in the long run then, but I knew I had to get to my post.

***

Months had passed since I discovered the journal, and spring was quickly approaching. I would periodically hear the whistling in the woods on evenings when I didn't have to work. The height of the fire tower probably just made it impossible for the melody to reach my ears when I worked nights, but I always assumed it was there. When the whistling would begin in the evenings, I would put in a pair of earplugs to block it out. It seemed to keep me from feeling that unreasonable sensation to follow the haunting melody.

Although it yielded no satisfying information, I shared the journal and its contents with Mr. Garland and Thomas. Mr. Garland explained that Gary Vincent had been a stellar employee for two years but confided in me that he had a history of mental illness. While they explained his complicated situation, Thomas handed me a photo of Gary.

He was a few years older than me, with bright red hair and a huge smile. They told me that Gary suffered from something similar to schizophrenia. It had been well controlled with medication for quite some time. Once Gary went missing, Thomas and the other rangers found months' worth of his medicine in the medicine cabinet of the cabin.

He had taken to traveling into the northern forest more frequently in the last few months. Thomas, Garland, and a host of other rangers had traveled to the location with Gary where he claimed to have seen the stairs and there was nothing unusual. Each unsuccessful search seemed to cause him to become a little more distant from them until eventually they all quit talking unless it had to do with work. The two of them implored Gary to seek help but he never did. And then he vanished into the woods.

The subsequent search for him only turned up his tattered uniform jack and his wallet.

For my part, I continued doing my job. I liked the night shift the best because there was no whistling. Staring out into the darkness for hours looking for fire soothed my worried mind. My phone ran a constant stream of music to keep me company. When I worked the day shift I would bring Gary's journal with me and study it as though perhaps I would discover some secret to his madness. I never did. It just seemed to provide a madness of my own. I was obsessed with what had happened to him.

I can't honestly tell you why I decided to do what I did next, but the mystery had become more than I could take. Thomas arrived to start my week off duty, and I told him I planned to do some camping. He seemed excited to have the cabin to himself for a few days. The day before he arrived, I had already loaded the ATV in the storage shed with camping gear and extra gas.

I was going to go find that damn staircase.

As soon as Thomas started his shift, I fired up the ATV and headed on the trail to the east of the tower so he would be less likely to discover my plan. I drove the ATV in a wide arc around the Tower 1 sector until I was about a quarter-mile due north of the tower. It took me a while, but after hours of searching, I found the rutted trail that Gary had written about in his journal. The trip was uneventful, and with the use of the ATV, I reached the tightly gathered copse of trees in no time.

I slid off the ATV and approached the cluster of trees with caution. They formed a tight circle with a three-foot gap facing toward the south. The canopy shadowed the interior, making it impossible to see what was inside. With a lump in my throat, I pulled the floodlight off of the ATV and aimed it into the circle of trees. There was nothing inside other than fallen leaves and a few dry branches.

My pulse relaxed and my body tension eased. The staircase wasn't there. I felt a mixture of joy and sadness. Gary had seemed so sure of what he had seen and now I felt sure he had been suffering hallucinations. Thomas said he hadn't taken it in months. A sorrowful picture of a man who had lost grip on reality filled my mind.

Walking inside the copse, I couldn't find anything out of the ordinary. Feeling content that the staircase was a fantasy, I decided to make the most of my days off and follow through with the camping trip.

The day was warmer than the seasonal average, so I chose to forgo the tent and camp under the stars. I was only going to be staying overnight so I opted not to dig a latrine and concentrated on setting up a comfortable fire after clearing the brush. Even with the unusually warm day, I still gathered an abundant amount of firewood just in case it took a substantial dip in temperature.

After a quick meal and a few chapters in one of my ragged paperback novels, I decided it was time to turn in for the night. I settled into my sleeping bag and enjoyed the heat from the stone-rimmed fire. It was only moments before I was fast asleep.

Sometime during the night, I awoke to a familiar sound. The melody I had avoided for so many months now was filling my ears, and it was coming from directly behind me. I rolled over and investigated the copse of trees. Standing in the gap between the oaks was Gary. I recognized his wide smile and fire-red hair from the photo Thomas had shown me. Gnarled tufts of hair sprouted in random directions, and his tattered ranger's uniform hung off his emaciated frame.

"Gary?" I asked in a daze.

He just continued giving me that unsettling smile as he stepped backward and was enveloped in the darkness of the circle of oak trees. I could hear what sounded like the thuds of hiking boots on wooden boards. Springing from my sleeping bag and grabbing the floodlight, I yelled Gary's name again.

"It's up here! Come see!" he replied in a manic voice.

I turned on the floodlight and aimed it into the trees expecting to see him hunkered inside, but to my shock, the beam of my floodlight gleamed off of a polished mahogany banister. There was a beautifully crafted circular staircase in the center of the trees.

Lifting my floodlight, I caught the bottom of Gary's boot as he ascended the stairs. Shouting his name, I sprinted inside.

"Gary, no!" I shrieked. My hand grasped the smooth, cold wood as I began to climb the stairs in their tight circle. "Come back, man! We need to get you some help!"

I could only hear the thuds of his footfalls as he continued upward. My pulse was racing as I bounded up behind him, clinging tightly to the banister. Leaves and branches traced the side of my face as we both climbed higher into the trees. The beam of my floodlight bounced and weaved between smooth mahogany wood and dense foliage. As hard as I climbed the stairs, I could hear that Gary was getting farther ahead of me.

My pace was beginning to slow, but I still clung to the banister, using it to pull myself up as I tried to reach the man racing ahead of me. The smoothness of the wood began to change under my hand as I climbed higher. What had been an unblemished surface began to feel bumpy and rigid on my palm. I was starting to breathe heavily through my mouth and knew I would need to rest soon.

In exhaustion, I decided to stop and catch my breath. The beam of my floodlight was pointed toward the stairs, but they looked different than they had when I first saw them. Where they had been a rich brown at the bottom, they appeared the color of half-burnt charcoal. I traced the light up higher to get a better view of my surroundings and discovered why the banister felt so different. The smooth wood had transitioned into what looked like an unending spinal cord. The bones curled upward, wrapping around the charcoal steps like a pale snake.

The foliage around me, which had been budding and green when I started my ascent, was now the sickly purple of a healing black eye with throbbing veins running through the leaves. Balls of black dew dotted the tops of the leaves. I noticed that anywhere this dew had made contact with my clothes, small holes appeared, and I could smell the light scent of chemical burn and hints of decay. The branches of the trees made sudden pattern changes from obsidian to ashen white.

I began to scream and turned to go back down when I saw the section of steps below me crumble and fall away into nothingness. There was no way I had climbed more than the equivalent of six flights of stairs, but I watched as chunks of the burnt charcoal platform and spinal cord banister drifted off in a hellish purple chasm. As I tried to gain my composure and figure out what to do next, I could feel the step below me beginning to crack and sink.

Without another thought, I began to run up the stairs as quickly as I could. All the while, I could hear the step just behind me crumble and drop off into the purple abyss below. There would be no more breaks to catch my breath. I couldn't even afford a glance backward unless I wanted to end up drifting off into whatever unknown hell ran below.

The air seemed to get thinner and had the tang of rotting meat.

I could feel my legs buckling and struggling to keep up with the stairs and knew I would soon fall back into the hellscape below. Just as I felt the last of my strength give way, my hand reached for another section of the spinal banister but found only empty air. My foot rose to find one more burnt charcoal step but instead extended forward and found no purchase. I fell forward onto level ground.

My floodlight flickered across the ground revealing a gray and writhing field before me. It was damp, and I could feel it pulse beneath my palms. I jumped up in a panic to get my hands off of the disgusting material. My hands shook violently as flecks of gray sludge flew wildly from my fingers.

I was wiping the rest of the muck onto my pant legs when I lifted my eyes to the hellish scene before me. The sky was a flowing haze of purple, full of a thick fog. There was no variation to this gray terrain. It writhed and shifted as far as I could see.

Dotted over the landscape were thin, leafless trees swaying lazily in the cold wind. As my eyes focused on the low, unearthly light, I realized they weren't trees at all. They were emaciated people. Thousands of them with bone thin arms raised, reaching toward the sky. Some of their feet were held in place by skeletal hands emerging from the ground, while others seemed to be growing into a gray mass like a plant. Their eyes glowed softly with the same purple light as the sky.

All at once, the numberless horde turned their heads toward me and spoke.

"We are many, but we are one in Him!" thousands of voices said in unison. "You have heard his beautiful song and now you will sing it with us forever!"

A few yards in front of me stood Gary. The same sick purple glow flowed from his eyes, but he stood with his arms at his side. He motioned with both hands to a spot just beside him and smiled that unsettling smile. On the ground where he pointed were two writhing, skeletal hands.

"You've heard the song," he said in a dreamy voice. "This is where you belong. With us."

I wanted to beg him to go back with me. To tell him it wasn't too late. We could help him if he would only let us. Staying there was madness. He had been twisted into something he was.

Before I could say anything, I started to feel it wasn't as twisted as it had first seemed. The melody I had heard so many times in the woods echoed everywhere now. The forest of skyward-reaching people produced an overpowering wave of sound as they all whistled the same hauntingly beautiful melody. I started to walk toward Gary and thought that this all made sense. Everyone here looked so happy. The purple of this world was evening beginning to become beautiful to me.

I was nearly halfway to Gary when I halted for a moment and looked over my shoulder. There was an opening in the ground where the stairs had been. My head darted from side to side, and I could see more of these openings on the ground between the swaying forest of humans. There must be hundreds of these staircases leading up to this world.

From my world, I realized. Bringing people from our world to this brainwashing hellscape.

Looking back at Gary, I could see that same smile as before but there was a nervousness to it. It was almost pleading with me to step beside him and accept those skeletal hands and allow them to wrap around my ankles. Then I noticed the tears running down his face and the ever-so-subtle shaking of his head.

He was trying to tell me no.

Before I could ask him to tell me where we were, to ask what the hell was going on or what was happening there, I was startled by the deafening sound. It was almost like a foghorn, but so much deeper. My bones shook violently. The ground beneath me quaked and the beautiful melody from the forest of people suddenly turned into a blood-curdling shriek. Their hands dropped from the sky and covered their ears, and I did the same.

A second boom of the foghorn came, and the writhing forest lifted their heads, mouths opening until their jaws nearly unhinged. Thin streams of blue and yellow smoke drifted out of them, swirling together into a twisting cloud above our heads. It began to funnel into a stream and drifted into the distance. My eyes followed the tip of the swirling stream until I saw something moving far in the distance. It was mountainous. Larger than anything I had ever seen.

The colossal silhouette was robed in fog, but I could still make out the shape. It towered above the field, blocking out the purple glow of the distant horizon. It seemed to sprout out of the ground into a thick torso with arms so thin they seemed like they would snap if made to hold any weight. At the end of these bony arms, I could see clawed hands scooping up people trapped in the gray ground in front of it. An oval shaped mouth with two ivory, protruding husks split open from its squat, stocky head. A cavernous mouth full of slender, sharp teeth gleamed in the sickening light. Two clawed hands shoved handfuls of screaming people into its mouth in between long drinks from the blue and yellow smoke that drifted toward it.

"They are blessed to become one with him!" The forest of humans shrieked. "He will welcome you too! Come and see!"

The appearance of the eldritch horror was more than I could bear. I stumbled backward and fell to the ground as the gray mass writhed underneath my hands again. Using my feet, I pushed myself back toward the hole I had emerged from and looked back at Gary. He was still crying, but he was nodding in agreement now as I got closer to the hole. I could see now that he was held in place by the same writhing hands he was gesturing toward.

Frozen in place, I thought for a moment that I would run to Gary and drag him with me. He must have seen it in my eyes. His smile faded as his brows furrowed and his lips pulled back in a pain filled grimace.

"Go!" he screamed, voice filled with agony. "It's too late for us! Go!"

I broke my gaze with Gary and looked into the sky at the impossibly large abomination towering over the forest of tortured souls. Its massive hand broke through the fog and reached for me. Without another thought, I pushed myself back into the hole and closed my eyes. Floating in an endless void was better than allowing that ageless horror to consume me or add me to its blasphemous garden of souls.

The sensation of falling was terrifying and my stomach began to ball up tightly. I could feel myself moving faster and faster as the sickening purple void swirled around me. My eyes closed, and

I prayed that I would die soon to spare me from the hellish nightmare. That is when I began to feel a sharp pain in my back as something began to strike me. I opened my eyes, but it was almost completely dark now. My body was slamming against solid objects, knocking the wind from my lungs.

My descent began to slow, and I could feel something soft and angular brush against my face as my body continued to be pummeled with blow after blow. My eyes were beginning to focus on the growing light and I could see that I was slamming into tree branches. Extending my arms, I was able to briefly grasp onto them to slow my fall.

After what felt like hours, I landed with a sickening thud on the ground, and everything went black.

When I came to, I was in front of the abnormal circle of trees. Dirt and saliva were caked to my face and my vision swam with ripples from the impact. I sucked in panicked breaths as I looked at the smooth mahogany stairs only feet in front of me. My entire body ached, but I pushed myself up and staggered to the ATV to retrieve the gas can. Fuel spilled out of the upturned can as I dumped the contents at the foot of those hellish stairs. I pulled a book of matches from my pocket and flicked it into the trees. A rush of warmth hit me as the fire swallowed the stairs and the trees surrounding them. My vision began to swim again, and I felt unconsciousness wash over me once again.

***

I woke up in the hospital in my hometown. Thomas was asleep in an armchair beside my bed. He awoke when I started shifting in the bed while attempting to make myself comfortable. My left arm was in a cast as well as my left leg. Reaching up to scratch my head, I could feel missing patches of hair. I was covered in bruises and cuts from head to toe.

Thomas told me that they had found me after he spotted rising smoke from the lookout booth in Fire Tower No. 1. When the rangers and forestry services arrived they found me at the foot of the blazing trees. I had been in the hospital for three days and had been in and out of consciousness. He asked me repeatedly what had happened, but I lied and told him I wasn't sure.

After Mr. Garland was informed I was awake, he stopped by for a visit too. It was pretty similar to my visit with Thomas. He told me what had happened from his perspective and asked what had happened. Already practiced at lying about the whole ordeal, I told him I didn't know. I had gone camping and woke up in the hospital.

I wasn't fired from my job, but I never returned to Fire Tower No. 1. The ranger service investigated the fire and while they were able to ascertain that it had been intentionally set, I wasn't suspected due to my battered state when they discovered me. Last I spoke with him, Thomas told me he had accepted the full-time position at Fire Tower No. 1 and I wished him good luck.

As for me now, I've taken a traveling position with the national forestry service. I travel the country performing survey studies of the national forests under our care. It's been nice to see the country and I still spend every available moment I have hiking and camping. My motivation is a bit different now. In every new town I travel to, I always ask the locals if there are any local legends about whistling in the woods. I'm always looking for staircases in places they should not be.

I'll never forget what I saw in that purple-tinted hell. What haunts me the most is remembering those hundreds of holes that I knew must lead to hundreds of different staircases. I always listen for whistling in the woods now. And I always carry an extra can of gas.

HEALING HANDS

The first time I saw Doc Hensley heal someone still haunts my dreams. I was only thirteen when I started working for him. Our family didn't make enough money after the coal mines closed. Appalachia is a difficult place to make a living. Most people I know daydream of moving away, but it's equally difficult to leave when you don't have the cash.

My Uncle Arthur had worked for the old man years ago to repay a debt. He had been sick for ages. Cancer ran in my family, but medical insurance didn't. Mom and Dad never said whether Hensley had healed him, but I figured that's the only way he managed to survive so long.

We didn't see a lot of my uncle, but when we did, he always looked careworn. I assumed it was the sickness, but now I know better. It was the work he did for the old man.

Arthur disappeared when I was eleven. My parents never talked about him again. The police didn't search for him. He was just gone and nobody cared. I think he just got sick of paying his debt to Hensley. He's probably dead now, but that could be better. Working for the old man is its own form of cancer.

The older I got, the harder times grew. My father explained to me that for us to survive, I would have to work to help support the family. Too young for a legal job, my father made an arrangement with Doc Hensley. I was terrified at the prospect. With my uncle two years gone, he needed a new assistant. He was a revered man in our region. Doc could provide healing that modern medicine failed to cure.

The old man agreed for me to assist him each day after school. I would make a small sum of money and Doc would use his influence to assist my family throughout trying financial times. From the moment I first arrived at his rustic cabin at the edge of town, I knew there was something dark about him.

Subtle hints of cedar, stale smoke, and dry herbs hung in the air. Shelves lined with poultice bottles and cans of ill-smelling salve covered every wall. Light from the fireplace cast bouncing shadows throughout the room as the old man spoke to the young woman in the chair. I sat on a stool by the door, watching with discomfort.

"Tell me, young lady," Hensley said in a gravelly baritone. "What can an old man do for you?"

"Justin and I have been married for three years," the young woman said softly, eyes sparkling with tears. Her hands were pressed to her abdomen as she spoke. "We've been trying to have a baby, but it never seems to take. We've tried doctors, but they all say I'm barren. I'm afraid he will leave me. Can you help?"

Hensley nodded his head as he shuffled toward a shelf by the fireplace. Rummaging through the tins and jars, the old man pulled a tall bottle from the back corner. Red liquid rippled with silver streaks sloshed inside as he made his way toward the back of the room.

"Over here," he said, gesturing toward a green cot. "Stretch yourself out and let me have a look. Doc Hensley'll get you fixed right up. Don't you even worry!"

Hesitantly, the young lady stood from the stool and made her way to the cot. She looked toward me for reassurance, but my terrified gaze couldn't comfort her. She stretched out on the cot before the old man. Doc had started mumbling under head breath and he shook the strange bottle violently in his hands. The young woman's eyes were filled with a mix of hope and terror.

"Will that bottle cure me?" She asked.

"No," he replied. "It just helps me understand the nature of the ailment. Ole Doc will figure out what to do after that. You just be still, now."

Doc reached his bony hands toward the bottom of the young woman's shirt and lifted it to reveal her navel. Discomfort joined the apprehension in her eyes as the old man peered at the flesh of her stomach. Uncorking the bottle, he poured the red liquid into her navel until it pooled at the rim. Dipping a finger in, he began to trace strange symbols across her skin.

After covering the young woman's abdomen in the strange red scrawl, Doc closed his eyes and tilted his head back. Spreading his fingers apart, he placed both hands on her stomach. His head swayed back and forth as a toothless grimace stretched across his face. Tears were streaming out of the woman's eyes as she watched.

"Can you fix me?" she asked, struggling to hold back a sob. "Can you help us have a baby?"

The old man's eyes shot open and he met the young woman's concerned gaze. He produced a rag from his sweater pocket and began to wipe the red liquid away from her skin. His smile had faded into an intense expression.

"I can help you," he said in a hushed tone. "It will cost a great deal, though. Old Doc can make it right, but can you pay?"

"We don't have much," she whimpered. "How much will it cost?"

The old man stroked his chin and stared away into the fire. "The tonic you need requires ingredients that are hard to find. I can make you better, sweet thing, but you'll have to take the medicine for the rest of your days."

"I will!" she proclaimed with excitement. "How much? We will pay anything!"

"Two hundred dollars a month," he said, eyes gleaming. "Two hundred a month and Doc will keep you right as rain. You'll have that fat baby and a happy husband."

The young woman nodded in agreement. The fear in her eyes washed away. She beamed at the old man.

"Know this," Doc declared, leaning over and placing his hands on her abdomen once again. "If you stop paying, even just once, the tonic stops. Without it, you'll die. Maybe the child too. I cannot say with any certainty."

"I'll pay," she said meekly. "Every month. I'll pay. Two hundred, just like you said."

"Be still," he replied with a smile. "I've got to draw out the sickness. It'll hurt both of us a great deal, but when it's over, you'll be mended."

Doc's hands began to press into the flesh of her stomach. His eyes closed and his head rolled back beyond his shoulders. They both began to shake violently and I thought he would fall from his stool. The young woman began to shriek in agony as the old man's fingers pressed deeper into her skin. After a few agonizing moments, Doc's fingers began to ball into fists as he lifted his hands away from her.

In his skeletal grasp, there was a wet pile of quivering black flesh. Drops of blood and flecks of viscera fell onto the young woman's exposed stomach. Against all reason, there was no wound where his hands had been. She stopped shaking and gulped desperately for air. Doc perched on the stool, sweat pouring from his skin, holding the tumor-like mound.

"Bring me a jar, boy," he said weakly. "Be quick about it."

I darted from the stool and pulled a mason jar from the shelf. Stumbling across the room, I removed the lid and held it out toward the old man. His hands shook as he leaned forward and dropped the black mound of flesh into the jar. I sealed it as soon as it hit the bottom. The weight was incredible for such a small thing, nearly causing me to drop it to the floor.

"Take it to the cellar," he barked. "Leave it on the table and I will take care of the rest."

Doc Hensley pointed to a rusting metal ring on the floor. I pulled at it and the hinges squealed wildly. A dark pit opened on the floor revealing a rough-hewn wooden ladder leading to the cellar floor. In the last bit of the dim firelight that fell into the opening, I could see an old table.

I moved slowly down the rungs of the ladder until my feet met with soft earth. The cellar smelled of mildew and rancid meat. Chittering noises and clinking of glass came from the dark edges of the room. My pulse hammered and my breathing became rapid. As I inched closer to the table, the rattling of jars and skittering noises intensified.

Dropping the jar to the table, I darted back to the relative safety of the ladder and clambered back up into the cabin. Doc Hensley was still sitting on the stool, breathing raggedly. The young woman was walking out of the door as I closed the trapdoor to the cellar.

"You'll go to her house on the first Monday of each month to provide her with the tonic," he panted. "She will give you the money and you will bring it to me. Keep ten percent for yourself. Work hard for me, boy, and your family will live a comfortable life."

I nodded in agreement.

"What do I do if she doesn't give me the money, sir?"

The old man lifted his eyes to mine and an expression of malice plastered his face. "If she doesn't pay, you bring the tonic back to me. I'll have something else for you to deliver in its place."

The young woman died four years later. When she stopped paying, Doc quit sending the medicine. Instead, he sent her a heavy black jar. No one lives very long once I hide one on their property. I hated delivering those damn black jars, but we needed the money. It's amazing the guilt you'll stomach to survive.

Each day after school, I would ride my bike to Doc's cabin on the outskirts of town. From Monday to Friday, I would fill my backpack with tonics, salves, and poultices before peddling from house to house. Each person would hand me a few crumpled bills. In return, I would find whatever medicine in my bag had their name on it. They thanked me and I would go on my way.

On rare occasions, someone would tell me they weren't able to pay. These people would always beg me to leave the medicine and promise to pay me the following day. I would try as kindly as I could to explain Doc's orders, but they still pleaded. It made my heart ache to see the desperation on their faces, but I was too scared of Doc to disobey.

He had never threatened or hurt me. Doc was kind-hearted and warm when I was there. If he cooked, I always ate with him. He would allow me to borrow books from his dusty old bookcase. During the holidays, he always sent me home with extra money for my family. Our lives improved greatly after I began working for him.

Regardless of how kind he could be to me, I knew there was a price for crossing him. When a patron didn't pay, I would peddle my bike back to the old cabin to give him his money. He would count it, setting aside my ten percent as he went. When he finished, if the sum was less than he expected, he would ask me who did not pay.

I would pull the undelivered bottles out and place them on the table in front of him. Refusing to say their name gave me the illusion that I wasn't responsible for their imminent death. He would carefully read the label on each and nod to himself. After placing them back on a shelf, he would crawl into the cellar and retrieve a black glass jar for each person who failed to live up to the bargain.

The first time I saw him make the descent, I was scared for such a feeble old man to use the ladder, but the anger I saw on his face seemed to strengthen his body. No matter how many times I offered to get those black bottles from the cellar, he declined.

"There's death down there, boy." He would say quietly. "Best let me handle that."

The only time I was allowed down there was to leave the new jars of tumor-like flesh on the table after he healed someone. Whenever I would go down next, the table sat empty. I never saw what he did with them, but he always took great care never to tend them while I was in the house.

Once he returned from the cellar with the black jars, he would take a white grease pen and write the name of the recipient on the lid. On the sides, he would draw intricate designs and runic symbols before wrapping each jar with cheesecloth. Tight bindings of twine were added to hold the cloth in place.

"Don't you give these right to the people, you hear?" He said firmly the first time I had to deliver the black jars. "You take 'em and put 'em in the bushes or up in a tree on their property. Has to be their property. If it's too far away from them, it won't work. Understand, son?"

"Yes, sir," I responded. "What are they?"

He smiled his toothless smile and slid the jars toward me. I placed them in the backpack cautiously. He patted me on the head as though I were a dog.

"I take away the illness and they pay me," he said in an amused tone. "They stop payin', I give 'em back what I took away. Fair's fair, my boy."

"Do you ever give anyone a second chance to pay?" I asked.

"No. You let one get away without payin' then they'll all say they can't pay. How's an old man gonna eat if he ain't got no money?"

"Just seems like you could let one slide sometimes, Doc," I replied in a half-whisper. "Give them a chance to catch up."

Doc smiled at me and pulled a wad of cash from his coat pocket. He unrolled it and dropped a one hundred dollar bill on the table for each black jar I was to deliver. Pushing it toward me, he began to chuckle.

"Doc Hensley's a fair man. You pay, you live. Stop payin', you don't. Unless you want to cover what they owe, deliver them jars."

I pondered the thought for a moment. It was tempting until I thought of my family. Mom and Dad both worked, but they didn't make enough. My job with Doc Hensley brought in more money than both of them combined. I could pay for someone's medicine now and again, but too often and my family wouldn't have enough money to sustain ourselves.

Feeling unfathomable shame, I slung the heavy backpack on my shoulders, slid the money into my pocket, and walked out the door.

"Smart boy!" I heard him call. "Smart boy!"

Each time I delivered those obsidian jars, I would see that person's obituary in the local paper a few days later. They always said *Passed away unexpectedly.* Their black and white photos showed smiling faces next to the column, but I always remembered the looks of horror on their face when they couldn't pay. Young and old. Men and women. It didn't matter. If Doc didn't receive his payment, they received the jars. No questions, no second chances.

The older I got, the more black jars I delivered. I lost count of how many I had hidden years ago. The weight of what I was doing was too heavy for a child. Numbness and apathy became my only solution. The jars became just another task, neither good nor evil. Just a means to help keep the lights on and our stomachs full.

During my senior year of high school, my mom got sick. Her weight began to drop rapidly and she was fatigued most of the time. It was like Uncle Arthur all over again. She was diagnosed with stomach cancer after a hand full of emergency room visits and consultations.

I bought an old car with some of the money Doc paid me and I used it to take Mom to the city to see an oncologist. Dad took her to appointments as often as he could. His job at the convenience store was the only thing allowing us to keep health insurance. Taking my ailing mother to most of her medical appointments caused me to miss a lot of days at school, but those kinds of things get overlooked in poverty-stricken areas like ours.

"Ma'am, your cancer has spread into your bones," the doctor said. "We can continue with treatment if you would like, but I think it is time to consider comfort measures. Make the most of the time you still have left."

My mother cried as the doctor described various methods to provide her relief in the coming months. She gripped my hand tightly as she sobbed. I tried to comfort her, but there was nothing I could do. As emotionally detached as I had become due to the nature of my work, the weight of my mother's imminent death was a sensation I couldn't shake.

"There has to be something you can do!" I shouted. "Don't tell me there isn't medicine that would help her. Tell us what it is! We'll pay anything. You've got to help her."

"Son," the doctor started. "If there was anything I could do for her I would, but we are out of options. The chemo and radiation aren't working We will do everything we can to keep her comfortable and give her the best quality of life we can. Short of a miracle, there is nothing left to be done."

We made most of the drive home in silence. At first, my mother cried and apologized to me. I reassured her that she had nothing to be sorry for, that none of this was her fault, but my words provided her with no real comfort. Tears streamed down her face until she drifted off to sleep. Her strength was so low that she could barely stay awake for more than two hours at a time. I let her rest.

Short of a miracle...

The doctor's words flew around my mind like a sparrow caught in a chimney. My hands clenched tightly on the steering wheel as the phrase echoed in my mind. I knew where to find a miracle. Dad and I had discussed the possibility of taking her to Doc Hensley countless times. More than once I had almost given in, but the price was so much higher than my father could understand.

My mother was the voice of reason.

"The doctors have said we've exhausted all of the treatment options," she said. "That's the end of the discussion."

"You know there is another option," my father said desperately. "Hensley can heal you! You don't have to die."

My mother smiled and placed her hand on my father's. They were both crying. I sat and watched, feeling helpless.

"I love you both so much," she replied. "This is how I want it to end. Being in debt to Doc is more than this family needs. Arthur made a deal with him and he's... been missing for years. I won't put us through that again. Let me go."

Her health continued its rapid decline. Most days she wasn't able to get out of bed. When she did eat, it never stayed down. Even the smell of food made her sick. The pain medication helped, but she tried not to take them often since they left her mind feeling clouded.

I continued with my work for Doc. Now that I had a car, I would drive people to and from his cabin for healing. The car expanded his reach. He was treating people from small towns across the region. My medicine deliveries increased rapidly, but so did my delivery of the black jars.

Our family had never been in a better financial position, but my mother's illness consumed any happiness that the money brought. The cost of our improved finances was paid in my more frequent absence from home. More deliveries meant more time away. I had taken this job to care for my family, but I saw them less and less.

"It hurts me a bit that you never talk to me about your mother," Doc said one afternoon as I cleaned the cabin. "You know I could help her, my boy."

I could feel hot tears building up. While he had never been cruel to me, it had sounded more like a taunt than an offer. I had told him she was sick, but he had never mentioned it until that day.

"If something happened and we couldn't pay, she would die anyway," I replied. Holding back the overwhelming urge to sob had caused my voice to shake. "If I ever had to take a black jar home..."

Doc Hensley pushed himself up from the bench and began to shuffle toward me. I watched as he padded across the cabin floor. The man was old, but it wasn't until that moment that I realized he didn't seem to have aged from the day I met him. His mind was still sharp, his mobility had endured, and his health never seemed to diminish.

When he reached me, he put his hands on my shoulders and stared into my eyes.

"There'll be no black jar for your mother," he said, his voice almost soothing. "There will be no payments. All I ask of you is one small favor."

"Didn't my uncle do you a favor?" I spat. "Look what it did for him!"

Doc sneered at me for a moment, but his face quickly softened.

"Your uncle made a deal," he replied softly, "that he had no intention of keeping. The fate that befell him was of his own doing. What I ask of you will change your life for the better."

"What do you want," I asked as I openly sobbed.

"Stay in my employ," he said. "Learn my trade, young man. I'm old. Much older than you know. I provide a service to folks around here, but I grow tired. If you learn to do what I do, perhaps old Doc can get some rest. What do you say?"

I agreed. How could I have turned him down? Working for him had always been a means to help my parents. Letting my mother die when a solution was so easily in reach was too much to pass by.

"Good," he said, tottering back to his stool by the fire. "Good. Bring her here tomorrow. You'll wait outside this time. I know watching my work makes you uncomfortable, but I won't make you watch as I heal your mother. Once she is well, you'll take her home but then return here afterward. Our lessons will begin immediately."

It took a great deal of convincing before my mother would agree. At first, she flatly rejected the offer. I tried to explain to her that there would be no financial cost and that she wouldn't end up like my uncle, but she thought it was a trick. My father echoed my pleas. She finally agreed to speak with Doc so she could understand his terms.

The next afternoon I helped Mom into the car. She was almost skeletal by then. Every bone and strand of sinew in her body danced under her taut skin when she moved. Dad and I had taken her to the car in a wheelchair. She barely had the energy to slide from the chair to the car seat.

"Let me come with you," my father said, heavy with grief. "I want to be with her."

I told him to stay home. The process was a horrible thing to see. I wasn't sure Doc would heal her if he came. The old man was secretive about his process and I didn't want to risk him backing out of the deal. My father reluctantly agreed and stood in the driveway as we drove out of sight.

We arrived at the cabin a short while later and she had already fallen asleep. Retrieving the wheelchair from the trunk, I put it beside the car and opened the door. Tapping her shoulder, she didn't respond. Her breathing was shallow. I put my index and middle finger to her neck and felt a weak pulse.

I picked my mother up and rushed her into the cabin. Doc was perched on his stool next to the fire. He turned his head toward me and he pointed toward the green cot against the back wall.

"Put her down quickly and leave," he commanded. "I can feel that she ain't long for this world."

I did as he asked. As I backed toward the door, I watched the old man make his way to my mother. Her chest was still, and her skin was the color of ash. I froze for a moment, fearing she was already gone.

"Go, boy!" he shouted. "Wait in your car. I will fix this, but you gotta leave."

Stumbling back, I pulled the door shut behind me. My stomach began to roar, and I vomited off the side of the old porch. The forest was silent as I walked back to the car. My hand was on the handle, but I couldn't open it. If my mother was alive, she would have been screaming by then. They always screamed.

All at once, the forest came to life with a piercing howl coming from inside the cabin. Birds scattered from the crooked trees all around me. My heart thundered in response to the sudden cry. Relief and agony gripped my heart as I crawled into the car and turned the radio up to block out the shrill cries.

After what felt like an eternity, I saw the door to the cabin open. While I had expected Doc to beckon me in, I was surprised to see the thin frame of my mother. She was smiling and waving happily. Her hand was grasping the door frame for balance, but she seemed healthier than I had seen her in months. I raced to the door and swept her into a hug. Even with all of her muscle loss, her arms wrapped around me and hugged me tighter than any embrace I could recall. She kissed me on the cheek but all I could do was sob in reply.

A leathery hand tapped me on the arm. When I opened my eyes, the time-worn face of Doc stood before me. He was covered in sweat and panting. A toothless grin pierced his exhaustion as he patted me gently on the shoulder.

"Take her home," he wheezed. "Your father'll want to see this wonderful thing. And you have the bargain to keep. Return here after you get her safely in the house. Our training begins tonight."

I returned to the cabin later that evening. It had pained me to leave my mother so soon after her recovery, but I couldn't risk breaking my deal with the old man. Doc was waiting for me on the porch when I pulled up the gravel drive. Smoke billowed from the clay pipe drooping out of his lips.

He beckoned me inside and told me we would head to the basement. While I pulled the heavy cellar door open, he grabbed a box of matches from beside his potbelly stove. Doc crawled onto the ladder and lowered himself into the darkness below. Once he was safely on the cellar floor, I crawled down to join him.

By the time my feet met the soft earth, Doc was swallowed in darkness. Mildew and rot filled my nostrils. A flame flickered to life as he struck a match before lighting a series of kerosene lanterns around the perimeter of the cellar. I had been down there countless times, but only to the wooden table in the center. I had never seen the entire room.

Dozens of wooden shelves filled the cellar. Each one was lined with black jars. Thick straps of leather were nailed into the posts of the shelf keeping the jars from falling to the floor. Each of them rattled gently in place. Scraping and chittering filled the air as the things inside the jars seemed to become aware of our presence.

"Back here, child," Doc said from behind a row of shelves. I walked toward him, gazing at the chattering black jars. "I have something for you."

When I rounded the final shelf, I saw Doc standing at another wooden table. Three leatherbound books were sitting on the edge and a clear jar filled with writhing black flesh. Next to it sat a mortar and pestle. He dropped a piece of charcoal into the bowl and poured water on top. He began to mash the coal and water into a paste. Once it was mixed, he dipped his hands into the stone bowl and scooped out the mixture before rubbing it onto the sides of the jar. His shaking hand took a lit candle from the table and held it to the black paste to help it dry.

"They don't move as much in the dark," he said in a low voice. "I coat the jars and keep 'em in the cellar so they remain docile."

"What are they?" I asked as I stepped closer.

"The illnesses I remove," he said. "They don't perish after they are removed. Can't be destroyed, so it seems. So, I place 'em here for safekeeping. Dark, ugly things."

My stomach turned as I watched the jar rattle in his hands. Cancer that had been inside of my mother only hours before writhed in the jar. Doc placed it on a shelf behind one of the leather straps before returning to me.

"They get more vicious with time. Hungry. Hateful. Damn things want to get back into the body they came from. If they break free and can't find their original host, they'll crawl inside the nearest person and start all over again."

A knot twisted in my throat. I had taken dozens, maybe hundreds of these things back to people over the years. Before, I was able to fool myself into believing that the deaths could be a coincidence, but now all I could see were these monstrous tumors carving their way back into the people they had been pulled from.

"Take these home and read 'em," Doc said, handing me the leather books from the table. "Lots to take in there, my boy. Generations worth of knowledge. Gonna take you a while to get through 'em. Tells you everything you'll need to know."

He sent me home that night and I began to read the books immediately. It wasn't long before I dropped out of school altogether. My grades were awful and it was clear my trade had been chosen for me years before. Mom and Dad argued against it briefly, but they signed the forms when I reminded them of the deal I made with Doc.

With school no longer taking up my time, my days were spent working at the cabin. Deliveries and healing sessions were performed earlier than in previous years. I was home by early afternoon and got to enjoy some time with my family. My evenings, though, were consumed with reading the leather tomes.

The pages were filled with nearly unbelievable information. Runes and prayers were provided to cure almost every ailment known to man. Diagrams showed where on the body to place the symbols and the cadence to follow as you spoke the chants. Chapters were dedicated to the study of the fleshing horrors that were removed from the bodies of the sick and dying. Hundreds of entries in different handwriting styles detailed attempts to destroy the creatures without success. Trial and error methods of containing them shifted through the accounts.

A fanciful cursive scrawl that I recognized as belonging to Doc Hensley described the current process of storing them in jars coated with dried charcoal and storing them unground in the dark. I wondered to myself if, in the future, once Doc was retired and I had taken his place, I would fill any of the space in these books with my studies.

Through the coming months, I read the books over and over. Some of the runes and placements I had even managed to commit to memory. As Doc would prepare to remove illnesses from our patients, he would often let me test my knowledge by telling him where to place the runes. He seemed pleased with how much I had learned, almost beaming with pride.

My fear of the future waned for a time. I had come to accept my position as a healer and concentrated on the things I would do for the community. The future looked bright for once until I realized something must be missing from the books. There was no mention of the tonics or elixirs that Doc prepared for after the healing rituals.

It was late in the evening, and I was readying myself to leave the cabin and head home. We were in the cellar coating jars in the black charcoal paste when the absence of the tonic recipes tickled the back of my mind.

"Doc," I said as the old man placed the black jar on the shelf. "When will I learn to make the medicine needed after the healing ritual?"

The old man froze.

"Eh?" he grunted. "Recipes for the medicines?"

"You said everything I needed was in those books," I stated. "None of the chapters mention needing medications after the healing is completed. There must be another book I haven't seen yet."

Doc ran his fingers through his wispy hair but didn't turn to face me. It was unusual that he didn't jump at the chance to fill me with knowledge. The old man loved the sound of his voice almost as much as he loved his craft. In recent months, he thrived on passing down the knowledge of his work. His silence was unsettling.

"Son," he muttered, almost sadly. "They don't need the medicine after I heal them. That's snake oil. Fake. I do that for the money."

"They… don't need it?" I stammered.

Doc turned to face me. He looked sad, almost guilty. He turned his head from side-to-side gesturing to the shelves full of black vessels. "Look, son. I give these people their life back. Most people here are so poor they hardly got a pot to piss in. You can't get much money for the gift upfront. This is my way of gettin' what I earned without charging 'em all at once. Medicine is like insurance. Makes sure they pay."

My head started to spin. I had delivered countless black jars to people over the last few years. The things inside had broken free to kill the people we had once healed. They hadn't even needed the tonics they couldn't pay for.

"What will you even do with the money?" I asked. "You live like a hermit and can't possibly have that many years left!"

"Do you think I've taught you all of my secrets, boy?" he chortled. "I haven't toiled all these years to wither away in this husk. If I can pull sickness from others, imagine what I can do with my own body. I don't know what's beyond that great black veil of death, but I don't intend to find out. A lifetime of work'll be traded in for another lifetime of leisure."

My stomach turned.

"I'm done here," I said and started walking toward the ladder. "I'm telling everyone what you are."

The old man began to cackle. His wails of delight made my face burn with anger. I wrapped my hands around the rung of the ladder. The splinters dug into my hand as I squeezed the beams tightly.

"You tell anyone what I'm doin' and your momma is going to have a really bad time soon if you follow my meanin'." he spat. I turned to face him, rage boiling. "They won't believe you, anyway. Even if they did, they want what I offer 'em. I'm a miracle man, boy."

Chittering and the sound of clinking glass filled the room. A lifetime of black jars rattled on their shelves as the old man laughed. The maddening sounds blended with my rage for the old man's deceit. I slammed my boot into the shelf closest to the ladder and watched as they began to fall like a row of dominos.

"What the hell are you doin'?" Doc Hensley shrieked. "They'll kill us!"

The black glass exploded across the floor as more and more of the vessels tumbled to the ground. Metal lids rolled like wagon wheels across into the dim corners of the cellar. I scrambled up the ladder and back onto the main floor of the cabin. Doc tried to make his way to the ladder, but his shuffling gait caused him to trip on broken pieces of the shelf. He sprawled forward into the broken glass.

The fleshlings began to quiver and crawl toward the old man. I pulled the ladder free from the trapdoor frame and pulled it into the cabin. A wave of writhing black flesh enveloped Doc Hensley as his blood-curdling screams filled my ears.

They began to burrow into his flesh, one by one until all of the damn things were inside. The old man's body became swollen and distended. His eyes burned red with rage as his body rippled and pulsed. Once more his mouth opened to scream, but only the chittering of the fleshlings came out.

Doc began to shudder violently before falling still. His skin mottled and turned black. Cracks spread across his now bloated frame. Inch by inch, Doc Hensley's body dissolved into dust. The remains drifted in the drafty air of the cellar.

I watched with delight as the old man faded into nothingness. For a short moment, I could see a light at the end of the tunnel. Free from the old man, I would never again deliver one of those damnable black jars.

As I made my way toward the cabin door, I felt something warm and strong wrap around my ankle. It felt like a snake was slithering up my legs and wrapping around my torso. Looking down, I could see a black mound of pulsing flesh push itself into my navel and I began to howl in pain.

My abdomen throbbed, bringing me to my knees. I could feel the vibrations as the thing burrowed deeper inside. As I collapsed in pain, my mind echoed the same harrowing thought on repeat.

I should have pulled up the ladder sooner.

OLD

I'm old now but I don't feel as though I should be. Not in a *"the ravages of time is a cruel fate"* sort of way. No, what I mean is I know now I wasn't supposed to be here this long. My 82nd birthday came two months ago, and it feels as though I've unjustly received 50 extra years when that simply wasn't the plan.

Not only that, but I've spent so much time in dread of the future that I didn't appreciate most of the time that I did have. All these toilsome years wasted puttering around wishing I had just died in 1972 just because I stopped in a diner for a cup of coffee back in '61.

In 1961 I was still a hell-raising young man with a steady girl and a shitty car. Sarah and I had been together since our senior year of high school and with her father's permission, we had gotten engaged just a few months prior. My grandchildren tell me what an antiquated notion that getting permission is but hell, it's what you did back then.

Sarah worked as a receptionist at the local pediatrician's office, and I was three years into an apprenticeship with a plumber named John Stevenson. Save your "crappy job" jokes for someone else. I promise that I've heard more than my fair share. Anyway, on a particularly gorgeous spring day, I had called Sarah to tell her I was stopping by for breakfast on my way to work. She was sweet that way. Even before we were married and still living with her parents, she insisted on fixing me a hot cup of coffee and a few fried eggs.

"I'm on my way, Sarah," I said into the receiver while I slid on my work coat.

"Oh, David," Sarah said and coughed into the phone. "Not today. I'm not feeling well, and I don't think John would care much for you bringing a bug to him at work."

"That's okay," I replied. "I'll stop by Lou's Cafe on the way in. The coffee's not as good as yours but a guy has to have something!"

"A guy had best tell a girl to feel better soon or he may not get any more coffee from her at all!" She giggled.

I smiled. "I sure do hope you feel better soon, Sarah. I love you."

"I love you too! Do call me after work, Davey boy." She hung up.

Feeling a bit sad that I wouldn't get to see Sarah that day, I trotted down five blocks between my cracker box house and Lou's Cafe. It was my favorite restaurant in town which wasn't saying much. You either ate at Lou's or ate at The Blue Fox. At Lou's, you could get a hot cup of joe, an open-faced roast beef sandwich, and a damn fine slice of pecan pie. The Blue Fox was likely to give you a lukewarm cup of sludge, bologna on stale rye, and a mild case of food poisoning.

When I got to Lou's I could see through the window that it was a bustling morning. Fortunately for me, there was still a two-seater near the window so my eggs and coffee wouldn't be standing room only. My knees were better back then but who the hell wants to stand up to eat and have a sunny side egg run down your work shirt?

"Mornin', Davey!" the big man behind the flat top yelled. At 6'4" and sporting a black eyepatch courtesy of the D-Day invasion, Lou was a monster to look at but gentle as a puppy. "Two sunny side and a hot cup?"

"Please!" I replied and waved in his direction. "Just going to read the paper over here, Lou!"

Lou waved back. "Margie'll have it out to you in a minute. Enjoy the funnies, son."

I laughed and smiled about the banter as I slid the chair facing the window away from the table and sat down. Reaching into my jacket pocket, I pulled the rolled-up new paper out onto the table and dove into the front page. All the main articles those few weeks had been news of The Bay of Pigs fiasco and I had become a little obsessed. Kennedy seemed like a pretty smart fella by my estimation, but this had been a mess. By the time Margie slid the eggs and coffee in front of me I was practically in a stupor.

"With Sarah fattening you up I hardly see you anymore as it is," said the waitress as she walked to the table. I looked up at Margie, a grin across her face. She tossed me a wink. "Glad to see you, kiddo, even if you've always got your nose stuck in the paper."

I smiled back at her. "Sorry, Margie. I'm glad to see you too!"

Margie pulled the paper out of my hands, rolled it up, and sat it on the table before sliding the plate of eggs closer to me. "Eat up. Paper'll be there when you're done."

She hustled off to the counter for another plate and I dug into my eggs. Lou had even thrown in a piece of toast that morning, big old softie that he was. I looked down at my watch and saw that I still had forty-five minutes before I was due at Mr. Stevenson's shop. Quickly polishing off the rest of my breakfast, I decided to get back to my paper for a bit before heading out.

The noise of Lou slapping away at the grill, the conversations of the other diners, and the paper had put me into a kind of trance. My family says I still get that way sometimes when I read. More so in my old age probably but I have always been that way. The written word had a way of hypnotizing me until I tuned out everything around me. When my kids come to visit sometimes, they will startle me out of a daze and tell me they had knocked on the door for five minutes before letting themselves in only to find me buried in a book.

That was just the unaware state I was in when a hand fell on my shoulder and made me jump in my chair. My ass must have come off the seat five inches, but the hand stayed firmly but gently in place. Once my heart had descended from my throat, I scooted the legs of the chair around and turned my head. An older gentleman who looked to be in his sixties or seventies was standing there, making intense and uncomfortable eye contact with me.

"Are you David West?" the old man asked. His voice was soft but gravelly as though he had a pack-a-day Lucky Strike habit. While his face held few wrinkles his ghostly white hair and beard gave away his age. The dark suit he wore was careworn with threadbare edges and finished off with scuffed loafers. Down on his luck, the old-timers used to say.

"Well, yes sir, I am," I replied politely but with a bit of confusion. "What can I help you with?"

"Your parents were Albert and Clara West?" he asked without making eye contact. The old man just shuffled around the table and slowly lowered himself into the chair across from me. "Lived in that nice old two-story colonial on Westmoreland Street, I do believe."

I was surprised and confused. This gentleman seemed to have at least some knowledge of me and my family but there was nowhere in my memory that I could locate even the faintest trace of him. I even tried to imagine him with darker hair and no beard but still nothing. He was an enigma waiting to be decoded.

"Yes, Albert and Clara are my parents," I stammered after an awkward pause. "Did you know them?"

"I know a bit about them and a lot about you, but no, we never had the pleasure of meeting before they passed." He smiled at me sadly and it looked as though tears were welling up in the corner of his eyes. "I meant to get here before they passed, David. I am so, so sorry."

My pulse rose and I could feel my face getting hot. This absolute stranger sitting across from me was making me extremely uncomfortable. My parents had both passed away in a boating accident when I was nineteen. Their boat had sunk in a freak accident and their bodies were never recovered. Mr. Stevenson had denied my request for a day off to join them or I would have shared the same fate. How in the hell could this man possibly have meant to come to see me before they died as though he expected it?

"Who the hell are you, mister?" I spat out with more anger than I intended.

"That doesn't matter, David." A single tear ran down his face and disappeared into the white hairs on his cheek.

He reached into his tattered suitcoat and pulled out an envelope and handed it to me. The flap was sealed with a mixture of gold and scarlet wax embossed with the impression of an hourglass. Looking at the hourglass emblem from my angle it appeared that the sand was almost completely tumbled to the bottom. A bit remained at the top, but it was almost out of time.

"Read that later tonight when you get home." said the stranger. He stood haphazardly from his seat and began his unsteady shuffle past me toward the door. "You'll have to make some choices."

"Wait!" I yelled but he just continued out the door.

Stumbling from my seat and trailing behind him, I pushed the door open and walked out onto the sidewalk to try and get an explanation. He was gone. A few folks were walking into the hardware store and Tom Vincent, the barber, sat outside of his barbershop waiting for his first high and tight of the day. With the old man's wobbly gait and unsteady balance, there was no way he had made it out of eyesight that quickly. Nonetheless, he was gone as if he had been nothing more than a mirage.

***

My workday finally came to a close and I hurried home as though all of Hell were on my hindquarters. The ridge of the envelope the old man gave me had been rubbing against me from my shirt pocket the entire day as if it were trying to remind me that I had an engagement after work. Distracted as I was, I phoned Sarah to check on her and give her my well wishes. I told her I wasn't feeling well, which was mostly true, and that I was going to bed early that evening. As soon as the phone was back on the hook I settled down in my hand-me-down recliner and stared at the envelope.

I rotated the letter from top to bottom making the hourglass appear full and then empty over and over. Turned the correct way the grains were almost all in the bottom of the glass. Fumbling out my pocketknife I slipped it under the wax and pealed up the flat exposing a yellow piece of paper and three smaller envelopes numbered from one to three. I put the smaller envelopes aside and started to read.

David,

Allow me to apologize in advance if any of this causes you any distress. I have performed this task countless times with varying degrees of success. What these envelopes offer you is the ability to make choices that may well alter the life that lay ahead for you. Few receive this opportunity so I hope you will consider whether or not this is the path you would choose to travel.

In each envelope, I have enclosed a single piece of paper with a date and a single piece of advice. You may choose to accept or ignore the message on the paper but there are certain to be consequences for either action. They are certain to help you avoid great tragedy. If you follow the advice, you may or may not be able to deduce what calamity you have avoided. Suffice it to say that if you accept the information and something unfortunate still befalls you, a worse fate had been in store.

Please follow the proceeding guidelines. Only open one envelope at a time. Read the information and determine if you will or will not adhere to the advice provided. If you opt not to, that is fine enough. But if you do adhere to the information then I only ask that you burn the note after the date at the top has passed you by.

Secondly do not open the following note until the date of the previous one has already gone by. I have been working on this system for an incomprehensible amount of time and I have discovered that too much information about one's future leads to incurable madness. For both your safety and sanity, do not open the next envelope until at least one day after the date of the previous one.

Last but equally important, do not speak to anyone about these notes. I care not about the privacy of my work, but I do care greatly for the safety of those around you. Anyone not affected by the information will likely laugh it off or think you mad. However, anyone who will be affected in some way by the information will suffer a similar fate as you would if you read the notes at the wrong time. I've yet to discover what causes this effect but the foreknowledge of events causes those in your orbit to become self-harming and suicidal.

If you decide against this then please burn the notes today. Don't throw them out. Destroy them.

If you opt to use this information, then store them away and keep them safe.

It had been my intention to reach you before the untimely passing of your parents and envelope number one would have helped you avoid this tragedy. A new option was added in its place since I did not make it in time. I will carry the weight of this missed opportunity for the remainder of my long years. I am so, so sorry.

Your life is still a path unrolling itself in a dark wood. A way has already been made clear, but I simply offer you three chances to remap its course.

Good luck,
Joseph

My head was swimming. Velvety paper rubbed against my hands, and I could feel warm tears pooling in my eyes. I wanted to think of this as the disturbed musings of a crazy old man but something in the pit of my heart urged me to accept it at face value. Even if it weren't true would there be any harm in reading the first envelope? The date and information would make it obvious whether or not this outrageous letter was true.

I stared at the stack of tiny envelopes and picked up the one on the top with a hand-scrawled *#1* in the upper left corner. My hand was shaking as I scooped up my pocketknife and slid it under the fold of the envelope and sliced it open. Sliding the tiny piece of paper, I immediately read the scant writing on the page

11/25/1969

Please choose the Teague job.

That was it. The letter of explanation clearly stated there wouldn't be much information, but I had still expected a bit more. I pulled my wallet out and slid the note in behind a picture of Sarah. Eight years was a long time to wait and see but what other choice did I have?

* * *

Let's jump forward a little bit in time but I'll catch you up on the scuttlebutt in between. Sarah and I married in '62 and lived in my little cracker box house until our first child, Tyler, arrived in '64. We upgraded to a larger place and welcomed our second and last child, Megan, in '66. Tyler and Megan were the apples of our eyes. They and the grandkids are still the only bright spot in the storm cloud that has been my life.

Old man Stevenson retired and sold me the plumbing business which had been pretty generous to us. I didn't mind working ankle-deep in shit for my apprentice and journeyman years, but it sure was nice to hire a few young bucks to handle the heavy lifting. We stayed steadily booked and I was often left to turn down more jobs than I could take. Such was a good reputation in yesteryear.

Still, the envelopes haunted my mind. I had been unimaginably happy all these years but the closer we drew to '69 the more I thought about it. The other envelopes were stashed safely in a lock box in my garage, but the first note still resided in my pocket. I would read it again occasionally when I noticed it and always pondered what the day may bring. Or for that matter if the day would bring anything at all.

On the morning of November 11th, 1969, I was sitting in my office chatting it up with my employees when the phone rang.

"Stevenson Plumbing," I exclaimed into the phone. My wife recommended we keep the same name since the company had become well known. "How can we help you today?"

"Yes, our new neighbors said to give you a call." the woman on the other end of the line replied. "My name is Darla Teague and we've just moved into town. There is a leaking pipe in our upstairs bathroom, and it has ruined my ceiling. Any chance you could send someone my way today?"

My eyes widened and my pulse rose. *Please choose the Teague job.* "Oh!" I finally replied in a burst. My mind darted around as I stammered through. "Yes ma'am. My assistants already have some work lined up, but I'll head that way myself immediately."

Mrs. Teague gave me her address and I got out of the chair, legs half like jelly. I slid my old toolbox into the work truck and gave a wave to my assistants as I pulled out of the drive. It was the moment of truth and I still debated whether it was a coincidence or providence.

I arrived at the house and knocked on the door. A sweet young woman introduced herself as Mrs. Teague and showed me to the upstairs bathroom. The floor was glistening with water and a steady stream was flowing from behind the toilet.

"Can you fix it?" she asked me with apprehension.

"Yes, ma'am," I replied in a certain tone. "It's likely just a pinhole leak that has gotten out of control. Give me about an hour and I'll have you fixed up."

She smiled and thanked me before leaving the room. I sat my toolbox down in the hall to keep it away from the water and surveyed the bathroom. It was the day stated on the note and there I was in the Teague household. Chuckling a little bit, I couldn't believe I had spent eight years with my thoughts dwelling on this date. There I stood in the bathroom of destiny. Maybe the old man could see the future, but I began to doubt that anything of consequence would be taking place there that day.

I straddled the toilet to try and find the source of the water and it took no time at all. The hose that ran from the tank to the wall was accordion-style copper tubing and there was the pinhole leak I expected to find. There was a box of replacement parts in the work truck, and I was satisfied this would be a cut-and-dry job.

Turning my torso to stabilize myself on the sink, I began to turn my foot to step out when I slipped in the water. My right leg slid between the toilet and the wall as I fell. The thundering sound of my tibia and fibula snapping in half echoed like a tree branch splitting in a windstorm. I howled in agony as the lightning bolts of pain radiated from my leg to the rest of my body.

Mrs. Teague had found me and called an ambulance. Paramedics took me to the hospital and the doctors ended up putting so many plates and screws in my leg that I could set off a metal detector from five feet away for the rest of my life. Well, maybe that's a bit of an exaggeration but you get the point. My leg was never the same again. A limp and my pessimistic outlook would become two of my most defining characteristics.

After a few days in the hospital, I returned home with the aid of a wheelchair. My mood had been sour, and I was probably pretty unkind to Sarah and the kids. I spent most of my afternoons on the front porch even though the developing December air was cold and unforgiving.

On December 2nd I was sitting on the porch puffing on my pipe when a black, four-door sedan pulled up to the curb in front of my house. Two men in military dress got out and made their way up the walk. Their stern faces made me uncomfortable.

"Hello, sir," the first man said. "We are looking for Mr. David Newsome. Is this his residence?"

I furrowed my brow. "That'd be me, gentlemen. What can I do for you?"

The two men looked at me and then down at my cast-wrapped leg. Their gaze drifted back to my face, and they returned my dismayed expression.

"Mr. Newsome, the conflict in Vietnam has escalated to a point that we as Americans must make bold moves in these uncertain times." the second man barked. "The Selective Service office performed a military draft yesterday and you have been selected to report for duty.

My face changed from confusion to astonishment. "You've got to be kidding!" I yelled. "Look at me. I'm not sure how much use you think I'll be in the jungle!"

The men conferred with one another with their backs turned to me. I sat in my wheelchair, blood boiling, waiting for them to tell me that some kind of accommodation would be made considering my state and that I was still going to have to ship off to parts yet unknown to me.

The first man turned to face me and said, "Sir, I believe an exception can be made here. Have a good day." They both returned to their black sedan and sped down the street. Of course they could make an exception. What good would I have been to anyone there? The doctors had already told me that the nature of the break was so severe that there was little to no chance I wouldn't walk with a limp for the rest of my days.

That evening at the dinner table after the kids had gone off to sleep, Sarah and I sat and talked.

"Vietnam draft, huh?" Sarah said half question and half statement.

"Yeah," I puffed. "Vietnam."

Sarah sent a heart-melting smile my way. "Well, look on the bright side. If you hadn't broken your leg at the Teague job, you would be off for basic training! There's a sunny side to everything, I guess."

I smiled back at her but as I looked into those eyes that I now miss so much I realized something. She was absolutely right. If I had sent one of the other boys to do that job, I would never have broken my leg. Without the leg, I would have gone off to that endless damn police action where so many men never made it back home. I likely would have died.

Please choose the Teague job.

The note was right. Somehow that damn note had been right.

***

Let's make up a bit of time here. Not every detail of my life is as interesting for you as it is for me. After Sarah unwittingly made the connection between the note and the draft notice for me, I knew instantly that I needed to read the content of the next note. If the first one had saved my life, then the second one must be equally as important. One day when she was out, I used my crutches to hobble out to the garage and retrieve the second note.

9/17/1972

You must not go to the grocery store.

It seemed simple enough. Three years to sit on one piece of advice. I just had to skip going to the grocery store. The first one hadn't been any more complicated, so I was relieved at the simplicity of that one as well. Even if I stayed home and broke the other damn leg, I could live with it. And so I did.

September 17th of '72 rolled around, and life was much as it had been for me three years earlier. The business was booming by then and I had hired a full staff. My leg healed but never quite regained the agility it once had, so I ran the day-to-day operations and had a team of plumbers who took care of the jobs. Both of the kids were out of diapers and starting to sleep through the night, so Sarah and I thanked God every day for the little moments of quiet in the evening. We even toyed around with the thought of just one more baby but that was not to be.

I was tapping the steering wheel with my hand and bouncing my head side to side to the radio. A new band called Looking Glass was singing about a girl named Brandy and what a fine girl she was. With the upbeat tune, I had been inclined to agree. My disposition at the time was pretty damn sunny. The last three years had been some of the best of my life. I woke up every day feeling like I had a new lease on life, and it was all thanks to those strange notes.

Pulling into the driveway I saw Sarah in the front yard with the kids. I got out of the car and started walking their way.

"Hey, sweetie!" Sarah exclaimed. "I am about to head to the grocery store. Think we ought to pack the kids up and go as a family?"

There it was. I had been waiting all day and had prepared myself for all of the eventualities. No grocery store for me that afternoon under any circumstances. The note had been right about the plumbing job. I trusted it for that one as well.

"I'm a little beat, hun," I replied, hamming it up for a little believability. "Mind if I just stay home with the kids so it'll be a little quicker for you?"

She kissed me on the cheek and started getting in the car. "That'll be fine, Mr. Lazy Bones! I'll be back in about an hour. Make sure everyone is ready to eat when I get home."

Sarah put the car in reverse and backed out of the driveway, waving at everyone as she did. I still remember that wave. That beautiful smile. I miss her so much it makes my heart ache. Sarah Archer Newsome was one of a kind and for a small number of years, I was able to call her all mine.

Pardon me for the sparse detail ahead, but even as I begin to tell you, I am already in tears. These days usually I'm mad but this just brings me a deep sorrow that I feel in my bones. I dwell on the details enough as it is so I will keep it as short as I can.

Here goes.

Sarah didn't come home from the store within an hour. No big deal. Another hour and she still wasn't there. I decided to go ahead and feed the kids and get them off to bed. Still no Sarah. I called Harlow's Market and the manager said he hadn't seen her but could have missed her. It had been a busy night. Something about a beef and poultry special.

I sat on the porch smoking my pipe as my children slept inside. It wasn't unusual for me to enjoy an evening pipe but my nerves waiting for Sarah to return had me so stirred up that I was working on my third round before I was done. Seems like I was about to go ask the neighbors to keep an eye on the kids while I went to look for her when I saw the blue and red lights flashing around the corner heading toward my house. The patrol car pulled into the drive and James Templeton, the chief of police, got out and started walking toward me.

"Evenin', David," James said. He took his uniform hat off and fumbled it around in his hands.

"James," I stammered. "Is she okay?"

He wouldn't look me in the eyes. "David, I'm sorry." He replied, eyes still downcast. "She was sitting at the railroad tracks over on Dixon Avenue. Guess she was headed to the store. Train came off'a the tracks and…" He stopped.

I collapsed back in my chair and began to weep. James started talking again but I don't know what the hell he said to me. The only thing that mattered was that she was gone.

***

So here I am now. Old, bitter, and angry. My kids and grandchildren come over pretty often, and it lifts my spirits. Don't get me wrong. I love them like nothing else in this world. The trouble is that every time I see them, all I can think about is how much Sarah would have loved those moments. But she never got to see it.

Why hadn't that damnable note said anything more specific? It just said "you". Why in the absolute hell couldn't it have said "no one"? Would it have been so damn hard to spare Sarah and me both? The first note had seemed like a Godsend, but the second note tortured me more than anything in the world ever could. I am relieved that the children weren't in the car that day, but if you want to know the truth, I wish I had died with her. I feel like I *should* have died with her but now I've dragged on all these fifty years and felt every day that I shouldn't be here anymore.

Maybe if I had just burned all the notes, I would have died in some jungle overseas like so many other young men I had grown up with. If that happened, then maybe it would have changed the course of everything for Sarah and she would still be here. I'll never know but it will haunt me for whatever wretched time I have left.

I bet you're wondering about the third note. Did I open it? The answer is yes, but not until last week.

4/3/2022

Go have dinner at Lou's.

I'm sitting across the street from the old diner right now in front of where Tom Vincent's old barbershop used to be. It's some damn vape shop or something now. The lights are on in the old diner. Some young fella bought it a few years back and restored it to its glory days. Looks just like it did when old Lou was still alive. I can see a hand full of people chatting at the tables and a young gentleman standing behind the flattop grill talking to a pretty young waitress.

I also see an old man with white hair and a long white beard sitting at a table by the window. His dark suit is tattered and threadbare just as it had been all those years ago. His hand is resting on the table on top of what looks like three small envelopes. He isn't making eye contact with me but I'm sure he knows I'm here.

Seeing him fills me with rage and fear. I don't want to go in, but I somehow feel bound to see this through. One note pointed me to salvation and the second filled me with despair. Perhaps the third will lead me to answers. If I'm lucky it will lead me to Sarah.

I'd best get going, folks. It's getting late and I need to get inside.

NEVER REALLY GONE

"I think I'm going to get the job as principal next year," I said to my husband as I ate dinner. He sat quietly as usual, unblinking and attentive. "The interview isn't until next week, but Superintendent Rance keeps talking to me about *when I'm in charge*, so that seems promising."

My husband, Walter, stares at me with a lopsided smile and I return the grin. Our son, Aaron, sits across the table from him with his usual mischievous grin. Dinner with them is the best part of my day and I hope they know that. No one makes me feel more special than they do.

"I'm not sure I'm ready, though," I continued. Both gazed at me with anticipation as I continued to discuss my future. "Being a vice-principal is already a lot of pressure, but running an entire school just seems like a whole new world of stress. The pay raise would be great though! The budget is getting kind of thin since we… I bought the new house."

My husband and son just continued to smile at me as I ate the rest of my dinner in silence. Their coal-black faces gleam cheerily at me as I collect my dirty dishes and carry them from the table to the sink. From their perch on the kitchen table, I can see the small soapstone carvings of my husband and son.

It was sad, but still, it was comforting.

Walter and Aaron died three years ago when our old house caught fire. While I was away in Orlando for an educator's conference, the electrical outlet in our kitchen downstairs had set the house ablaze and trapped them in the upstairs bedrooms. The fire investigator had tried to tell me what had happened, but I fell to pieces as he tried to explain how Walter had tried to save Aaron.

I just couldn't listen. Those two hung the stars in the sky for me. When they died, I lost everything in the world that I loved most. Our entire life is filled with grief of one variety or another, but in one fell swoop, an entire lifetime of grief fell in my lap.

It almost broke me, too. But then I found the statues.

Friends and family were kind enough to try and salvage what little bit could be found in the charred carcass that was our home. After the top floor was demolished to make the remains safe to enter, they went to work searching for keepsakes and salvageable pieces of our lives together. By the end of the effort, there was less than a shoebox full of memories.

I'm eternally grateful for the people who sifted through the ashes of my life and for the few precious things they found. More than anything, I'm grateful for the statues.

Walter owned a company digging water wells across the country. He spent countless evenings trying to tell me about his work, but I was so often preoccupied that I don't recall many details. I did my best to listen to him but thoughts of upcoming staff training or forgotten tasks always haunted my mind when he discussed work.

Man, if I could turn back time to hear just one more story about a Texas ranch water well, I would hang on to every word.

What I do remember clearly was the numerous amount of trips Walt would take overseas to dig wells in developing countries. I always teased him that it was a tax write-off to see foreign lands and he would laugh it off. Walt was kind-hearted. We lived an exceptionally fortunate life, and it was important to him to give to those who hadn't lived the kind of life we were afforded.

Three years ago, Walt traveled to Niamey, Niger. It was an African country I didn't know very much about, but Walt was over the moon about the trip. For all of the work-life discussions that I drifted out on, hearing him talk about traveling for relief work always kept my attention.

Aaron hung on to every word, too. He idolized his father. Rightfully so. Walt was one in a million. And Aaron was too. I was so lucky to have had them.

Walt was gone for three weeks. Aaron, seven years old and crestfallen that his hero traveled overseas without him, stayed home with me. We talked daily about what we thought his father was doing and all the amazing things he had seen.

Evening text messages kept us up to date on his location and sent messages of love. We missed Walt, but as any mother with a son knows, time with a little boy is precious. You have to take in those innocent years before they grow into serious men.

Each night before bed, Aaron would pull a piece of paper out of his pocket and read it intently. He would wander the house as he glanced down at the folded note and nod occasionally. Once he had made a full trip around the house he would sit next to me in the living room and slide the note back into his pocket.

"What's that, buddy?" I asked him.

"It's a list Dad gave me before he left," he said with a serious look on his face. "He said I had to do everything on the list every night to help you."

"May I see it?" I asked with a chuckle. "It must be very important!"

Aaron smiled and handed me the list. I unfolded it and started reading.

Dear Stinker,

I'm going to need you to take care of some things while I'm gone. Please follow all of the steps each night before bed until I get back. I'm counting on you!

Check all of the doors and be sure they are locked.

Turn off the lights in empty rooms.

Make sure the dog has plenty of food and water.

Keep Mom safe! She gets scared when I'm gone, so be brave!

I love you, buddy! Sneak a cookie when Mom isn't looking. She'll catch you anyway, but I bet she'll let you finish it! See you soon.

Love,
Dad

When Walter returned from Africa, he told Aaron and me of all the amazing places he had been and the wonderful people he met. All through his stories, I could see Aaron's eyes transfixed on the duffle bag by his father's feet. He knew there were gifts inside and did his best to listen patiently.

After Walter finished telling us about his trip, he kneeled on one knee and unzipped the tattered duffle bag. Fishing around inside, he brought out a colorful beaded necklace and handed it to

Aaron. His eyes sparkled with a fascination for the trinket his father had brought back from overseas. With a quick thank you, Aaron darted to his room to add it to his collection of items his father had brought back from his travels.

"And for you," Walter said as he pulled a box from the bag. "I have something handmade and one of a kind."

Walter placed the box on the counter and gestured for me to open it. Sliding the lid off and pulling away pieces of crumpled pieces of newspaper, I could see three stone figures nestled at the bottom of the container. A man, a woman, and a little boy. Cut from blue-gray stone and polished to a high gleam, I marveled at how much they looked like us. Our family.

"Our translator showed us a stone carver when I asked about a custom gift for you," Walt said as he brushed a scrap of paper away from the figure of our son. "The craftsman said that the carvings will watch over our family when any of us are away and keep them safe. Seemed like the kind of thing you would enjoy."

***

I stayed in bed the majority of the time for the first six months after Walter and Aaron died. Initially, I lived with my sister and brother-in-law. They did their best to help me through the grief, but they rarely left me alone. No doubt my attempts to withdraw alarmed them, but grieving with an audience was difficult.

The homeowner's insurance policy allowed me to purchase a modest home in the suburbs outside of town. My sister begged me to stay with them longer, but I declined. The healthier thing to do would have been to stay with them longer, but I needed space.

Boxes of unassembled furniture, home decor, and kitchen necessities filled the new house for months. Family and friends had been kind enough to take me shopping for new things, but once they arrived, I could never muster the willpower to begin putting the pieces of my life together. My old life had been so well-built. Our future was certain. We were blessed.

No one prepares you to lose everything and be left behind to start from scratch.

At the six-month mark, some unusual things started happening. The box of mementos from the house fire had been sitting on the kitchen counter since I moved into the new house. While I had already looked through the assorted photos and knick-knacks that had been collected, I hadn't unpacked them.

I had just gotten out of bed and headed into the kitchen to fix a cup of coffee when I saw that the lid of the box was sitting to the side. As I walked closer, I could see that some of the contents had been shuffled around. I was puzzled but assumed that I must have looked through it recently and forgotten to close it. Lifting the lid to put it back in place, I was startled by the two obsidian figures sitting on the counter.

Black eyes gazed at me from beneath the lid. The lopsided smile and mischievous grin I was so familiar with sent a cold chill running up my spine. The soapstone statues of my husband and son sat on the counter, oriented in my direction as if they had been waiting for me.

My mind raced. I had no memory of opening the box or looking through the contents. There was little chance I had taken the statues out and placed them on the counter. My new house had a security system that I armed each evening, so the odds of an intruder rummaging through my things were equally as unlikely.

Palming my cell phone, I considered calling my sister and brother-in-law to ask if they had been to the house recently without my knowledge. My thumb was scrolling through my contacts when I decided against it. The two of them had spent such a great deal of time worrying over me that I didn't want to give them any additional cause for concern over my mental state.

Scooping the two stone sculptures up, I prepared to place them back into the box when my eyes met those belonging to the statue of Aaron. Even made of stone, the eyes still sparkled with wonder and amusement. The mischievous smirk made me smile even as the tears of despair filled the corner of my eyes.

I knew at that moment that I couldn't place them back in the box. Hiding them there would no more heal my spirits than the months of dwelling in my darkened bedroom had. While my heart ached as I looked at the two stone carvings, I also began to feel a sense of happiness, almost as if I had them back in some small way.

From that moment things began to improve slowly but surely. Boxes that had gathered dust for months were opened. IKEA furniture was assembled and put in place. My husband and son sat atop the kitchen counter where they had a view into the open dining room and living room. Their intricately carved eyes kept a watch as my new home slowly came together.

I even found myself beginning to talk to them. When I completed a piece of furniture, I would ask the carving of my husband where he thought I should place it. A small voice in my head that sounded so much like his would give me an opinion. More often than not, I adhered to the imaginary answer. Walter always had a good sense of how to put a room together.

After a lot of internal struggle, I decided to end my bereavement leave from school. Returning to work lifted my spirits as well. The students and faculty were extremely kind and welcomed me back warmly. My grief wasn't gone, but the weight was becoming manageable.

When I returned home from school, the carvings of my husband and son were always waiting for me on the kitchen counter. It didn't seem to matter whether I entered the kitchen from the garage door or through the living room from the front door. Walter and Aaron always seemed to be facing the door I walked through as if to greet me.

Exactly when I started eating dinner with them on the table, I can't be sure. I spoke to the statues daily about my experiences and feelings. In my mind, I knew they were only sculptures of my family, but treating them as if they were my son and husband comforted me. There is no doubt in my mind this wasn't a healthy coping mechanism, but it got me through my days with a greater deal of ease.

A year after their deaths and I was functioning on an almost normal level again. Where initially my every waking moment was filled with thoughts of them, I was now able to focus on required tasks again. Walter and Aaron always crept back in, but their memories were a source of joy and motivation rather than an anchor dragging me farther under. And I always knew the end of my day would result in a quiet dinner with their effigies.

It was also around this time when unusual things began to happen more frequently with the statues. Nothing overtly terrifying, but unsettling, nonetheless. One morning I misplaced my car keys. School started in less than half an hour and I was dangerously close to being late. Usually, I left them sitting on the kitchen counter, but this morning they were nowhere to be found.

After more than ten minutes of frantically searching for my keys, I was startled by a loud noise in the kitchen. It sounded like a bowling ball had fallen onto the tile. Heavy clacking like the sound of stone on stone echoed down the hallway followed by the jingling of metal.

Rushing into the kitchen to see what happened, I saw the statue of my husband sitting in the center of the kitchen floor. Next to it were my car keys. I had walked through the kitchen at least a dozen times during my frantic search for them but there they sat. Scooping the keys from the floor and placing the statue of my husband back on the counter, my mind raced.

As I looked toward Walter's statue, I was transfixed by the lopsided smile. It almost seemed to say, *"You've got to keep up with your keys, Emily. What would you do without me?"*

All the doors were locked. No one could have come inside. Even if they had, what burglar would locate your car keys and move a keepsake into the center of the floor?

It consumed my mind for the entire workday. Were the statues moving? Was I losing my mind? The thought terrified me.

Since their removal from the box, the statues of my family had either been on the kitchen counter or the dining room table when I ate dinner. While I would occasionally move them to clean the kitchen surfaces, they kept their watch from there. Over time, though, they could more frequently be found in different places.

One evening, I was awoken by the sound of the squealing of door hinges. A habit from college when I had too many roommates, I had always slept with my door closed. When my eyes focused in the dark, I could see that the door was only ajar, maybe five or six inches. The light from the security system panel blinked green in the darkness of the room, showing that the exterior door alarm was still armed.

I moved my arm to the nightstand to turn on the lamp when my forearm unexpectedly bumped into something hard. It fell over onto the wooden surface of the table and the noise made me jump. Bolting up in bed, I again reached for the lamp and turned it on. The statue of Walter lay on its side, smiling and gazing at me. Aaron sat just behind him, smiling as well.

As I walked to the kitchen holding the two stone effigies, my mind retraced my steps before I had gone to bed. I ate in the dining room with the statues, took them to the kitchen while I washed dishes, and went to brush my teeth. There was no memory of having brought them to the bedroom. The thought had crossed my mind thousands of times to leave them there to watch over me as I slept, but I had drawn the line there.

I spent so much time talking to the inanimate objects that I knew there had to be a limit somewhere. Still, I must have moved them into the bedroom with me. Perhaps I had spent so much time talking to them throughout the day that I was inadvertently picking them up and placing them in different places throughout the house.

A cold chill still rattled my bones as I placed them back on the countertop. They smiled at me as always, but now, those smiles filled me with fear and discomfort.

***

Two years after the house fire and I had agreed to go on my first date. It was a strange sensation on so many levels. Life doesn't do much to equip you for the thought of reentering the dating pool when you're nearly forty years old. It wasn't something I had done intentionally. A few gentlemen here and there had expressed interest, but I had politely declined.

Dennis was unexpected. A colleague from my first years of teaching, Dennis had moved to another school in the district nearly eight years ago. Our classrooms had been next door to each other for my first three years on the job and we both taught freshman English. He was handsome and witty.

We reconnected at a district-wide meeting the year before. During one of those annoyingly childish group exercises, I was shocked to see him smiling at me from across the table. His dark hair had gone to salt and pepper, but that rogue smile of his was the same as it ever was. We finished the meeting, and he caught up with me outside.

"Emily," he shouted from behind me. He smiled widely. "Hey! Good to see you! How've you been?"

"I've been better," I said with a forced smile. "Things are getting… better, I guess."

"Oh, damn," Dennis replied, smile melting away to a look of shame. "Walter and Aaron… I'm so sorry. I meant to call, but it always felt like a bad time."

I raised a hand to his shoulder and gave him my best attempt at a comforting squeeze.

"Life gets hard sometimes," I replied. "As I said, it's getting better. Slowly. How are you and Samantha?"

Dennis' eyes dropped to the ground, and he ran a hand through his shaggy hair.

"Yeah, Sam and I split up a few years back," he muttered. "Seems like I wasn't the only one for her anymore."

"Damn, myself," I replied sympathetically. "We know how to start a conversation with an old friend, don't we?"

He laughed. I smiled. Everything happened quickly from there.

We went for coffee that day and it seems like we were rarely apart from one another unless we were at work. Dennis cooked dinner with me almost every night. Bottles of wine vanished rapidly. I was intimate for the first time since my husband passed away.

For the first two months, the statues of Walter and Aaron sat silently. They watched our meals and listened to our conversations. Dennis had asked me about them, and I had told him they were some of my few mementos of life before the fire. What I failed to tell him is how the statues had been companions to me almost every night since my family had died.

I grew increasingly uneasy with them watching me live my life without them. Dennis would happily talk about his day at work and the various events he had scheduled in the coming months. Nodding along agreeably, my eyes would lock with the statues. They continued their whimsical smiles, but my sense of guilt continued to swell.

Dennis never noticed when I moved the statues to the small table in the entryway of my house. I couldn't bear to have them watch me fall in love with another man. They weren't my dead husband and son. I knew that. It still felt wrong. Almost voyeuristic.

While the first five months of my romance with Dennis had swept me off of my feet, warts began to show themselves soon after. The turn was sudden and unexpected. Dennis had become such a source of comfort and warmth for me. It was jarring to see how quickly he changed.

Where he had once been talkative and attentive, he had grown quieter and reserved in the evenings. Dennis had started to rearrange things in my house without asking me. When I asked him why he would look at me with contempt and explain condescendingly how much better it looked.

There were also off-handed comments about my appearance. I didn't wear makeup or dress to impress every day, but my appearance was always tidy. He never said I was ugly, but a point was made often that I could do more to "look pretty" for him.

On at least two occasions, I'm certain he was trying to through my cellphone. I kept it password locked. As a school teacher, you learn hard lessons about leaving an unlocked cell phone on your desk. A few times when I tried to unlock the phone, a warning appeared on the screen that it was locked for a certain period of time before I could try my password again.

The phone was set to allow for 10 attempts before the time-out went into effect. When I asked Dennis about it, he looked at me as though I had accused him of murder. We didn't talk for a few days after the second conversation, but it blew over eventually.

We stopped cooking dinner together and he began to question me when food wasn't ready when he came to visit after work. I initially teased him about it and joked that he could come to give me a hand.

"Samantha always had dinner ready when I got home from work," he said dismissively as he read a newspaper at the kitchen table. I was standing at the stove stirring ground beef in a skillet for tacos. Turning my head toward him, I stared in disbelief.

"Walter would have offered to help," I quipped in return before returning my attention to the skillet.

"Well," he said briskly. "It really is too bad he burned in the house instead of burning dinner like you frequently do."

I dropped the spatula onto the stove and turned to face him. His face was as solemn as a gargoyle and his eyes were piercing. He smiled cruelly in my direction and began to read the paper again.

"Get the hell out of my house," I said in a shockingly calm tone.

Dennis continued reading the newspaper.

"Did you hear me?" I asked. He didn't look up.

"I'm sorry," he replied without much emotion. "That was unkind. It's been a long day and I'm hungry. Can I help you finish cooking?"

He dropped his newspaper to the counter and began to walk toward the stove. I lifted my hand to his chest and held it firmly to stop him from continuing forward. He looked at me in astonishment and brushed my hand aside.

"I said get the hell out of my house!" I shouted. "Do you not understand what I'm telling you?"

Dennis' surprised look turned to one of shame and disappointment. He continued to the stove and picked up the spatula. Stirring the meat quietly, he still didn't respond.

"Leave now." I spat and jerked the spatula from his hand. "You will not talk about my husband that way. You won't have the chance. This is through. We're done. Leave."

Red rage filled his cheeks and he continued to peer down at the sizzling pan of ground beef. His hands clenched into fists that began to turn a pale white. The corners of his mouth began to twitch as he turned toward me. His face looked rigid and cruel. Without warning, his hand shot out and grabbed my wrist forcefully.

"I said I was sorry," he said through gritted teeth. His grip on my wrist was getting tighter and I could feel the loss of blood in my hand. I drew my free hand back to strike him, but he caught the blow before it landed. "Samantha even knew when to accept my…"

The sound of breaking glass and the blast of a car alarm exploded into the kitchen. We both turned our heads toward the window to the front of the house where flashing headlights and turn signals now erupted. Loud wails from the car horn filled our ears.

Dennis released his painful grip on my wrist and darted for the front door. I followed behind him and watched as he approached his car in the driveway. Shards of glass were scattered across the hood and onto the concrete. His windshield was shattered and one of the planters from my porch sat clumsily on his dashboard.

"Emily, call the cops." He said as he looked over the damage. "My phone is on the kitchen counter."

I went back to the kitchen and picked up his phone. Walking back to the front door, I was still in shock at how he had just treated me. Looking at him standing in my driveway caused my rage to overflow.

I threw his cell phone out the door and into the front yard. He watched it sail from my hand and bounce into the grass. Darting toward the phone, he looked at me in disgust.

"Call them yourself," I said flatly. "Once the cops finish their report, leave. Don't come back."

I watched from the porch as he dialed the number for the police and asked for a unit to come to my house. He paced in the front yard, looking from end to end in case the vandal was still in the vicinity. Looking down where the planter had been, I saw something that I couldn't quite make out in the dark of the evening.

Squatting down, I picked up the smooth object and held it up in the path of the streetlight. A mischievous grin and sparkling eyes full of wonder met mine. The statue of Aaron reflected the abrasive light from overhead. I clutched him to my chest. Tears flowed down my cheeks as I headed back into the house.

Locking the doors behind me, I scooped the statue of Walter off of the foyer table and carried it to my bedroom. Gently, I placed both carvings on my nightstand and crawled beneath the blankets. After an hour, I got out of bed and looked through the dining room window to see that Dennis and his car were gone.

The driveway was still covered in broken shards of glass and the discarded planter. I would clean that up tomorrow. For now, I was just relieved that he was gone.

I crawled back into bed and looked at the statues on the nightstand. The tears had stopped, but I felt worse than I had in months. At least I had them.

"I love you both so much," I said quietly as I closed my eyes.

A voice in the back of my mind seemed to say *"We love you too…"*

***

Things were calm for around a month after I kicked Dennis out of the house. Phone calls and text messages bombarded me throughout the day and night. I couldn't make it through an entire day of school without hearing my phone vibrate in a drawer at least a dozen times.

The voicemails and texts all implored me to call him back. I just needed to hear him out. He could explain if only I would give him a chance. That single bad night didn't represent who he was.

I would have been content to never answer his calls or texts for the rest of my days. That had been my goal. It was easy enough to manage for a while, but eventually, his persistence and deception caught me off guard.

As I sat on my bed beside the carvings of my family reading a book, my phone began to buzz beside me. When I picked it up, I recognized the number. It belonged to the central office of the Board of Education. It was after hours, and I was confused but hit the green button to accept the call anyway.

"Hello, this is Emily Clark," I said in a slightly confused but pleasant tone of voice. "Kind of late to be working, isn't it?"

"Why won't you answer my calls, Emily?" a rough voice said. "I just want to explain myself, but you won't give me the chance."

"Dennis?" I asked.

"Yes," he replied. "You're a hard woman to get ahold of. Look, I just want to explain what happened that night and clear the air."

His voice was different than usual. His tongue sounded heavy, and his words slurred.

"I don't want to talk to you," I said. "Please stop calling me."

"Please," he responded. I could hear him crying. "Just let me explain myself. Can I come over?"

"No," I said angrily. "You've been drinking. Why are you in the board office?"

I could hear three loud *whacks* from what I could only assume was Dennis slamming the receiver of the phone on a desk.

"I took a key from the school before I left work," he said loudly after the banging had ceased. "It was the only way I thought I could get you to answer your damn phone."

"Goodbye, Dennis," I said sternly. "Don't come to my house and don't call me again."

I was about to end the call when I heard him scream.

"I tried to do this the nice way! When I get to your house, I'll kick your door in and…"

I hung the phone up and immediately called 911. Veins throbbed in the side of my head and my heart thundered in my chest. After two brief rings, someone spoke from the other end.

"911. What is your emergency?"

***

Dennis was arrested as he drove to my house. The emergency dispatcher sent out the description of his car and the potential travel routes that I provided. Officers made contact with him three blocks from my house. They found a handgun in the passenger seat of his car.

In addition to his charges of terroristic threatening and DUI, the board of education also pressed charges against him for breaking into the board building. He was terminated immediately and held in county jail. I nervously checked the county detention center website multiple times per day to make sure he hadn't been released. It surprised me that he hadn't bailed himself out, but day after day he remained there.

The mystery of his failure to make bail was solved when Dennis' ex-wife, Samantha, called two weeks after the drunken phone call. Through tears, she told me of her abusive marriage. Dennis had never hit her, but the mental and emotional abuse was immense. She apologized for not reaching out to me sooner to warn me, but I assured her no apology was necessary.

Samantha confided in me that Dennis had a gambling addiction and lived in crippling debt. She had endured years of emotional abuse, but it was the near-poverty state they were living in that finally prompted her to take the children and leave. He was six months behind on child support and the court system had started to garnish his wages.

A sliver of me felt sorry for him. I also felt a little bit of shame that I knew wasn't fair. His financial situation wouldn't allow him to afford bail or an attorney. None of it was my fault, but some black tendril of emotional manipulation tried to anchor itself in my brain. Those kinds of thoughts can grow like cancer.

Mental and physical abuse can cause even the strongest person to become numb and hollow. Samantha had survived her ordeal and managed to escape. I was proud of her, though I never told her. While I may not have allowed it to continue, so many people are manipulated into accepting it, or worse, believing they deserve it.

With the assistance of a local domestic violence advocacy group, I was able to receive a protective order against Dennis. A kind advocate walked me through the process and assisted me with the court filing. The process was uncomfortable as our state allows both parties to be present in court to present evidence, but this amazing group was with me every step of the way.

Life returned to the shattered version of normalcy that I had achieved before Dennis entered the picture. The events caused me to withdraw again, but my sister and brother-in-law were a constant source of comfort. They stayed with me for a few weeks. My brother-in-law even slept in a chair beside the front door for the first few nights. A bit overzealous, perhaps, but amazing nonetheless.

After a few weeks, I grew more comfortable, and they returned home. It was lonely but also nice to have a bit of space to myself. My sister, ever the worrier, insisted on leaving a handgun for me. I tucked it away in my nightstand, hoping never to use it.

Honestly, I didn't even feel completely alone. The obsidian carvings of my husband and son kept watch over me day and night. I moved them from room to room with me throughout the day when I was home.

The carvings soothed me but also concerned me. I could never fully come to terms with some of the strange events surrounding them. The car keys. Showing up on the nightstand. Dennis' broken car window. Mentally, I knew they weren't moving, but I could not remember moving them on some occasions.

I returned to work three weeks after the night Dennis was arrested. The support of the faculty and students humbled me again. Never let anyone tell you that community isn't important. The kindness and comfort received from them were invaluable to me.

I finally stopped checking the detention center website religiously.

Dinner time had returned to the unusual format as before. Each evening when I returned home I would cook myself a meal and move the statues to the dinner table to keep me company. I would share the events of the day and the two of them would smile politely as their carved eyes almost seemed to glitter with life as they reflected the overhead light.

In the evenings I would place them on my nightstand. I would say goodnight to them and tell them how much I loved and missed them. In the back of my mind, I always heard them say it as well. It was unsettling but comforting.

***

It was 3:05 AM and I heard something move in my bedroom.

My eyes burst open and struggled to adjust to the darkness. A sensation of being watched flooded my body and the hairs on my arms stood on end. I felt like a gazelle barreling through the savannah, knowing all the while that lions perched in the high grass waiting to pounce.

I brushed my arm to the nightstand and felt shocked when I didn't make contact with the soapstone statues. In a panic, I turned and pulled the chain on my bedside lamp and blinding illumination flooded the room. A figure stood in front of my bedroom door.

"Hello Emily," Dennis said, his eyes cold and piercing.

I broke loose from my frozen state and pulled the nightstand drawer out. Pulling too hard, the drawer fell out of place and slammed to the floor. The contents were dumped onto the floor and scattered across the carpet. Terrified, my eyes darted from side to side trying to find the handgun my sister had left me.

It was nowhere to be found. I looked at my nightstand and my cell phone was gone as well. Somehow, I was most startled to see that the carvings of Walter and Aaron were missing.

"Looking for these?" Dennis said with amusement. He dropped my cell phone to the floor and stomped it. The cracking of the screen made me cringe. After destroying the phone, he pulled up the tail bottom of his shirt to reveal the handle of the gun that once rested in my nightstand drawer. "I figured you may have gotten a gun since I was last able to see you. Thank God you're a heavy sleeper, baby. You could have hurt me before we got to talk!"

"The alarm…" I muttered. "The cops will be here soon…"

"Cut the phone line," he said without pause. "Should have spent the money on a better system. You can be so silly sometimes. That's why you need me."

Dennis began to step toward me slowly. Still wrapped in the blankets, I began to push myself backward. As I tried to slide my legs out from under the blankets and onto the floor I became tangled and fell from the edge of the bed.

"Emily," he said with surprise. "Are you okay? Let me help you up!"

He walked around the corner of the bed and stared at me. I pushed myself into the corner in a panic reflex and stared at him, fear swelling. My eyes watered with rage and disgust.

"Dennis," I whimpered. "Please leave. I have a protective order. You'll go to jail."

"Sweetheart," he said as he stood over me. "I just want to talk. I don't like how things ended and I just want to try and make it right."

"No!" I said more forcefully. Dennis smiled in amusement as he looked at me. My eyes were drawn to the outline of the gun under his shirt. I only had to wait for him to get a little closer to me and I would make a move for it.

He ran his hands through his messy hair and sighed.

"Look here," he said, almost exasperated. "You got me thrown in jail… and I forgive you. We can work this out. You've just got to be smart about this. Are you going to throw this away over one bad night?"

"You hurt me, Dennis," I replied. "I'm not going to let you hurt me."

The amused smile slid off of his face. A mask of pure rage replaced it. The look of malice and contempt from the night he grabbed me in the kitchen presented itself.

No, this face wasn't a mask. This was the real Dennis. The mask was the kind and genial man who had wooed me over coffee. The man who melted away my defenses. That man was a lie. This hateful thing before me was Dennis.

"If you think that was me hurting you," he said in a low tone. ", then you are about to learn a difficult lesson."

As Dennis began to close the short distance and reach toward me, I prepared myself to fight back. Bracing my feet against the wall, I knew I would only have one shot to take the gun. Just one shot to make it out of this alive.

Five feet away…

Four feet away…

Three feet away…

Two feet away… This was it…

As Dennis stood a foot away from me, there was the sound of stampeding footsteps in the hallways. Heavy thuds resounded and shook the room. The reverberation was so intense I could feel it in my bones.

"Who the hell is here?" Dennis said, head snapping toward to door to the hallway. "Tell me who…"

His sentence was cut off and I pushed off against the wall and wrapped my arms around his waist. I pushed him backward with all of my strength and he began to stumble. Feet tangled, Dennis twisted his ankle and began to fall backward, smacking his head against the floor with a sickening thud.

Before pushing myself off of the floor, I pulled the shirt away from the waistband of his pants and pulled the gun from his waist.

Switching off the safety, I took a step back and aimed the gun at him as he lay sprawled on the carpet.

It took him a moment to collect himself. By the time he did, he was looking into the barrel of the gun. The rage returned to his face for a moment, but fear danced in his hateful eyes. He held his hands up in a gesture of defeat.

"Get up," I spat. "Keep your hands in the air and walk five feet in front of me. We're going to the neighbors to call the cops."

"And if I don't?" He asked.

"The first shot goes in your leg," I replied. "If that doesn't work, we'll move on from there. Get moving."

Dennis wobbly lifted himself back onto his feet and put his hands in the air. He limped clumsily toward the bedroom door. His pace was slow, and I made sure to keep a safe distance between us. The ankle may not be as bad as it seemed, and I wasn't taking chances.

Dennis passed through the bedroom door into the hallways, hands still raised. Without warning, the bedroom door slammed shut. His hands were visible above his head, and I knew that he couldn't possibly have moved that quickly.

"What the hell?" I heard him say through the door. Rushing forward, I began to turn the knob, but the door wouldn't budge. No matter how hard I tried to turn it, the handle wouldn't rotate. "Hey! Hey! Get off of me!"

Dennis began to shriek like a wounded animal. Thrashing and thuds penetrated the door. The floor shook and the sound of something being dragged across the floor filled my ears. Dry cracks echoed in the hall and Dennis' wails grew louder.

It was the snapping of bones.

"No! Please!" he begged. "I'm sorry! I'll never bother her again! Just don't…"

Silence.

I backed away from the door and raised the gun toward it. There was no noise coming from the hallway now. Unnerving silence filled the space where the desperate screams had been only moments earlier. My heart jumped into my throat when I heard the *click* of the light switch from the other side of the door. Bars of illumination filtered in from the space beneath.

The latch clicked and the hinges squealed as the door slowly opened into the bedroom.

Dennis was gone.

Sitting in the center of the hallway were two small stone figures. Even from this distance, I could see the lopsided grin and mischievous smile that I loved and missed so much. Their eyes sparkled, almost alive. Underneath the base of the smaller effigy, there was a scrap of paper.

Venturing carefully into the hallway, gun still leveled, I approached the carvings of my husband and son. I pulled a scrap of paper from below the carving of Aaron. The paper was yellow and crinkled with age and the edges were blackened and flaking.

Tears streamed down my cheek as I read the words.

Keep Mom safe!

ACKNOWLEDGEMENTS

The funny thing that occurs to me as I finish putting this collection together is how many hands were in the mix throughout the process.

To my wife and sons: You supported me in this strange endeavor and let me hide away in a dark office for hours longer than I should have. I couldn't have done it without your love and understanding. It's time for playing Legos and taking evening walks now.

To Travis, Jessie, Deco, Jess, Poppy, C.E., Grant, and countless writers: You've read countless pages and let me take time away from your busy lives. Thank you.

To Dr. NoSleep, Full Body Chills, and Lighthouse Horror: You fine folks gave me my first taste of what it was to be a working author and I'll be forever grateful for my start. Thank you for helping to build my confidence.

To Velox: Thank you for giving me a platform to share my work and the opportunity to collaborate with you.

To my readers: I wouldn't be able to do this strange, unbelievable thing I get to do now without you. My imagination made me a writer, but your support made me an author. I will be forever grateful.

9 781963 107043